D0381313

DO OR DIE FOR DIXIE!

MAJOR AUBREY LEE QUIDLEY III
True blue to his aristocratic Southland, but blind to what people will do for power.

SHARON SUE HUNT
A plantation belle who can wrap any man around her little finger . . . for motives they never suspect.

COLONEL EARL SAWYER
The redneck intelligence officer who'd die for the Confederacy . . . as long as his kind rule.

VYRY LEWIS
Virtually enslaved in a white-man's cat house, she'll use her beautiful body in the cause of freedom.

JOHNNY LEWIS
He's fought all his life to free his people. Now he's ready to sacrifice his life.

Avon Books are available at special quantity discounts for bulk purchases for sales promotions, premiums, fund raising or educational use. Special books, or book excerpts, can also be created to fit specific needs.

For details write or telephone the office of the Director of Special Markets, Avon Books, 959 8th Avenue, New York, New York 10019, 212-262-3361.

THE SHILOH PROJECT

DAVID C. POYER

AVON
PUBLISHERS OF BARD, CAMELOT, DISCUS AND FLARE BOOKS

THE SHILOH PROJECT is an original publication of Avon Books. This work has never before appeared in book form.

AVON BOOKS
A division of
The Hearst Corporation
959 Eighth Avenue
New York, New York 10019

Copyright © 1981 by D. C. Poyer
Published by arrangement with the author
Library of Congress Catalog Card Number: 80-69982
ISBN: 0-380-78733-4

All rights reserved, which includes the right to reproduce this book or portions thereof in any form whatsoever except as provided by the U.S. Copyright Law. For information address U.S. Licensing Associates, 123 East 54th Street, Suite 2-F, New York, New York 10022

First Avon Printing, November, 1981

AVON TRADEMARK REG. U.S. PAT. OFF. AND IN OTHER COUNTRIES, MARCA REGISTRADA, HECHO EN U.S.A.

Printed in the U.S.A.

WFH 10 9 8 7 6 5 4 3 2 1

For all my Tidewater friends

"As a historian, my daydreams often take characteristic shapes; and often they return to that fatal day in July, 1863, when Lee faced Longstreet across the ramparts of the Pennsylvania hills.

"What, I ask myself, would have happened if that heroic and nearly disastrous charge of Pickett and Pettigrew had failed? Might not a defeat before Gettysburg have postponed or even cancelled British recognition in August, the Palmerston Alliance, and the large-scale Empire aid that later turned the tide? I shudder at the thought that the South might now be, instead of a proud and solid Confederacy over a century old, merely the downtrodden stepchild of a victorious and vengeful Union.

"Futile such daydreams may be . . . but it is fascinating indeed to speculate on *what might have been. . . .*"

JOHN DARDEN WOODARD, Vol. I,
*THE CONFEDERATE EXPERIMENT:
THE FIRT CENTURY*
Government Press, Richmond, 1983

One

"Riot, looting, arson," said Colonel Earl Sawyer softly, staring out through the thick windows as the Bentley's tires crunched on shattered glass. "Even rape—though not white women yet, they say. They've learned that lesson, at least."

Major Aubrey Quidley, sitting easily erect beside him, nodded, without words. He was staring down at his hands, seeing them, yet not really there. The colonel's words had illuminated, like a suddenly lit and frozen single frame of film, a horrific picture within his normally unimaginative mind. It was a picture of Miss Sharon's slender legs, pale, naked under her torn-open dress, spread wide in his vision to allow . . . he caught Sawyer looking oddly at him and recalled himself to reality. "Yes, sir," he said.

The fat colonel rambled on. "This is the worst I've seen since the riots in Alabama, back in sixty-eight. Those were some bad weeks, let me tell you. Took a full division of Regular Army to pacify Birmingham. There wasn't much left." Sawyer shifted his heavy body slightly in the seat, bringing his chest up; a small red decoration came into the edge of Quidley's view, and he knew what the colonel wanted him to ask.

"Is that where you picked up the wound badge, sir?"

"Only a scratch," said Sawyer modestly.

1

Quidley suppressed his initial urge to gag, murmured something polite, and then the two officers fell silent, looking out as the gray staff car crept along. The thick dark smells of smoke and plaster dust, quenched ashes and roasting meat filtered slowly in past the scents of leather and cologne and good tobacco. A pall of dark oily-looking smoke rolled across the road as Sergeant Roberts, the darky driver, slowed at the corner of Hampton and Little Creek, and Quidley caught his breath and leaned over Sawyer to look.

Their own neighborhood. Burned, all of it, the great tract of Richmond-subsidized housing, designed to move Norfolk's half-million coloreds from squalor to healthy, if spartan, accommodations. The first of the great Renewed Colored Areas, four years in the building. Destroyed in one night. He leaned back, feeling sick. Flakes of soot blew across the road as Roberts accelerated, sounding the siren as they swerved to the right to pass a squat gray Johnston tank.

"That's Railroad work, burning those houses," said Sawyer.

"Do you think so?" said Quidley, looking at him curiously. The colonel, just in from Richmond, outranked him; but the man's rumpled, obviously off-the-rack uniform, the cheap cigar he puffed, the shocking way he had run to fat, all made him conscious of the fact that Sawyer was a social inferior. And then, after all, he was from Mississippi.

"Hell, yes, I think so. Who but niggers would've done this? They don't value decent housing the way whites do. Why, I always said all this fancy new housing was a waste of good Confederate tax dollars. More police, that's what we need for those conditionally emancipated loafers—not fancy-ass bathrooms and hot runnin' water." He waved toward the sky with the end of the cigar. "Hadn't been for this rain your whole downtown would've gone up, Major."

"We've got a good fire service, Colonel."

"Loyal? Or niggers?"

"There are Negroes, yes, sir, but with white officers. Like the police. They'd have done just as well." Quidley raised his voice a trifle, though he knew that Roberts, in front, could hear every word they exchanged. "Sergeant,

2

can you go a little faster? The colonel was delayed at the station, and we'd like to arrive on time."

"Yes, sir." The Bentley's motor purred instead of whispering; the Stars and Bars, fixed at either side of the staff car's grille, began to flutter in the breeze. Shattered storefronts, broken street signs, burned-out hulks of cars streamed by them. Quidley saw that most of the stores had been looted, with glass and scattered, dirtied merchandise littering the sidewalks. Looting—despite curfews, patrols, and orders to the police to shoot lawbreakers on sight.

Something out of place (even in that desolation of ruined homes and hopes) caught his eye and he frowned. Men—white men—lounged in front of a block of broken-in storefronts. Each carried a weapon—rifle, shotgun, or at the least a length of pipe. Guards? But they wore no uniforms. "Who are they, I wonder," he murmured, and felt Sawyer turn his head beside him.

"Who? Them? Look like patrollers."

"Don't look like them. And I don't think they patrol out here."

"Aren't they—"

But he'd seen it too, at the same time Sawyer had. One of the men had turned, and the white armband with its red flaming-cross symbol came into view. "Kuklos," he said, finishing Sawyer's sentence. As the speeding car left the block behind he saw another armbanded man step from the dark gape of a broken window, lugging out something heavy in both hands.

"How much longer, Major?" said Sawyer, shooting his cuff to expose a large gold English wristwatch.

"Half an hour to the beach. A little more to the fort."

"I see. Well, let's not waste the ride. Can you go over the local situation for me again? There was a briefing at the Castle before I left, but I understand you've been on the scene since it began."

"Yes, sir, I have." Quidley drew a breath, looking out of the window at destruction. "The first hint of trouble occurred about nine last night. The government and most of the private factories had let out for Secesh Day, and the city had some free entertainment and oratory laid on —the standard sort of thing. The biggest thing was a speech by the Mayor and a fireworks display down at Town Point, on the river. That drew a crowd of about

3

twenty thousand, mostly colored, but in good spirits—a holiday crowd. The fireworks started a little late and there was some booing, a few fights; nothing the city police weren't handling well.

"About nine-fifteen some of the pyrotechnics seemed too loud. People began falling, and those near them began to scream. Some alert police—Chief Mays' people, not Army—had been placed atop buildings nearby as security for the Mayor, who was down below, on an elevated grandstand over the river. They later reported that they saw figures on the roof of one of the warehouses along Waterfront Drive. They were armed and were firing on the crowd."

"On their own people?" Sawyer was incredulous.

"Correct. The police took them under fire, of course. Meanwhile the crowd panicked and began to stampede. Squad cars were unable to reach the scene. And then someone started to rock a parked car."

"Started that way in Alabam' too. Coloreds seem to hate them cars somehow."

"Maybe because they can't own them," said Quidley. "The crowd turned ugly. Several policemen were beaten and their weapons taken."

"What about the snipers?"

"They disappeared, according to the police officers, in the midst of the uproar. And they're still at large. It all happened very quickly."

"Anyone killed? Whites, I mean?" said Sawyer.

"None. Fortunately, there aren't many downtown that late at night. Still, there was a lot of damage done in the business district."

"And what about all this?" said Sawyer, pointing his cigar out the window.

"Well, it—the riot seemed to expand. The news came in through Army channels about ten-thirty. I ordered the Fort patrols out at eleven. All key military points were defended by one A.M., with roving patrols at the shipyard perimeter, the docks and ordnance works, Sewell's Point, and—key civilian neighborhoods. This was coordinated with Commander Channing at the Naval Base. Now, the fires—they started early that morning. *This* morning. In widely scattered neighborhoods, but all colored. I had local radio stations pass the word for all citizens to stay indoors. The looting peaked just before sunrise; after that

4

there was no organized resistance to the police or patrols. General quiet was restored by about eight. Nevertheless, I thought it best to keep them indoors for the day—"

"Yes," Sawyer said, nodding. "You seem to have handled this all pretty well, Major. I'll relay that to Richmond when I get back."

"Thank you, sir," said Quidley.

The gray car presently slowed, and flashed its lights twice, Quidley and Sawyer returned the sentries' salutes as the Bentley purred through gates and barbed wire into Fort Davis. "Port Control," said Quidley to Roberts. To Sawyer he said, "You'll want me at this briefing, sir?"

"I sure do, Major. You won't be directly involved, but I want you to know what's going on. After all, you're— what is it?"

"Port Security Officer," said Quidley.

"Right. We'll be depending on you to keep this all under wraps. It would definitely cause . . . problems . . . if even one whisper of Shiloh . . ." Sawyer glanced significantly forward, at Sergeant Roberts' close-cropped head.

Quidley nodded, tensing. *Shiloh.* It was a word, or a name, that he had heard before. As security officer of Hampton Roads, the Confederacy's largest seaport, he was the center of a net of operatives and covert police personnel and officials in factories, military units, and service organizations. Army Intelligence at Castle Thunder considered it his duty to hear all and know all, at least as far as southeastern Virginia was concerned.

And of recent weeks a strange word, almost a code, had been reported to him as in use at establishments as diverse as the Marine Corps Amphibious Planning Office at Little Creek and at the oil-transfer piers in Portsmouth. The word, his people had reported, invariably occurred only in conversations between high-ranking managers and officers, and even then was used with great caution. Quidley had even heard General Norris use it once . . . overheard it, rather, as he was stepping into the general's office, and had seen Norris start and lower the phone as he ordered him out to wait.

That word was *Shiloh.* Meaningless . . . as the name of one of the first great battles of the War of Secession, fought on the Tennessee, ending in Johnston's death and mutual heavy losses. But what did it *really* mean? In half an hour or less, Quidley knew, he would understand.

The Bentley braked; he felt Roberts ease off at the last instant so the car would roll gently to a halt, rather than jerk, and he half-smiled. Roberts was a good driver, if a little forgetful in matters of his uniform. Both he and Sawyer sat stiffly as Roberts opened first the colonel's door and then the major's, and saluted. Quidley nodded. "Up here, sir."

Port Control, near the center of Fort Davis, was ten stories tall, high enough for its upper levels to serve as observation posts for seaward firing. The lowest levels were of heavy concrete, with tall windows barely a foot wide framing a colonnaded entrance way. Sawyer sighed audibly as the doors swung closed behind them. "Air conditioned. Thank God."

"Would the Colonel like to freshen up? We have a few minutes left, and——"

"Yes, I sure would. I've been sweating like a pig ever since I got off the train."

"Follow me. sir."

OFFICERS ONLY, a discreet sign advised. The attendant, old, colored, bowed and brought towels and a small tray of toiletries. Sawyer disappeared into the black; Quidley ran a moistened cloth over his face, selected a touch of French cologne, and turned to check his appearance in the full-length mirror.

Aubrey Lee Quidley IV, Major, Confederated States Army (CSA), was tall and thin as a saber. The tailored gray melton army tunic was severely cut save for three stripes of thin gold braid that intertwined gleaming from cuff to elbow. The gray trousers, or jodhpurs, were traced along the outer seam by a single inch-wide buff stripe that disappeared into soft brown knee-height riding boots; their hue was matched by a polished leather Sam Browne belt that crossed his tunic, supporting a holstered .455 Leech & Rigdon semiautomatic. A gold needlework star gleamed at his collar. He nodded in satisfaction; the uniform was right.

And so, too, was the face. It was a typically Quidley face. High forehead. Sandy-dark hair, beginning to recede and to gray slightly at thirty-four. Eyes too of cadet gray, steady and, as he thought of them, forthright; actually they protruded slightly, but this was only visible in profile, and even then not so much unsightly as striking. Except for a barely visible auburn moustache he was

6

smoothly shaven; even without sleep there was time for that. The receding chin alone (which all the Quidleys, a family old and well respected in Raleigh, had) seemed out of place, almost petulant.

The old man was back, flicking subserviently at his shoulders with a stiff brush. "Get that dirty thing away," said Quidley sharply. "Is the Colonel—"

"All done," said Sawyer, emerging from one of the stalls. He sniffed the air, looked at Quidley, looked at the tray, and contented himself with washing his hands.

The staff meeting room, where the briefing would take place, was on the fifth floor. Several other men, officers and civilians, joined them in the elevator. Quidley recognized some of them. Commander Channing, his opposite number for the Navy; they nodded as their eyes met. A Coast Artillery colonel from Battery Davis, whom he'd worked for when he was an observer, several years before. Two dark-suited civilians; Confederate Bureau of Investigation. He didn't know them but they looked like Richmond boys. At the second floor the elevator stopped for a short square man of middle age in Royal Navy uniform, with the gold-encrusted sleeve of an admiral. Moving to the rear, Quidley matched his weathered face with pictures he had seen: Sir Leigh Vickery, the British Empire's liaison with its staunchest ally, and commander of the Allied Western Atlantic Fleet. If he was here, Shiloh must be . . . *important.*

The elevator slowed. Fifth floor.

"After you, sir."

"Identification, please, gentlemen."

"I'm Colonel Sawyer—"

"I need to see your ID, sir." The marine was polite but inflexible. Quidley noted that he carried his sidearm loaded and cocked.

"Here it is, then," said Sawyer, holding out the gray military ID.

"Pass, sir."

The table had places for twenty; when they were all seated it was almost filled. Quidley glanced around at the room. A quiet green carpet. A lectern. A few prints on the paneled walls, mostly War of Secession battle scenes: Sumter; Manassas; Chancellorsville; Gettysburg; the "pivot of victory"; Harrisonville, the famous truce scene after the Brady photograph, Lee and Meade shaking hands warily,

7

an anonymous farmer smirking in the background. Facing north, wide floor-to-ceiling windows overlooked Thimble Shoals Channel and the mouth of the Chesapeake. From his seat Quidley could see all the way to Cape Charles and to the rolling green of the Atlantic to the east. And to the west, a dark stain on the horizon, the buildings and battlements of the enemy.

"Atten*tion*," said one of the guards, and there was a scrape of chairs as everyone rose.

"Seats, please, gentlemen," said General Norris. He paused on his way to the head of the table to shake Vickery's hand and say a word of welcome, then sat down. He glanced at the marines, who stepped outside and closed the door. He looked around the table and played with a pencil for a moment before speaking. "Pardon me, gentlemen, but it's been a bad night . . . we've had a bit of trouble recently, in town . . . but police authorities have assured me it's now under control. Military involvement will be minimal." Short, white-haired, worried-looking, Norris spoke in a stammering, high-pitched voice. "We can, I think, disregard it and proceed directly to the purpose of today's meeting." He smiled briefly at Sawyer. "Earl, I'm glad to see you. I should get up to Castle Thunder more often."

"You're always welcome at the Puzzle Palace, Gen'ral."

"Gentlemen," said Norris, "I'd like to introduce Colonel Earl Sawyer, CSA, Military Intelligence branch, who will present today's briefing. Earl is a good old boy, but I happen to know that under all that Mississippi he is damned sharp . . . and cheek by jowl with the General Staff. Earl." Norris smiled again, looking relieved, and sat back in the chair as Sawyer heaved himself up, opened the briefcase, and began laying out papers.

"Good mornin', all. I'd like to start out by saying that this briefing is *most secret*. As you all understand. Even the name of this project—Shiloh—should be considered vital to the security of the Confed'racy."

Quidley frowned, leaning forward. Sawyer seemed to change on his feet—the drawl thinned out, the cracker manner changing to something more rapid, more efficient. But his attention was not on the man's manner but on his words. Shiloh. At last he would find out what it was.

"I'm going to begin quite a ways back," said Sawyer,

8

looking at Vickery, "for the benefit of the Empire representative. I'll make it as concise as I rightly can.

"For the last hundred and twenty-some years, the Confederacy has been face to face with a powerful foe. Sometimes it's been real war, like it was durin' secession and out West in the 1880s; sometimes, just been a face-off, like in this century. But always we've been facing a powerful and, in the main, hostile North.

"Probably started right during partition. If Lincoln'd let us out peaceful, we might have got along all right afterwards. If we'd lost the war . . . well, who knows. But all through the nineteenth century we were neck and neck, expandin' territorially. The North went west and north, into the midwest, Alaska, West Canada. We went west—till the Arizona war—and then south, into Cuba and the Yucatan and Coahuila. Till today there's seventeen stars in the Stars and Bars."

Norris coughed impatiently, but Sawyer would not be hurried.

"The Palmerston Alliance—eighteen and sixty-four—has been the cornerstone of our security. And we carried our share, too, in the Quadruple Entente, winnin' the Great War in 1916. This Confederate-Empire friendship has stood like a rock amid changin' world events—and made the Yankees and the Czar think twice about attackin' either one of us.

"Today, however—" his voice dropped, and he leaned forward over the table—"that alliance, and our security with it, is bein' threatened. Again, from Philadelphia."

Quidley concentrated. He knew the history. But what could threaten the strongest alliance on the planet?

"As you all know," Sawyer went on, "the Union has just concluded the Japanese war. It was a long one—ever since 1975, the surprise attack on Los Angeles. But last January it ended—with the Union usin' a new weapon."

"The new shell," murmured someone.

"That's right. One of them—fired from a battleship sixty miles at sea—completely destroyed the port city of Yokohama. It's a weapon that is, well, irresistible once it's fired. No armor can withstand it. Its explosive power is terrific. But that's not the worst of it." Sawyer tapped the table for emphasis. "The worst of it is—that the Union's the only country got one."

"Research is proceeding at London and Capetown,"

said Vickery. Heads turned at the dry Dartmouth accent, and the whispers that had punctuated Sawyer's remarks ceased; the Empire liaison carried a lot of weight, in Richmond and elsewhere. "If you don't mind my making a remark—"

"Go right ahead, Sir Leigh."

"As to the new shell . . . our, ah, scientists have been able to duplicate some of the, ah, effects. Others elude us. We might have had our own device by now but two years ago there was an—accident—at the Lochboisdale facility that destroyed most of the equipment and many of the best men in the field.

"What we badly require at this point is certain information on the internal construction of the explosive portion of the shell."

Sawyer nodded. "You're gettin' a bit ahead of me, Sir Leigh, but you're right. So that brings us to the sensitive part of this briefing." He tapped one of the papers he had spread on the table. "The Castle, of course, has got intelligence people in Philadelphia. They've been tellin' us some interesting things. For an example—we thought they had only one shell, the one they fired, and that makin' more was a lengthy affair. Now we come to find out that there's one bein' made a month—turned out of a top-secret plant in Thief River, Minnesota. So they've had time to accumulate a few."

"That's bad news," said Norris.

Sawyer nodded solemnly. "Yes, sir, it is. Real bad. Get into that in a minute. But there's another piece of intelligence bears on it too—a piece we just recently got."

"Go on," said Vickery.

"The Yokohama device was a shell for a naval gun; twenty-four-inch, Yankee battlewagon caliber. Apparently the first six shells were of this model. But now our source in Philadelphia is tellin' us that a new model's being produced. A thirty-inch."

"Union coast artillery," said Quidley.

"That's right, Major. And the first of those thirty-inchers has come off the line—and is earmarked for shipment to Fort Monroe."

"Damn," Norris muttered. Similar words came from others at the table. Sawyer unfolded a map of the area and laid it in front of Vickery. To the admiral he said, laying a finger on Old Point Comfort, "This is Fortress

10

Monroe. By terms of the Treaty of Montreal, 1864, the Union retained this fortified position in Southern territory in order to guard the mouth of the Chesapeake and the Bay cities. Later we built this fort, Davis, across the channel from it. We swapped shots all through the war of '88 but the Yankees held. Since then they've continually modernized and strengthened it. The present thirty-inch disappearing batteries were installed in 1964."

"We have thirty-eight-inch Tredegar rifles on this side," said Norris.

"Yes, sir," said Sawyer politely. "And they've been a powerful deterrent to Yankee adventurism. Up to now. But the whole picture is changin' now. The power balance is still working. But pretty soon it's going to be overturned—in the North's favor."

There was an uneasy stirring about the table. They knew what an upset of that uneasy balance could mean. A renewal of the perennial confrontation in the divided city of Washington. Pressure for concessions in Venezuela and Mexico, just as the oil fields there were reaching peak production under the aegis of Confederate corporations.

And, most dangerous of all, stepped-up Railroad activity among the coloreds.

"Now," said Sawyer, "Shiloh.

"Today is—" he checked the large watch ostentatiously —"The seventeenth of July. Three days from today, on the twentieth, a Union ammunition ship will depart the Colts Neck, New Jersey, arsenal for Hampton Roads. The—cargo—will be aboard. It's scheduled to dock in Phoebus Channel, near Monroe, at 0730, on the twenty-third of July.

"It will never make it. During the night, as it approaches the capes, it will be boarded and sunk by Railroad terrorists. The shell will, presumably, go to the bottom in well over a thousand fathoms of water."

Quidley stroked his moustache nervously. The pause grew too long for him and he said, "Will it, Colonel?"

"Of course not. Oh, the ship will, sure. But the shell won't. We'll have it. It'll be immediately transshipped by rail to the Arsenal and Weapons Laboratory at Columbus, Georgia. There, a group of Allied"—he glanced at Vickery, who nodded slightly—"and government experts will disassemble it for study."

11

Quidley frowned. Something was nagging at his mind, some obscure fact.

Sawyer went on. "That, in brief, will be the project that we've been callin' Shiloh. The General Staff has approved it—our Allies know about it—and, I might say too, it has the personal approval of the President."

*Something obscure—a ship—a fort—*Quidley struggled with his memory. Meanwhile, amid murmurs of surprise and interest, Sawyer passed stapled sheaves of paper around the table. Quidley eyed his. It was the opertion order for the project.

There: He had it. A piece of moldy history, exhumed from his mind, where it had lain since his school days. Hadn't it been an ammunition ship—Union, of course, named the *Star of the West*—that had tried to reach Fort Sumter, in Charleston harbor, and been driven off by the South Carolinians. . . .

. . . Starting the War of Secession?

He glanced up, opened his mouth, but Sawyer was talking again. "That's the general idea, then," he was saying. "I'm sure you've got lots of questions.

"So now, let's get down to details. . . ."

Two

The bouillon was ready. Vyry Lewis turned off the gas
and poured the liquid carefully into a cracked china cup.
The hot steam, beef-redolent, curled up into her eyes,
and whether because of that or for some other reason
she blinked back tears as she walked into the small bedroom of her flat and knelt by the sleeping man in her
bed.

He was powerful even in sleep. Great thick muscles
bulged smoothly beneath the tattooed walnut-brown skin
of his arms. His chest, broad and massive, was covered
with a thick mat of coarse curly hair, strangely exciting
to her as she remembered its abrasiveness against her
nipples. His neck was thick and sinewy; his jaw, broad,
and scarred from numberless waterfront fights; his nose,
mashed almost flat by bottle, fist, or police truncheon.
His hair was cut short in the standard government-worker
haircut.

Vyry set the cup down carefully, trying not to wake
him. *Sleep, now, that's what my man needs,* she thought.
That do him more good than food.

Cautiously, she lifted the worn sheet that covered his
lower body. His chest rose and fell gently with his breathing. The bandage, still in place on his upper thigh,
showed only a small stain of blood. *Thank the Lord,* she

thought, and then smiled at a familiar sight. He was naked underneath the sheet, and his manhood moved and stirred slightly as she watched. . . .

"You rascal," she said, dropping the sheet and smiling into his opened eyes. "Ain't nothing else ever on your mind?"

"So who's stealing looks?" said Johnny Turner. He tried to move his leg and the smile went out of his brown eyes, and Vyry saw that it hurt him. "What time's it gettin' to be, Vy?" he said, looking toward the drawn shades of the window.

" 'Bout the middle of the afternoon. Near to three. You feel like eating, Johnny?"

"Oh, yeah."

"I made you some bouillon."

"Boy-yon?" He took the cup and sniffed at it distrustfully. "Looks like tea. You know I don't like this fancy English whitey shit, Vy."

"That ain't tea, Johnny. It's like beef soup. Go on, try you a little; if you really hungry, I'll cook you up something more."

Eyes on hers, he drank the cup down, then looked into it. "Say, that wa'nt bad."

"Want more?"

"No."

"You want some real food?"

"I want to get up, that's what I want. I shouldn't be here." His eyes moved around the tiny, dingy room. The exposed, rusting radiator; the water-stained ceiling; the small window, cracks patched lovingly but unavailingly with cheap yellowing transparent tape; the few sticks of scarred second- and third-hand furuniture. It was clean, but the neighborhood was poor and in the night he had listened to the furtive scurrying of things in the walls. "I shouldn't be here, in your place. They catch me here, and—"

"Hush, hush your mouth now." She pushed him gently back down on the bed and nailed him there for a moment with a kiss. "You going to stay here with me for a day or two at least. Till you can walk. And I will admit" —she straightened, and smiled—"it sure is nice, having you here all to myself."

She watched him close his eyes and exhale slowly and then she got up and went back into the kitchen alcove.

It's not a bad apartment, she thought, filling a coffee-pot; *not for a CE.* A tiny living room, the bedroom, and then this snug little half-kitchen. Running water and a flush toilet down the hall. Not bad for West Main, the crowded Colored Area of the city. It was nice to be able to share it with Johnny. If only he weren't hurt—she shoved the fear, fear of his dying, fear of his or their capture, out of her mind for the moment and took a packaged meal from the shelf. They were insipid and the food was all starch or fat, but they were issued free to every workcard holder and on her House salary she was glad to have them. She opened it and poured in water from the tap and put it in the oven and then began to set the table. Her dishes, like everything else she owned, *like my life even,* she thought, were mismatched and cracked, patched together. Makeshift.

It's hard, she thought, *being black in this Confederacy.* A long time ago, her mother had told her when she was little, down in South Carolina, when their people had not been Conditionally Emancipated but *slaves,* they'd had a legend that someday, someday, would come the Jubilee.

Ain't been no Jubilee, Mama, she thought, opening the stove and checking the meal with a fork. *President Lee "freed" us over a hundred years ago; but still slaves in all 'cept the name. Free on paper; but we can't vote, can't go no place without a pass. Can't get a job outside the government factories or the government farms. Got to carry the green workcards, got to say "sir" to every white foreman, got to live in the Colored Areas, got to be off the streets ten at night. Got to do what you're told, or you go to the Hospital.*

Vyry shivered. The Hospital. They didn't whip you like they did in the old days. It was far worse, what they did to you there—the machines, the drugs, the "conditioning," they called it.

She'd been lucky. They'd caught her in Charleston, out after curfew with a bulge in her blouse. The patrollers had torn her clothes from her and the pamphlets had fallen to the sidewalk in a white-and-black cascade—Railroad propaganda, carried for a friend she never saw again.

That was a Hospital offense, but she'd been underage, only fifteen. First offense; juvenile; relocate and assign work, said the white judge. She had never seen Charleston or her mother again. She'd hoped once to be a nurse, had even studied it a little, as much as a CE could; she was smart, top of her class in the colored school. But with conspiracy in her file, her life held only two choices. Take the work they assigned, no matter how low, how degrading . . . or turn in her workcard.

And starve.

When she went back to the bedroom to check on Johnny he had his eyes open again, the sheet off, and his fingers were under the edge of the bandage. "You let that alone," she said, too sharply.

"Don't tell me what to do, woman. I got to see it for myself."

"Here, then." She forced the anger out of her voice; that riled him, she knew. "Let me do it."

She pulled a chair up to the bed and wet the blood spot with the dregs of the bouillon. With careful fingers she pulled at the tape until only the clotted blood held the cotton to the wound. She stopped then, and looked at him.

"Go 'head," he said, closing his eyes.

When she had it free and had cleaned the dried blood from the leg she helped him to sit up. "Now, don't touch it. It ain't real serious. See here, the bullet just like scraped you, came in here and out here. This flap of skin might shrivel up, come off."

"Don't look too bad to me," said Turner thoughtfully.

"You go down to the docks like that too soon and you lose your leg. Now I'm going to pour some this whiskey on it and fix you a new dressing. Then we going to eat."

His face tightened when she poured the cheap brown liquor into the gash, but he made no sound. She taped a fresh cotton pad down securely. "There. Now, lean on me, my man, and we'll get you to the dinner table."

Meat loaf, mixed greens, starchy potatoes. Turner asked her for catsup but there had been none in the colored store when she last went. She turned on the radio to get his mind off himself but the first thing that came on was the news.

"*Secession Day festivities interrupted by shooting!* The big news in the Tidewater area today, and the subject of intense police activity, occurred at Town Point late last night. A party of terrorists fired at random into a peaceful, biracial crowd, enjoying Secesh Day fireworks provided by the city and presented by His Honor Mayor Driver Etheridge.

"The terrorists—whose identities are as yet unknown, though Police Chief Richard 'Dick' Mays intimates he has several suspects—fired indiscriminately from the tops of nearby buildings, wounding six and killing two, including a thirteen-year-old child, Williams Burwin Jefferson, of Portsmouth. City officials and community leaders from all walks of life, including influential colored churchmen, have condemned this act as a cowardly and—"

She had watched Turner as anger invaded his eyes but she was not expecting it when he reached out suddenly and knocked the radio to the floor, where it tinkled, squealed briefly, and then fell silent. "Johnny—there's no call to do that!"

"That's lying whitey shit, that's all that is. Their radio. They even jammin' the North so they can't send the truth through. True Negro got no business even ownin' a radio in this country." He chewed angrily, eyes distant, and she put her hand over his.

"Johnny-Jo . . . you tell me the truth, then. I ain't asked you up to now. What all did you and them others do? Did you kill them people last night?"

"Me?" He held up a fist; immense, powerful, the knuckles seamed with bluish-black scars. "You see this fist? This a Railroad fist. This fist for whitey. It's not for strikin' against my own people." He took another mouthful and then continued: "That's a whitey lie we killed them people. Want to know how it really was? Shit, yes, we had guns up there, me and Finnick and Sammy—got 'em from a shipment for Turkey. But we was after whitey, girl. After that fat Mayor, sittin' up there so sleek on the grandstand above all his poor devoted grateful niggers, givin' 'em shows and fireworks. We would have got him, too. Finnick had a clear shot at him."

She waited. He continued, sopping up gravy with a piece of the dry issue bread. "But some cops—they been putting cops on the rooftops now since somebody got that Wallace down in Alabama—they saw us and started shooting before we could. They was shooting down at us and every bullet missed us went right down into the crowd. Well, shit, we haul ass out of there, but them cops kept on shooting. Even when they could see we gone."

Hatred gleamed in his eyes. "And now they blamin' it on *us*."

"Johnny—"

"I don't know, Vy. Sometimes it seem—they ain't no way to do it—no way to fight the cops and the Army and the patrollers and all them fuckin' Toms like their tame Jesus-lovers." He shook his head. "But by Christ I ain't going to stop trying."

She felt sick, and crossed her arms over her stomach. She felt his hand, large and warm, on her neck. "Ain't you hungry, Vy?"

"No, Johnny. I ate while you were asleep."

The whole world, she was thinking. Was the whole world crazy? Or was it only this little corner of it, only the South? The papers all said up North it was no better. But they were all government papers, all white; whatever they printed was probably the opposite of truth.

The North. Used to be once the Underground Railroad was for getting you there. Now the Wall was up—wire, lights, concrete, the dreaded dogs—and "escape" was a euphemism for death. If they didn't shoot you as you crossed, as you hung crucified on the wire, the guards took you right back, to be "conditioned" and put back to work, a zombie, your brain half dead. She had seen them, able to follow simple orders often repeated, able to say little more than "yassuh."

She looked at Johnny Turner, at the ripple of smooth muscle in his arms as he spooned the last of the food into his mouth. Johnny Turner—uneducated, tough, a child of the city. He was a common laborer, a longshoring foreman on the Norfolk waterfront, by day. But by night he was a fighter. And for that—as well as for other things, far more intimate—she loved him.

"That's pretty good," he said at last, leaning back so that the rickety chair creaked alarmingly. "I was powerful hungry. You got anything to drink round here, girl?"

"Just that shine."

"Let's have some." He tried to get up, forgetting his leg, but went suddenly rigid and sank back into the chair. "Whee-oo," he whispered. "That hurt."

"I'll help you. Lean on me."

Together they tottered back into the bedroom. She handed him the bottle, and he poured the teacup full and

18

drank it down and sank gratefully back against the patched pillow.

"Come over here, Vy."

Obediently, she slid closer to him on the bed. His hand, big and rough with callus, slid inside her dress and she felt the strength and yet the gentleness of his fingers on her breast. She leaned forward and their lips met in a kiss but when his hands moved downward she shook them free and stood up. "None of that stuff when you're hurt, Johnny-Jo. Besides, it's five o'clock, and I got to get ready for work."

"Vyry." She had expected him to be angry—when Johnny wanted her, he wanted her *now*—but instead his voice was low, and serious. "Vy—this thing last night, that didn't work. I could have shot back at them cops—killed them, prob'ly—but I didn't want for any of our people down below to get hurt."

"I know that, Johnny."

"I'm going to carry off something big someday, girl. Something really big, that'll make all the white piss-ants in the South shake when they see a black man. Something really big."

"I know, Johnny-Jo." She bent to kiss him a last time, gently, and reached for her purse.

"I wish you didn't have to work at that place," he said, his eyes following her to the door.

"Yes," said Vyry, feeling the familiar numbness begin in her belly, feeling the cold under her heart. "I wish so too. I'll be back in the morning, Johnny. You rest comfortable. Keep it warm for me. And don't answer the door."

Three

Quidley, his mind busy with the implications of Shiloh, was descending the steps of the Port Control building when he felt the hand on his elbow. He turned to shake it off—he had never liked men's hands on him—and found himself facing a smiling, obviously much-excited Sawyer.

"Great meeting!" the Mississippian said. "Great! General Norris—he's first rate. I knew him before this. Smart staff, too—and that Brit admiral's no dummy. This is all going to go right accordin' to plan!"

"I surely hope so, Colonel." Quidley looked at Sawyer's hand until the other man dropped it, and looked around; where the devil had Roberts got to? "Have they assigned you a vehicle, sir?"

"Don't think anyone has, come to think on it."

"The general must have overlooked it. Why don't you take mine, the Bentley? My man will drive you over to the club, and he'll stay at your disposal for as long as you need him."

Sawyer looked startled and a little displeased. "Sure grateful, Major, but I—well, I sort of thought you might be willin' to show me around the town a little. Been a coon's age since I've seen this part of the country."

Quidley sighed inside. He understood. Sawyer wanted to be entertained. Next—in the crude way of his class—he would offer to buy the drinks.

"Why don't we do the town together, Major? Hoist a few? I'll take care of the check."

"To tell the truth, sir, I'd like to. But I have a previous engagement. Dinner, with my fiancée—you understand. Any additional time tonight will have to go into reading this," and he lifted his own briefcase, "—the operation order. And preparing my own activities to mask our intentions and confuse the enemy."

"I see." Sawyer looked disappointed, but only said, "I'll make myself at home at the club, then."

"Again, sir, I'm sorry."

"That's all right, Major, that's all right."

The Bentley appeared at last. Roberts, in the front seat, was hatless. Quidley motioned for him to stay inside and opened the door for Sawyer himself, then leaned in the driver's window. "Take the colonel to the Officer's Club, Sergeant. Remain at his disposal tonight. Pick me up at eight A.M. tomorrow, at home."

"Yes, sir," said Roberts, smiling. Quidley ignored the grin and fixed the top of his head with a long look of distaste and disapproval until the sergeant understood and groped for his cap on the seat beside him and jammed it on. He saluted quickly, but Quidley was already turning away, stepping up to the curb.

He saluted Sawyer as the car pulled away, then straightened and walked briskly toward the nearby fort motor pool. *I'll get a small car,* he thought, *one of the Tredegars or a Dallas.* As he was saluted and scurried after at the pool office his slight anger with Sawyer and with the colored driver dissipated. They were only minor annoyances, and though it was wearisome to have to cope with them it was something a gentleman learned to do without showing strain. He was assigned a new white Dixie Traveller two-door and as he tossed swagger stick, briefcase, and cap on the seat and slid inside he was thinking: *Sharon.*

She had been twenty-three, he thirty-three, when they'd met a year before. Met, of all places, at a dance at the club. As he slowed for the gate he smiled, remembering his first sight of her, radiant in a clinging black silk sheath and pearls. The black silk had made her blonde hair seem to glow and the pearls had seemed darker than her skin, and she had been surrounded by young officers eager to dance.

Hurtling east, toward the beach, he smiled again to think how he had walked away from the party with her. She was fascinated by him. *Fascinated*, he thought. By his poise, his obvious breeding (the Quidleys, orginally of Raleigh, on his father's side; the Lees and the Dardens, of Virginia, on his mother's), by the importance of his billet as Security Officer.

Fascinated. He smiled as he made the turn south on the road that led to her home. Ah, well. There were some things about Sharon Sue Hunt that he did not understand, and a few that made him admiringly frustrated . . . but he had to admit, she was the most beautiful woman that he had ever met; and she was in love with him.

At precisely six he pulled the car into the twisting, gravel-surfaced road that led from the main highway back to her house. Like most of the homes in Lynnhaven —an expensive and, of course, exclusively white area set back from Virginia Beach—it was isolated, set far back from the approach road in a vast stretch of near-virgin forest. He stopped the car where he usually did, halfway off the drive, directly in front of the house.

It was a house that he always had to stop for a moment and admire. Tall, brick, two-story in the colonial style, it stood near the banks of a picturesque inlet of Hampton Roads, surrounded by shrubbery and by an immense lawn that demanded two Negroes to keep up. She owned it, had bought it just before they had met. A good Tennessee family. He began to lock the car, then shrugged, picked up the briefcase, and took it with him up the short brick-surfaced walk. The door opened as he lifted his hand to knock, and he smiled; but it was only Ella, the maid.

"Miss Shar'n be down directly, Mist' Quidley. You please to come in?"

"Yes, thank you, Ella. How are you?" he said, keeping the smile. He took great care to be nice to Ella. One never knew when or how the goodwill of a domestic could be useful.

"Take your hat, sir? An' that bag?"

"I'll keep this."

"Jus' put it in the hall closet here, get it out of your way."

"Oh, all right, Ella." The briefcase disappeared behind a door. *Well, it's locked*, he reassured himself. *Besides, this is Sharon's.*

"Get you a drink, Mist' Quidley?"

"Perhaps a small one before dinner, yes. A sherry?"

"Yes, sir. Why don't you sit yourself down in your favorite chair there and just wait for Miss Shar'n to come down."

"Thank you, Ella."

He sank gratefully into the deep soft leather of the chair. It had been a long day, since the emergency call late the night before, when the riots had broken out. Since then he'd been on the move nearly every minute, investigating the riot, getting patrols out to protect federal property, reporting hourly to Norris, who was nervous as a cat in heat, then having to pick up Sawyer on ten minutes' notice. And then the briefing . . . Ella came back with sherry in a fine cut-crystal glass and he thanked her absently and slid back into his thoughts of Shiloh.

His first impression of the plan had been that it was incredibly dangerous—seizing a Union ship was nothing less than an act of war. But that could well be an advantage, though a hidden one. Certainly it was risky, but the very Confederacy had been born in risk and incredible danger. What if R. E. Lee had played it safe at Gettysburg? What if Wilson had decided to watch and wait and had stayed out of the war in 1914? It would have dragged on . . . would have ended years later in some draggled bloodied stalemate, leaving Europe exhausted. And then what might have happened, to Germany, to Russia? And McAdoo, and Dixie socialism in the thirties. . . .

"Daydreaming again, Quidley?"

He rose, and turned. She was poised on the stair, smiling mischievously; she was stunning, and knew it, in a long dinner dress of dark green satin, subtly interwoven with a pattern of silver.

"You're lovely," he said, and moved across the carpet to catch her up in his arms.

"Oh. Careful, my makeup—you're so strong, Aubrey." His chin brushed her cheek as she turned her head skillfully from his lips, and he smelled jasmine. He had meant to hold her but somehow found himself walking toward the dining room with her, and she was calling, "Jesse! Serve, please. The Major's hungry!"

Over a candle flame, over glowing old silver and damask and marinated steak with sautéed mushrooms and wild rice and Hopping John and corn pie and a delicate scup-

23

pernong wine, her face floated opposite him. She talked almost without pause, maneuvering her fork rapidly with pale delicate blue-veined fingers; he found the weird West Tennessee nasal twang of her speech strange and sexually exciting at the same time. She talked about her work, some volunteer duty, useful but respectable, out at the Portsmouth Military Hospital; talked about her "daddy," as she called him, a lawyer, one of the Brownsville Hunts, a man of bourbon and horses and money; talked about her troubles with Jesse and Ella.

He was not really listening. Much of what she said did not interest him, bored him even, though he nodded at the right places and made enthusiastic or condemnatory sounds when her glance and pause seemed to demand it. He felt comfortable, though, felt that he belonged. He understood her; that was it, he felt; she was like him, one of the better people, the more refined, and she understood him, too. He finished the last spoonful on his plate and patted his lips with the napkin and caught her glance and recalled the tone of her voice on the last word she had said and nodded in agreement.

"It's not as if I asked them to do very much, you know . . . but it's different, as Daddy says, now that any of them can count on getting a soft government job and free meals, too. And it's so *hard* to replace them when they go." She pouted slightly. "Not that I really *need* them, in this little place, but it's the convenience, when I come home at night after *slaving* in that *awful* hospital. . . ."

He nodded again, agreeing in monosyllables. Jesse cleared the plates away. He was happy just watching, watching her thin triangular face, the wide slightly empty blue eyes, the mouth rich and pale and tense. The gown was loose and was cut low, and he could see blue veins in the candlelight leading from her thin neck to the slight swell of her bosom.

"Aubrey, darlin'! I asked you a question! What are you thinkin' on, anyway?"

"I'm sorry, Sharon Sue. I was really . . . just thinking on how beautiful you look by the candlelight."

"You go on. But I love to hear it. You know *that*, Aubrey." She giggled and then looked toward the kitchen and picked up the little silver bell and tinkled it. "Jess-*ee!* Are we going to have that dessert any time tonight?"

"Yes, Miss Shar'n."

"Well, hurry up."

"Yes, Miss Shar'n."

When it came, Quidley toyed with the strawberry confection. Jesse hovered nearby, waiting for him to taste it. "Say, this is quite tasty," he said.

"Miss Shar'n made that herself, Mist' Quidley."

"You don't say. Well, it's really good."

"I can cook when I have time," she said. "There's more in the kitchen. No, thank you, Jesse, I'm watching my weight this week."

"Mist' Quidley, do you want coffee?"

"Thank you, yes. I've been up since eleven last night."

"Since eleven! No wonder you're so quiet. I bet it was those riots, wasn't it, Aubrey?"

"Partly," he said.

"I know it. Are the nigras going to come burn me out here at Lynnhaven?"

"Not much danger of that."

"Well, then, what is it, Aubrey?" She had dropped the bantering tone that she normally used with him and he looked up, surprised. "You *are* looking awfully serious tonight. What's it about?"

"Nothing. Nothing really."

"Something at the fort."

"You might say that."

She looked sharply at him and then rang again, and when Jesse came out said, "Jesse, the Major and I will be alone after dinner."

"Yes, Miss Shar'n. Me and Ella got some things to dust upstairs we ain't got to yet." The old man withdrew, bowing.

She turned back to Quidley, her eyes suddenly gay. "Will you sit with me, Aubrey? That useless old Jesse has finally fixed the swing, and—"

"I'd love it."

"I'll get us something wet. Some lemonade? I'm having something a bit stronger, I think."

"You can include me in that if it's your father's stock."

"Oh, yes, sir. He sent me up a fresh case. Would you like a bottle or two to take back with you later?"

"Don't want to impose—"

"Oh, bullcrap. There, now I've gone and shocked you. Are you shocked, Aubrey? Properly shocked?" She was

25

up now, laughing, swaying against him as they stood close. "Up west Tennessee we're not so refined as your fine Virginia families. But we're good folks and loyal Rebels anyway, even if there were bluebellies there through most of the War. Here, now, you go on out back and unbutton that tight collar and I'll get us a little drink."

He turned to leave the room, and did not see how, behind him, her eyes lingered on his back in a long, opaque, impenetrable stare, lasting for several heartbeats before he was out of her sight.

The garden was dark and, except for the distant sounds of insects, silent in the July night. A sliver of moon silvered the leaves of the ginkgoes that shaded the swing. Lightning bugs flickered coldly in the hedges, between which, farther down the long lawn, he could see the gleam and ripple of water. The swing creaked as he settled himself into it and obediently unhooked the tight collar and exhaled. Several hours in dress uniform made his head feel like a ripe plum sometimes.

She was not, he mused, a demonstrative girl. Not physically. She could be affectionate in a kittenish, playful way, but he had never been allowed, even after the ring, to do anything untoward.

You have to respect that, he told himself. That was, after all, good breeding, the standards he would expect for a wife. And it was not as if he had no other outlets. Still, it could be frustrating. She was so beautiful—her waist so small and fragile, those long legs so exasperatingly curved, feet so tiny in the high heels he had never seen her without. When she stood close. . . .

He stared at the wandering insect beacons and waited for his drink and dreamed hopelessly of lowering himself between her damp and waiting thighs.

"Here you are, Aubrey." She rustled as she sat down, so close that her perfume was overpoweringly sweet. It nibbled at his self-control like subtle acid, and to restrain himself he gulped at the drink. There was very little water but he enjoyed really good bourbon that way. No gainsaying it, her father had excellent taste in whiskey.

"Damned fine bourbon."

"It is." She laughed softly. The west Tennessee was still there, but mellowed in her near-whisper. He reached out his arm and she slipped under it, and he felt the warmth of her body through his tunic.

26

"Now you can tell little old Sharon Sue what's bothering you. You say it isn't the nigras."

"No. They're under control. Nobody hurt but their own people."

"How strange."

"Yes."

"It's not the coloreds? The Railroad?"

"No, really it's the Yankees, if you have to know."

"I don't *have* to know." She turned her face up to his, reminding him of a pale blossom in the moonlight, and he could see her lips parted and eyes faraway and half-closed. It was only the third time he had kissed her and he was surprised and pleased when her lips parted for him.

It was strange; it was very strange, he thought, his lips on hers. Here he was with the woman he loved; a woman of his own class, almost of his own aristocratic breeding; a woman, moreover, of undeniable beauty and charm; a woman who was capable of arousing him with a hundred subtle tricks and wiles, but who drew back with that strange high shrilling laugh whenever he tried in his own way to grow closer with her. Perhaps if he had what he wanted, he would no longer—no, he could not allow himself to think that. Not about the woman he would someday marry.

But if only, he thought, feeling guilty even as he thought it, *if only she was not quite so witless. . . .*

"Yankees?"

"Mmmm. Yes. Over't Fort Monroe."

"Making trouble?"

"Might say that."

"Kiss me some more, hm?"

The dress was low and now that his eyes were adapting to the dimness of the garden he could see the sweet thrusting of her breasts against satin. Her head was on his shoulder, and he was rigid within and soft as wax without as he traced the line of her neck gently with a finger.

"Your hands are cold."

"From the glass."

"Is it empty? Can I get you another, Aubrey?"

"Why, sure enough it is," he said, genuinely surprised.

When she came back with the glass she hesitated, then set it on the lawn table beside the swing and raised her hands to her head. Golden waves of hair spilled down in the moonlight.

"Sit here," he suggested.

"Well—all right. For a little while."

With her head on his lap she seemed helpless, crumpled, like a limp drowned body thrown up by a wave. He stroked her fine soft hair gently. From somewhere in the distance came a low humming sound that gradually swelled to a vaguely menacing chorus. "What's that?" she said, stirring.

"Cicadas."

"Cic—?"

"Locusts, they call them. But they're really cicadas. They swarm every—I think it's every seventeen years. You're probably too young to remember—"

"*Locusts,* Aubrey?"

"Not the kind in the Bible. These are harmless. Oh—listen."

The unearthly humming of the insects had changed, merging into a distant harmony that rose and fell, rose and fell. Quidley felt her stiffen in his arms. "Aubrey—it's *weird.*"

"I remember when I was small," said Quidley. "On my great-aunt's farm in Carolina. They came one summer, crawling out of the earth under the trees."

"What are they like?"

"Like big bugs, or moths, maybe inch and a half long, with fat bodies. Oh—and wings." He had almost forgotten his great-aunt, a small angry woman who held him tranced for hours with stories. "She had to catch one to show me; I was frightened. They have"—he traced the letter in the air with a finger—"a bright red W on their wings. She said it was a warning."

"Of what?"

"War."

"Was there one?"

"Of course not." He laughed. "She scared the dickens out of me, too. That night—when they started that humming—she told me they were calling me. Out in the woods. Au . . . brey. Au . . . brey. I believed her."

"Oh, Aubrey, what a horrible thing to say to a child." She shivered.

"No lasting effects," said Quidley. He stroked her

neck, long, white. Her breasts, rising and falling slowly with her breathing, beckoned him.

"What kind of trouble?"

"Beg pardon, Sharon Sue?"

"What kind of trouble the damn Yankees making over't the fort?"

"Oh, they're shipping in a new kind of shell. Don't tell anyone about it."

"Of *course* not, Aubrey. I wouldn't—"

"I know. But it's secret. Just so you don't repeat it."

"I feel honored that you tell me things like that. I really do. But after all, we're engaged. That's almost married. And there aren't any secrets between a man and his wife, are there?"

"I suppose not."

"And I do feel—tonight—as if we were really close, Aubrey—"

"Oh yes," he breathed. Only a little move now of the hand—

"This shell, darling—"

"Oh—well, it's coming in on a ship. Army's going to capture it, and then we'll be able to copy it, make our own."

His hand, moving as gently as a man catches butterflies, slipped underneath the edge of her bodice. He felt the trembling softness beneath. Oh, God, he thought. She lay quiet, eyes closed. "Sharon—I—"

"Aubrey," she said.

"Yes?"

"It's cold."

"I can warm you—"

"And there are mosquitoes coming out. I hear them. And that creepy sound—"

He knew the tone of her voice and what she meant. She had let him have this much and now she meant him to stop. He swallowed, half-angry, but admiring at the same time, and slipped his hand out from underneath her clothes.

"Another bourbon?" She sat up, shrugging her dress back in place as if his hand had never touched her. "Really we should go back inside. The bugs are all coming out and I get so bit up—"

"All right," he said unhappily.

She laughed, high, and leaned against him for the

space of a moment and kissed him chastely on the cheek. "Don't be tiresome, darling. Another year, you know, and we'll be married. I've told you how Daddy feels about short engagements. If not for that I might—well, bend the rules."

"Hm."

"Though I know that if I did you wouldn't respect me."

"Well—"

"You're not so hard to figure out, Aubrey. I know what you want. But more than anything else I want my husband-to-be to respect me. The way I want to respect him."

Quidley stood and took several deep breaths to quiet the trembling in his legs. He had never felt like this. No, he had, but years ago—as a cadet at Virginia Military Institute, parading the Post after dark with—what had been her name?—murmuring in his ear. He felt weak.

"Come on inside, Aubrey."

He swallowed the last bourbon down quickly and looked at his watch. It was nine o'clock—early yet.

"What's the matter? Do you have to go?"

"I'm sorry. I really ought to get back to the fort."

"Ella. Ell-*al* The Major's things!"

"Here you are, Mist' Quidley."

"I had a briefcase, too."

"Find his briefcase, Ella."

"Yes'm. Here it is."

"Well, good night, Sharon Sue."

"Good night, Aubrey. It was so nice having you. Tomorrow?"

"Depends on work. I'll try. Good night."

"Good night," he said, pressing her hand one last time.

He sat in the car for a long moment and thought. He was as hard as a gun barrel and there was only one place to go. After a moment he decided that as long as he was going there he might as well swing by the club and see if Sawyer had gone into town yet.

"So this is the famous Chicken's," said Earl Sawyer, leaping out eagerly as Quidley steered the Traveller into a space marked "reserved." "Even up at Castle Blunder we've heard of this place."

"I think you'll like it," said Quidley, joining him on the worn brick sidewalk. They looked up at the narrow building for a moment, each savoring his own anticipation of pleasure.

Bute Street was narrow, tree-lined, not far from the waterfront, yet still genteel. The homes were brick, most of them over a century old, with leaded glass and intricate wrought-iron and shaved-brick lintels. Chicken's was set back from the street a few feet and their boots echoed from the darkened houses as they mounted the steps. Sawyer glanced around uncertainly. "Say, Major—are you sure this here is the place?"

"This is it, all right, sir," said Quidley. He pointed to a tiny brass plaque beside the door. It carried four letters in discreet continental script: CSAB. "The official officer's brothel for the Hampton Roads Military District."

The first floor was narrow but long, dimly lit, with patterned velvet wall hangings in shades of deep red and burgundy; but not, for all that, very different from the bar in the officers' clubs in every fort. Quidley checked his and Sawyer's hats, decided to keep his briefcase with him, and steered the colonel to the long polished walnut bar that lined the entire length of one wall.

"Major Quidley! How you doin' tonight, sir!"

"Fine, George, fine. Colonel, they take bourbon down in Mississippi, don't they?"

"When they can afford it, Major, when they can afford it." Sawyer laughed short and hard. "Otherwise we make do with the mountain dew. But say, whyn't you call me Earl? Hey? No need to be so stiff-collar long's we're workin' together."

Quidley nodded, wincing as Sawyer tilted the double shot of straight bourbon up and set it down empty. Already he was regretting that he had thought of bringing the man. He could have had a quiet drink, burned out his lust with one of the girls, gone home quietly . . . now he would have to endure all kinds of drinking and poor-white camaraderie. Well. That was part of what breeding meant: courtesy under pressure. And after all, through whatever oversight, the man *was* a Confederate officer.

"Sure, Earl," he said, and smiled. He raised his own glass, still nearly full, as Sawyer signaled for another. "Confusion to the damn Yankees."

"Damn Yankees," echoed Sawyer. The bartender smiled into the mirror. They drank, Sawyer swiftly, Quidley still sipping at his first. George had given him the house's best—*he knows me,* Quidley thought—but as he rolled it behind his tongue he had to admit that it wasn't quite as good as Old Man Hunt's.

"This is damned good liquor," said Sawyer, gesturing to George. "One good thing the planter class left us. Right, Aubrey?"

"I'm not sure I know what you mean, sir."

"Earl, man!"

"Earl."

"I mean our precious upper classes." Sawyer finished the third double bourbon and stared at Quidley, his broad face flushed, his eyes sparkling. "Say, where'd you go to school?"

"The Post."

"That so? Thought you was a ring-knocker from the way you dressed. Say, that reminds me of a story." The bartender paused with the drink and Sawyer threw a twenty-dollar piece on the bar. He took Quidley's elbow. "Say, you listening?"

"Yes," said Quidley.

"Seems there was this Mississippi Guard officer—I came up through the Guard—who goes into the latrine with this VMI fella. They use the, you know, the john, and the VMI fella is standin' there washing his hands. Well, the other fella zips up and starts to leave and the Post officer says in this high-and-mighty tone, 'At VMI they teach us to wash our hands after we use the can.' and the guard officer says, "Well, in the Guard they teach us not to piss on our hands.' " He threw back his head and laughed, spilling some of the fresh drink. "Let's move to a table, Quid."

"All right, Earl."

Their sitting at one of the round tables, away from the slightly more brightly lit bar, was the signal for two of the girls to leave the long table where they sat together. Quidley looked around the room as they approached. It was a quiet night on Bute Street, apparently; the only other men there were four Navy types, ensigns and lieutenants, playing "ship, captain, and crew" with the house dice.

"Hello, Colonel, Major. Looking for company?"

Two women, one dark, one mulatto or quadroon, both in standard House long dresses. Quidley nodded to the tall dark one, but he felt the man beside him stiffen in his chair. "Something wrong, Earl?"

32

"I don't drink with niggers," said Sawyer loudly.

The women's faces froze, and they turned to leave. "Wait, please," said Quidley. "Look, you"—he looked at the tall one—"you sit down over here, by me. Earl, do you mind?"

"You do what you like. But I don't—"

"And please send over a free employee for the Colonel."

The woman who arrived was undoubtedly the fattest woman at the House, and Quidley was hard put to keep from staring at her; but the fact that she was white seemed to satisfy Sawyer, and they were soon talking and drinking together like old friends. Relieved, Quidley turned back to the woman beside him, and almost spilled his drink.

She was breathtaking; that was the only word he could find. She was as tall as he was, even sitting down; tall, but with a magnificent shape. Her neck was curved, long, inviting, with the velvety dark skin set off by small curved circlets of gold (a CE was permitted the use of jewelry during working hours at the CSAB).

It was her face that made him decide to start breathing again. She was not what he could have called beautiful, but in her presence something seemed to happen to him. The lines of her face were flawless and regular, like a black cameo, with high, almost Asiatic cheekbones, a fine wide chin, and a long sensuous mouth. Her hair, thick, glossy black, and long, was piled high, as Sharon's had been.

"You're new here," he said.

"Not so new. I was working the weekends before."

"Yes—that's right, I'm usually in on weekdays." He cast about for something more to say, to make her talk; he liked her voice, low and purring, with a hint of reserve or pride or anger. She kept her eyes in front of her, on the table; her hands were folded in her lap. Beside them Sawyer and the woman chattered on.

"Would you like a drink?"

"No, thank you."

"You gentlemen satisfied? Oh, it's Mr. Quidley. Nice to see you, sir. Your regular night, isn't it?"

"Madame Chicken. Hello." It was the manager, a short wide motherly woman. "Yes, we're enjoying ourselves immensely. I'd like you to meet Colonel Sawyer, from Richmond—Earl, Mrs. Rosen, the housemother."

"Pleased," said Sawyer, not rising; nor did he take his hand from the large woman's breast. "You got a hell of a nice cathouse here, ma'am."

"You like her?" said Chicken to Quidley. "You take to her? Go upstairs with her. Do you both good. Use number ten."

"Shall we?" he said to the girl.

"That's what I'm here for."

He eyed her from the back as they moved between tables to the rear. Sawyer shouted a lewd suggestion after him; the naval men laughed. She had nice hips, he thought, narrow but well rounded under the dress. He yielded to temptation and put his hands on them.

"Not here," she said, coldly. He dropped his hands, feeling vaguely ashamed, and then felt a wave of anger. What right had a colored to tell an officer, and a gentleman, what to do?

Nevertheless, he controlled himself and kept his hands in his uniform pockets till the elevator stopped and she led him down the hall and opened the door of number 10 for him. He stepped inside and looked around. It was a small room, but a cut above the ordinary, with deep carpet, wood furniture, long blood-scarlet curtains that framed the same moon he had seen in the garden, but higher, now, in the sky. And a large, brilliantly polished brass bed.

"Nice room."

"You've seen lots like it, haven't you."

Again he caught the edge of contempt, of disrespect. She had not even bothered to call him "sir." This time he let himself go. He pinioned her arms, shook her hard, and then threw her on to the bed, which creaked dangerously. "Let's have the proper respect from you," he said, standing over her. "Let's not forget your place."

She stared up at him. Her eyes were dark and had nothing for him but hate. But she said nothing more, only lay and watched as he unbuttoned his tunic and unbuckled the Sam Browne and the holster and hung them carefully over a chair back, smoothing the wrinkles from the tunic. When he stepped out of his boots she got up reluctantly and let her dress fall. She wore nothing underneath.

34

"What does the Major desire?"

"Don't be sullen, girl. Just do your job."

"My job," she repeated, and the bitterness was still there, though no longer directed against him. *All right, bitch,* he thought. *I don't care what you think as long as you keep your mouth shut.*

They were both naked now and he pushed her back down on the bed. He lay beside her for a moment enjoying her nakedness. What a lovely body she had, he thought, running his hand lightly over her breasts and the soft mound of her belly and the warm wiry thicket between her legs. She lay motionless, head turned away, but he felt her shudder as his fingers slipped inside the damp.

"Does the Major want some dope?"

"Some what?"

"Mary jane. Jimson weed. Dope."

"They have that here?"

"It's mine. Not the House's."

"I'll pay," he said.

She seemed a little friendlier now as she got up and searched in some arcane pocket in her dress. He watched, feeling his blood rise as she bent naked and then came back to the bed. Damned nice. An image of Sharon as she might be nude rose unbidden to his mind but was sharply suppressed. Thoughts of her did not belong here. Not here, not with this colored whore, this servant of his animal pleasure.

"You smoke this before, Major?"

"On post out West. A lot of it gets up there from Mexico."

"Is it cheap there?"

"Well, there seemed to be a lot of it around. I suppose it was."

"They say it's illegal up in the Union."

"I wouldn't doubt it. They're even down on tobacco now. The puritans never knew how to live. It took the cavaliers for that." He heard the smugness in his own tone and was almost ashamed.

"You a cavalier?" she said. "You from some high and mighty old family, Major?"

"Don't talk about my family."

"Sorry." She licked cigarettes together expertly and

35

placed one carefully between his lips. She lit it and then her own.

She smoked steadily, sucking it deep, burning the herb recklessly. Quidley smoked more slowly, wondering if it were true that the stuff was illegal up North. He remembered they were down on amateur whiskey, too. He felt suddenly glad that he was free and southern, and not some dull anonymous citified Northern bourgeois.

Her breasts were cool as he stroked them. She lay back, still smoking, as he rolled over onto her and forced her long legs apart with his knee. Her eyes were becoming glassy and as he slid himself inside, gasping with the pleasure of her she blew a ring of liquid smoke over his shoulder into the cool dark moonlight.

When he was done with her he lay on his back and looked at the moon. It was red and shimmering and he knew the stuff he had smoked was strong. Already he wanted her again, but he remembered Sawyer downstairs and that he had to be back at the fort at eight, six hours from now. He struggled up and pushed his legs into his trousers.

Dressed, he turned. She was still lying there, legs apart, as he had left her. He could see a gleam of his moisture on the inside of her thigh.

"You're not getting up?"

"I'll lie here for a minute. Major."

"What do I owe you?"

"Five for me. Two for the grass. Plus—oh, fuck it. That's all you owe me, Major. Major Cavalier."

He thumbed several dollars from his wallet and laid them on the sheet beside her. Money and her musky smell mixed with his. The pink-and-gray bills curled noiselessly over the endless space of a second. He turned to go, but stopped by the door. She lay dark in the moonlight, a pool of shadow in the tumbled sheets.

"What's your name?" he said.

"I'll be here, Major. It's my job. Remember . . . my job."

"What if I like you? Want to see you again?"

The shadow moved slightly. He could see that she had put an arm over her eyes, as if to block out the world, to block out him.

"Ask for Vyry," she said.

36

Four

She had left again, and he was alone. Alone in her bed, staring at the flies circling near the ceiling and pacifying the ache in his leg with an occasional pull at the bottle, which was now close to empty.

"Shit," said Johnny Turner to the four dingy walls.

He was bored. And on edge, in a remote kind of way. He was safe here at Vyry's, he knew, unless the po-lice made a house-to-house search. And even then, if they tried that through the whole West Main area of the city, he'd be seventy years old before they ever got to him.

But he didn't like being cooped up.

Around noon thirst moved him and he got up carefully, easing most of his weight to the good leg, and hobbled into the kitchen. He drank a glass of cold water, staring out the edge of the window.

He stiffened as someone rapped at the door.

Three knocks. A pause. Two knocks. A pause. One.

It should be all right. That was the Railroad knock. But if the white law had captured one of them in the wild flight from downtown . . . he limped quickly to the sideboard and selected one of Vyry's kitchen knives, a serrated six-inch meat blade with a sturdy pressed-wood handle. He approached the front door warily, standing to the side in case they fired through it.

"Who there?"

"Hey, it's Bo, Johnny, lemme in."

Turner slid off the chain, but kept the blade ready until the small black man in the faded green work clothes was inside and the door had been locked again. Then he lowered it, and they looked at each other and clenched their fists and touched them and then grinned.

"How you doin', Johnny?" said Bo Finnick.

"Oh, jus' middling. How you?"

"Jumpin' to whitey's tune, brother."

"Not for much longer, man. Somethin's got to give."

"Well . . ." drawled Finnick. He had a twisted, wiry, beaten-looking face, and thin whitish hair, though he was only about forty. He could be, Turner knew, a clown—on the docks, he could turn the toughest longshoring job into a lark with his shanties and his wry mocking jokes behind the white supervisors' backs. At the same time he could act the perfect Tom. He was the smallest man on Turner's crew—but he could be, with the proper leadership, a killer.

"What's happenin'?"

"Come to tell you about a meeting," said Finnick, looking at Turner's leg. "But I guess you be out of it for a while."

"What, this? This just be a little gnat bite. What meeting? Where? Here, sit down, man. Here, sit down. I got a little of this corn left—"

Finnick looked into the cracked cup, sniffed at the liquor, and downed it with a quick jerk of his head. "That's good," he said, licking his lips.

"Want 'nother?"

"Nah," said the smaller man, "I got to go. I got me a hidey-hole till night. Then I'm going down to the meeting."

"Where is it?"

"You know the R R Smith warehouse, down the Elizabeth? Where they unloads them little German cars, puts 'em on the Norfolk and Western spur?"

"Yeah."

"We're meeting round the back, on the river side. Word is they's a man from higher up in the Road goin' to be there."

Turner stared at him, and Finnick nodded. "Must be

pretty fuckin' important for the road to send a man down here in the middle of a crackdown," said Turner.

"Hear tell it is," said Finnick. "Well, man—if you can make it in on that leg we sure do need you."

"I be there, I said."

"Take care then, bro'."

When he had rechained the door Turner sat down, scratching absently around the bandage, and thought. After a time he put the cap back on the bottle and went back to bed.

It began to turn dark outside the window about nine. No one other than Bo had come by all day, and Vyry, he knew, would not be back from the House till three or four in the morning, this being a Friday night. He got up and limped into the kitchen and drank some more water and looked at the kitchen knife. It would fit so well inside his shirt . . . but no, it was insane to carry a blade. A routine search by a patroller, and . . . there would not even be a hearing. CEs were not allowed to carry weapons, though the longshoremen had work knives that were kept at the docks. And firearms . . . for a colored to be caught with one was a capital offense. He left the knife where it was.

Okay, Turner. So you going to the meeting. Then let's go. He pulled on the green waterfront work pants and shirt and clipped his workpass to his left pocket. It would not be good being out after curfew but maybe if he talked Tom he could convince any curious patrollers that he was on the night shift. He eased the door open and slipped out, hearing the lock click shut behind him. Now he could not return. Vyry had the only key.

West Main was a maze of narrow, poorly paved streets and refuse-littered alleys. In the previous seventy years hundreds of thousands of farms and plantation Negroes from farther south had been sucked toward the growing government industries of the Tidewater. It was not a free life, nor a luxurious one, but there were no other choices for CEs reassigned from farm chores in Tarboro or High Point or Lawrenceville to the new factories; and it was better than starving when the white landowners turned you out and brought in tractors to till the land. They would have gone north, to Detroit or Phillie or New York, but the border barred their way. So they migrated—to Atlanta, to Selma and Augusta and Charleston and Macon, and especially to Tidewater and to the sprawling war-born Tredegar Works in Greater Richmond. And were everywhere channeled into the downtown slums— the Colored Areas.

Now Turner walked in the shadows and felt at home. No white patroller would enter West Main after dark. Black families sat together on sagging unlighted porches and talked softly; a radio blared a hymn from a darkened alley; a swaying female form called to the limping man, who joked back, taking no offense and giving none.

He walked south, down unlit zigzag streets, toward the waterfront district of the East Elizabeth River. Faintly he could already hear the sounds of ships in the channel. Three short whistles; there was a ship backing out into the stream, getting underway, filled perhaps with North Carolina tobacco, or pulpwood, or coal; or heavy machinery or weapons from Tredegar, bound for India or South Africa or Borneo. A longshoreman saw them going out, the heavy wooden boxes like long coffins. The Confederacy was the arsenal of the Empire; and all of it, Turner reflected, keeping the black and yellow and brown man down. . . .

Shit, Johnny, you gettin' to be a motherfuckin' philosopher, he thought, smiling at himself. *Let's keep our 'tention on gettin' to the meeting on time.*

The streets broadened gradually and became straighter and better paved as he crossed the eastern end of the downtown area. Here and there a bar spilled music and colored light out into the street. Street lamps began to appear as he turned onto Highland Road and crossed the Norfolk and Western tracks. He was beginning to feel relieved when the sound of a motor came from behind him. He stiffened but forced himself to walk on as the light swept over him and then brakes squealed.

"You there! Nigger!"

He stopped and turned. An old two-tone Dixie. Four white faces, pale behind the windshield. A shotgun's double barrel draped out the rear window. A beer can in the driver's hand.

Patrollers.

Turner grew suddenly shorter by a couple of inches. His arms hung foolishly. He shuffled closer to the car, and smiled.

"Yassuh?"

"Git that shotgun inside the car," said one of the men, in a tone of authority.

"Fuck you, Billy, and the horse—"

"You, nigger," said the man on Turner's side, the man they had called Billy. Johnny could see him in the light of the street lamps; a thirtyish man, running to fat, in a dirty, short-sleeved white shirt. Narrow suspicious eyes over a wide mouth, fixed to an unshaven face with a cigarette. "What you doin' out after curfew been passed? Answer up quick, boy."

"Suh, I's gwine to de waterfront. I works down dere, suh," said Turner. He grinned. The muscles of his back and neck were rigid with hatred, but if he had to play Tom to survive—to strike that blow he dreamed of some-day—he was willing to grin and shuffle and sweet-talk like any old coon just in off the farm.

"Lemme see your workpass."

"Yassuh. Here 'tis, boss."

"Says you work at the docks."

"An' that's where I is goin' to now, suh. Got me the night shif' this week. Right now. If the gennulmans will let me, suh."

"They working you boys at night down there now?" said the patroller, holding out the card. Turner reached for it. The man dropped it in the road.

He bent, slowly, and as he came up he smiled and said, "Yes, boss, they sure is."

"Let's go," said one of the white men. Turner stepped aside as the Dixie's wheels shrieked. He looked after the car with the anger almost uncontrollable in him and his big hands fumbled with the card and dropped it again. He almost left it there.

Some ten minutes later he faced another barrier: the twelve-foot chain-link fence that surrounded the warehouse and dock area. The "night shift" story, he knew, would not fool the security guards at the yard gate, so over the fence was the only way in. Well, it would hurt, but . . . he found a part of the fence shadowed from the streetlights by a power substation shed and began to climb it. His weight bent the steel mesh outward, and he clung tight, fearing that it, and he, would fall; but it held and at last he was over, and running crouched down for the rows of shipping containers that lay like giant dominoes stacked in the freight yard. When he was safe from

41

view among them he stopped and felt his leg, and cursed; it was wet. Climbing the fence had torn the half-healed wound apart again.

But it wasn't far now. He took a short cut through one of the warehouses and found himself at R R Smith's. A dim glow came from one of the rear doors of the warehouse. He waited for several minutes, watching it, and when nothing happened he moved up to it and gave the Railroad knock. The light went off and a moment later the door opened.

"It's Turner," someone said.

"Hey, Johnny, come on in. We was just starting."

Inside the warehouse office eight oddly assorted men sat or stood among the desks and filing cabinets and worn hand dollies. Most of them wore working greens and had their hair cut government short. A few were in civilian clothing, almost like the free white workers, and one wore the uniform of a noncom in the police. But one among them stood out: a wiry young octoroon—he looked almost white—who stood easily in the center, watching Turner.

"Who's this?" said Turner.

"This a man from the Road, Johnny. Says his name's Leo."

"Leo what?"

"Just Leo," said the octoroon. He was tall, very thin but well-built, almost too carefully dressed in anonymous-looking cotton twill pants and a mismatched work shirt. His voice sounded odd and then Turner realized why: His accent, too, was almost white.

"What you want with us?" he said, trying to keep suspicion out of his voice.

"Something very important," said the man, Leo, looking Johnny up and down. He seemed to like what he saw; he smiled and held out his fist. Turner touched his fist to it warily.

"You the leader of this bunch?" said the light-colored man.

"Yeah."

"Good; I'm glad we waited, then; this man"—he motioned toward Finnick, who nodded at Turner—"said that you were hurt, might not show up. Say, is that blood on your leg?"

"Don't pay that no mind. Let's get on to what you

42

came for." Turner looked around; one of the men in work clothes quickly got up from his chair. Turner sat down, put his hands on his knees, and looked at Leo, waiting.

"Here's the situation, then," said Leo, looking around the room. "The Road, as you know, has its own sources of information. Some outside the Confederacy, and some inside."

"Go on," said Turner.

"Here it is, in a nutshell. The Yankees are sending a ship to Fort Monroe. On that ship is a very powerful new weapon. A new kind of shell."

"I heard of that," said one of the men, in tones of awe. "Blew up a whole Japanese city in one go. Man! That be the day of judgment, sure enough!"

"Let him talk," said Turner.

"You've heard of it, then. Now—we've found out that the Confederate Army is going to try to take that ship. Board it and capture it, on the way in."

"What's that got to do with us?" said Turner.

"Just this. Those Army people are going to be disguised as coloreds. They're going to tell the Yankees we did it."

Turner nodded. He was beginning to see what the man was driving at. But he had the feeling that he was not going to like it. "Go on, then, brother."

"So here's the plan. Railroad wants that shell. Using it can get us what we want. Freedom."

"How?"

"Load her on a truck," said the man called Leo. He grinned. "Drive her up to Richmond. Park her, right between the White Mansion and the Tredegar Works. Then —make our demands."

"Shit," said Turner. He looked around at his men, who stared back, blinking. Some of them had their mouths open. He turned back to Leo. "Okay, man. That might work, maybe not. Guess that's up to you and the Road. But first you got to get it. How you going to do that?"

"*I'm* not going to," said Leo.

"Who is?"

"We hope your people will."

"Oh, hey now, slow up. We've done a few things—set a fire or two, put some sand or ground glass where it'll do the most good—but hijack a *ship?*"

"The ship will already be hijacked," said Leo. "The

Confederate Army will take care of that. All you have to do is take custody of one little piece of cargo."

"That's all?" said Turner. "Look at these men here. Ain't one of them ever done anything like that in their life. All they know is longshorin'." He shook his head. "Won't work anyways. The government never give in even if you got that thing up there. They too stubborn, and too dumb, too. You'd have to blow up all of Richmond to convince 'em."

"So?"

Turner stared at the thin man and laughed a little. "Say, you're a real fire-eater, ain't you, boy?"

"I've been called worse," said Leo, returning the stare. "At least I've never been called a whitey-lover."

Turner rose to his feet, very slowly. "Are you callin' me that, nigger?"

"No. Now sit down. We have things to plan," said Leo. "Here, you—hand me that lunchbox. Thanks. Now, this here is a chart of the Hampton Roads area. Turner, you see this line?"

Johnny leaned forward. His leg burned, but he put it out of his mind and traced the lightly penciled line with a finger. "This one?"

"Yes. That's the ship's path coming in."

Turner followed it with his finger. Dates and times were penciled in lightly where turns were shown. "So this —Yankee ship'll be comin' in from out in the Atlantic. Morning of the twenty-fourth. Makes this turn in toward the channel at two-forty-five. Goes past Fort Davis out on Cape Henry, at about four-thirty. Then goes on in to the Union fort."

"That's the plan."

"What's this X here?"

"That's where the Army plans to take it over."

Turner studied the chart. At that point, at three in the morning, the ship would still be over fifteen miles out at sea. "Then what they going to do?"

"Continue on in for a short time, long enough to meet a CSN boat . . . here. They'll offload the shell into the boat, which will then take it in to the Navy base at Sewell's Point. From there it goes to Georgia by rail, under guard."

"What will they do to the ship after that? Union don't like having their ships taken."

"They have that figured out," said Leo. "They'll take it back out to sea after the shell is offloaded. The idea is that black terrorists—us—took over the ship to escape, without knowing what was aboard. They have radio messages prepared to give the Yankees that impression. The Confederate Navy will supposedly have a destroyer on patrol out there and will try to do the Union a favor and recapture their ship for them, from the 'pirates.' The terrorists resist, set fire to the ship, and it sinks in water too deep to salvage from. The terrorists and, as a neat incidental, all the ship's crew go down with her. In reality the destroyer will take the Army boarding party aboard and then shell the ship until it goes down. If the Union gets suspicious, they can even put into a Northern port and let them search the destroyer. There won't be anything aboard."

The men looked at each other and nodded. Turner looked at the chart. "Okay, man. That's what they're going to do. Now, what are you asking *us* to do? And how? This better be one fucking good plan, Mister Leo."

"I know," said Leo. His young face suddenly became very serious. "I know. It is a good plan, we think, but it will be dangerous, too. We need men who know boats, who know the area—and we need strong men, too. That's why we came here, to Johnny Turner's longshoremen."

"We're still waiting," said Turner. "Forget the compliments and tell us how we going to get this shell away from the Army, the Navy, and the Union, too."

"Look here," said Leo, pulling back a corner of the chart, which had started to roll itself up again. "Up to this point—four-thirty, off Fort Davis—we go along with whitey's schedule, let them take out the Northerners, the ship's original crew. Now, see, they're steering in toward land, and the boat that's waiting to take the shell off before they head back out.

"The boat is waiting . . . here. Two miles offshore. It'll be dark that time of the morning. We know the recognition signal; two red lights, same as for a breakdown at sea."

"We know," said Turner.

"If the boat meets the ship at four-thirty, that means, standard military procedure, that the boat's crew will have to get it out there by at least one A.M. And then they'll sit there and wait.

45

"While they're waiting, we take 'em."

"Kill them?" said Turner.

"That bother you?"

"Killing white soldiers doesn't bother me."

"Good. That leaves us waiting in the boat. Ship heaves to, they lower down the shell, and we head on off into the dark. They turn around and carry out the rest of their plan. Meanwhile, we go into Lynnhaven Inlet, not Sewell's Point. That's miles shorter and we'll be ashore well before they expect the boat back there."

Finnick cleared his throat. "No piers back in Lynn-haven," he said. "Only white folks' places."

"Correct. That's where the muscle comes in. We'll have to run in close to shore, get the boat as close to the truck as we can, and then carry it."

"Man, that could be mean," said Turner. "Mud—this will all be in the dark—how much does it weigh?"

"Not sure. Anywhere up to two tons. Standard North-ern thirty-inch weighs two and a half, but this is supposed to be a lot lighter."

Leo straightened and the map rolled shut with a snap, and some of the men started. Turner rubbed at his chin and looked at the floor. There was a long moment when no one spoke or even breathed.

"Well?" said Leo.

"You right, it's dangerous. Men in that boat might be armed."

"They probably will be. The Road can give you guns if you want them. New, fresh from the factory."

"What do we do afterward?"

"Go to work in the morning. If we work it right, no one will be left alive who's seen us. Why should whitey suspect you when the shell turns up later in Richmond?"

"How you going to drive a truck through town?" said Finnick. "Nigger can't drive no vehicle. Not legally. You know that."

"I have a blue workpass, false papers for a shipment of coffee, and an ID for a trucking company. We made them up in Richmond. I can drive, and,"—he pointed to his face—"in the dark, at least, I can pass for white."

"You boys well organized up there," said Turner.

"You're part of the Railroad yourself," said Leo. "You know how long we've been in business."

46

"What about the boat?" said Finnick. "Wait—don't tell me. We going to steal one, right?"

"That's right. Got one in mind?"

"I might."

"Any more questions for now?" said Leo, looking round the warehouse office.

"Just one," said Turner. "You really going to blow up Richmond if the Government don't give in? Lot of black folk in that town."

"What would you do, Turner?"

"I don't know, Mr. Leo." Turner looked at his big, scarred hands. "I'll kill whitey's soldiers . . . I'll kill his cops . . . but I don't think I could kill my brothers."

"You leave that decision up to the Road," said Leo confidently. "We'll handle our end. The President and the legislature will give in. They'll have to. Just the shock of finding out we have it instead of the Army will scare the pants off of them." He looked at Turner. "So. Are you with me?"

Johnny Turner looked at his men one by one. Their faces did not quite reflect the Railroad man's enthusiasm. "Bo, what you think?"

"Maybe it'll be dangerous . . . but I been spoilin' for a fight for a long time," said the little man.

"Ben?"

"I guess, Johnny. Yeah. If you're going."

"Willie?"

"S'pose so."

"Sammy?" A nod. He continued around the room until everyone, each in his own fashion, had had his say.

"Okay, Mr. Leo. You got eight strong backs to hump your shell for you."

"Good. Now, we'll meet again tomorrow night—"

"No."

"Look, Turner—"

"You look," said Johnny. "No more meetings. The cops are scrambling all over each other after these Secesh Day riots. Patrollers are out—I met four of 'em on my way here. All they got to do is to catch one of us comin' in or out, and that put the quietus on the whole thing. Boys here and I works together all day. You got more to say, see me—I'll pass it on. You see, Mr. Leo, if you is askin' me to do it, then I'm the man got to be in charge."

He stared at Leo. The man was angry, but Turner

didn't much care. These were his men. He would lead them. There could be no question about that and he was quite willing to have it out with this whitey-looking kid right now, wounded or not.

But finally Leo relaxed and nodded. "All right, Turner. You win; I'll get with you later. Where can I find you?"

He gave him Vyry's address. "I'll be there two, maybe three more days—till this leg's healed up. Finnick, you cover for me at the dock."

"Sure, Johnny."

"All right, then," said Leo.

"That's all you got?"

"All for now."

"That's good." Turner stood up and stuck out his hand. "We'll do this right."

He watched Leo's face as his big hand closed. The kid didn't wince. Good. He turned to the others. "Okay, boys, this meeting seem to be over. Let's start going out, two at a time. Sammy, cut off that light."

When they all had gone he rolled up his trouser leg. The blood gleamed dark against his skin. The pain had dulled to an ache. *Have to clean it out again with that corn,* he thought. *Wonder if Vyry's back yet.*

Time to go; the men out before him must be over the fence and beyond the tracks by now. He rolled his trouser leg back down and slipped through the door, pulling it to behind him.

Quiet outside now; the river sounds were muted with the lateness of the hour. He started for the fence, taking it slowly; no sense in running at this hour. He reached the fence and clambered painfully over it and dropped to the ground. Too late, he saw the old Dixie parked in the shadow of the substation shed.

"Jus' come on over slow," came the same oily voice. "Night shif', huh? Don't make no sudden moves or this here twelve-gauge likely to jus' go off of hitself. Billy, search him up good."

Hands ran over him as he stood still. "Built like a damn truck, but he's clean. Hey—looks like he hurt here in the leg. Lotta blood."

"He going to hurt a lot more than that," said the man with the shotgun. "You got them cuffs? We'll just put him in the trunk. It's only a half hour ride over't the fort."

"Fort? Why you takin' him to the fort? Police station the place for this buck."

"Now, hit obvious you ain't heard," said the man called Billy, with great patience, "but bein' you is about as stupid a bastard as they come I ain't surprised. They got the military and everybody out lookin' for the people started this riot. Some of them, Baylor says, might be shot up. So we find this here nigger scurryin' round in the dead of night, and he hurt—why, we jus' give him a little ride down to see that Major Quidley, thass all."

"Oh, fuck you, Billy," said the other man. "Okay, nigger. Get in the trunk. Don't bleed on my spare."

Five

He stood stiffly, almost painfully, his arms locked behind his back.

Before him the tall windows, overlooking the Roads from eight stories up, showed early morning mists still softening the outlines of the lower reaches of the Chesapeake. The sun, only a little above the sea to the east, was already a blazing fireball; the fog would not last for long. It would be another hot day.

Aubrey Lee Quidley IV turned from the window and sat down stiffly at his desk. He pressed his fingers to his eyes, then rubbed cautiously. So early. And after such a late night, and so much bourbon. For the second night in a row he'd gone back to the narrow house on Bute Street.

Vyry. The name brought it all back; the smoothness of her skin, darker at armpit and thigh; pert musky nipples, brownish-purple and rigid against his tongue; the lovely sweetness when he plunged himself into her; the strange anguished moan he had finally, after many minutes and two returns, coaxed from her as her mouth opened under his.

He smiled. He had had many colored women but none of them like this Lewis. Still, he would tire of her. One always did of low women. Sharon, now—he would never tire of her.

He felt suddenly guilty for thinking of two so different women in the same context of his own lust. *You're hung over, Aubrey,* he said sorrowfully to himself. He slid open his desk drawer and swallowed an aspirin and washed it down with the coffee that had been waiting, hot, on his desk when he arrived. He pressed the button on his intercom. "Jeannie? I'm in. Got the night reports?"

"In your basket, sir."

"Any calls?"

"General Norris. Wants to see you as soon as you come in."

"Oh." That didn't sound good. "Is he in yet this morning?"

"He's been here all night, Major."

Even worse. "Thank you," he said, and reached for the black Night Reports folder. Best to take a minute and be ready for Norris's questions. He skimmed the reports quickly; not much; the usual odd hiatus in individual violence that followed a riot had begun. Police reported the robbery of a Granby Street liquor store by a white man with a gun; Chief Mays' men could handle that. Quiet in the fort area. Attempted break-in at a city building in Portsmouth; shot by a guard when he ran, colored, no investigation necessary . . . the citizen's patrol in the Elizabeth River area had brought in a curfew breaker. Quidley read this one in full, since for some reason they'd brought him in to the fort. The man was hurt . . . might look in on him later down in the tank. That was it; not a heavy night at all. He dropped the folder into his briefcase for reference along with the Shiloh operation order, closed it, and stood up. On the way to the General's office he paused at a mirror, adjusted his Browne belt, flicked a speck of dust from the fresh tunic. He knocked, entered, and saluted so smartly that his head hurt.

"Good morning, General. You wanted to see me."

Norris looked up from his desk. The thin officer's face was haggard and his white hair was tousled and lifeless. He motioned to a chair. "Major. Sit down. We have a problem."

"Yes, sir?"

Norris tapped a gray-and-black Confederate Bureau of Investigation folder. "This came in at midnight; urgent, secret. It's been routed to us via Castle Thunder.

51

I've been trying to get hold of you since it came in. Where in the devil have you been?"

"Ah, at my fiancée's, sir."

"All *night*, Major?"

"Well, sir—"

"Never mind. I'd reprimand you, Quidley, but frankly I'm too tired right now. You've got to leave a number even when you're off duty, while this Shiloh thing is pending. Understand?"

"Sir."

Norris pushed the folder across the desk and leaned back, closing his eyes. Quidley read it quickly.

"My God," he said.

"That's right, Major. Somehow, there's been a leak. From Norfolk. Fortunately, the CBI says they found it out from a Railroad informant. So the Yankees don't know. Yet."

"From *here*," Quidley repeated.

"Yes, Major. That doesn't make me look very good. But if you can find that leak and stop it, we both might come out of this with our current rank." Norris's eyes narrowed, and his voice, always high, went up almost to falsetto. "Now, you're Port Security Officer, Quidley, and that includes counterintelligence functions on my staff. I want a report on what we're doing on this by five today so I can get it out to Richmond. No excuses. No unexplained absences."

"No, sir."

"Get going."

He saluted, pivoted, and left. Outside Norris's door he stood still and breathed deeply until he stopped trembling. His first thought was to delegate the job, but he knew he couldn't. He'd have to give it his personal attention. He marched back to his own office, seething.

"Jeannie. Get me Commander Channing. Then Chief Mays." He spent several minutes with each on the phone, then sat staring at the empty coffee cup on his desktop. Now what? He had no leads at all. From Norfolk . . . how could anything that had been as carefully guarded as Shiloh get out? He had no immediate ideas. *Got to at least look busy, though,* he thought. *Till I feel a little better. Maybe I'll think of something then.*

"Jeanie, I'm leaving the office. I'll be down at the tank,

talking with a curfew breaker they brought in last night."

"Yes, Major."

The tank was deep in one of Port Control's subbasements. Thirty separate cells, three well-equipped interrogation rooms. It doubled as a bombproof shelter, the thick concrete walls and ceilings making it ideal for that role. Quidley asked the soldier in charge, a colored sergeant, to bring the prisoner to IR #2 and to stand by.

He was an unexpectedly big man, big and scarred-up. He was in handcuffs but looked neither cowed nor defiant. He looked resigned. Quidley waited for him to be seated, then nodded to him. "Do you smoke?"

"No, sir." A deep voice, a little hoarse. Quidley noted bruises on the face, recent ones, and the bulge of a dressing under one trouser leg.

"I understand that you have a hurt leg."

"Yes. The man on night duty dress it for me."

"Are you comfortable? Would you like coffee? Breakfast?" The standard start for any interrogation was friendly. If that failed, then one moved on to other techniques.

"No, sir."

Strange. He was used to colored men, to CEs, who fawned. Most did it badly—too obviously deferential, almost to burlesque—but there it was. A few of the really bad ones he had seen were defiant. But this big man seemed different. He had an odd sense of dignity about him, yet without . . . fear. That was it. He suddenly saw that this man did not fear him.

That could not be allowed.

"What's your name?"

"Johnny Turner, sir."

"Where do you work? Do you have a pass?"

"Yes, right here. I'm longshorin' foreman down at the docks."

"Sir," added Quidley, sharply.

"Sir."

"Citizen patrol found you climbing the fence around a warehouse area on the waterfront a little after midnight. Long after curfew. What were you doing there?"

The man looked at the floor and smiled slightly.

"How were you hurt?"

The man did not answer. The sergeant stepped forward, but Quidley waved him back. Time to get rough

53

later. There was still a chance of talking it out, and he intended to try it. "I think you mistake your position, Turner. You're in the custody of the Confederate Army. You were caught breaking the law. We want answers, and we'll get them. Make it easier on everybody. Now. We'll try again. What were you doing there?"

After a moment he shook his head and looked at the sergeant. "All right, he won't be reasonable. We'll need a medic. Get Sanchez. He's good at this." He looked back at Turner. "You won't enjoy this, my man. Tell me now. What were you doing out on the docks at night?"

"Sir—I tell you. I was in a fight."

"Go on."

"That's all. Me and this other nigger had a knife fight. That's how I got cut."

"What were you fighting about?"

"Woman."

"But why in the dock area? Why couldn't you fight where—wherever you live? Or at some bar, the way you people usually do?"

Turner was silent again. Quidley saw that he was lying. He sighed. The sergeant came back with Sanchez, the Cuban medic, who set a case on the floor and began to lay out drugs and a few items of equipment. He looked up at Quidley. "Hello, Major. What you want to start him with?"

"What do you recommend?"

Sanchez looked Turner over. "Jeez, he's big. Hey, man, you don't want to talk to Major Quidley? Hey, you ought to. He really won't, huh? Well, case like this, we try a hypnotic first. Generally easiest."

"Do it," said Quidley, and turned away as the Cuban began to prepare the injection.

Turner pulled at the handcuffs behind his back. They dug into his wrists and he knew they would not give. He looked at the door but knew he could never make it out . . . not with three men, two of them armed, to stop him. He watched the medic fill the needle.

I'm not afraid for me, he thought, watching. *But there's no way I can let myself talk about that Shiloh. The Road can do the job without me. Finnick's mean enough to kill. Leo will lead them. If only I was better at lying . . .* he winced as Sanchez wasted no gentleness giving the injection.

"I want the polygraph," he heard the white officer say.

"Right, sir. I'll connect it now."

Turner felt a dulling fog begin to creep into his mind. *I can maybe rush them—maybe that soldier would shoot me if I got this Quidley—* but it seemed to matter less, somehow—

"Can you hear me, Turner?"

"Yes, sir." Damn; he hadn't meant to answer at all . . . he would stay silent . . . but he was becoming confused. And dizzy.

"Steady him up, sir. They get woozy."

"Would he be better on the cot?"

"I think so, yes."

"Move him, then. Sergeant, lend him a hand."

He felt himself being lifted—it took both the sergeant and Sanchez to drag him, and left them breathing hard —and laid on a bare cot along the wall of the interrogation room. He felt sleepy. So terribly sleepy that his eyelids fluttered and closed.

"Is he out?"

He felt Sanchez open an eye, saw the two faces close over his. "No, he's just under. Go ahead, Major, ask him what you want. Wait a minute. Turner, listen to me. We're your friends. We just want to talk to you about a few things. Talk to us and then the Major will leave and pretty soon we'll let you go."

He heard the Cuban's voice, soft, persuasive. He wanted to believe it. He did believe it. But there was something else. Had been something else . . . was it Vyry?

"Go ahead, Major. He's ready."

"Turner. What were you doing at the docks?"

Blankness.

"Damn it, he's out, Sanchez."

"Ask him again, sir."

"Turner. What were you doing at the docks at night. Answer me!"

"Uh . . . boss."

"What?"

"He's pretty groggy, sir, pretty deep. I think maybe his resistance is low on account of his injury."

"Turner!" He felt a blow rock his head, but there was no pain. He felt wrapped in cotton, the fluffy dirty cotton

55

that blew about on the warehouse floors when bales burst.

"Turner, answer me!"

"Uh . . . Leo," he said.

"What?"

"Lee, I think he said, sir."

"What's that supposed to mean?"

"Means at least he's starting to talk. Keep on with it, Major. Takes a strong stomach sometimes."

I going to tell them, Turner thought, somewhere deep in his mind. *Can't help it. They going to get it all out. If I could move . . . can't get up. . . .*

"Turner. Who is this 'Lee'?"

Deep down, in the tiny isolated self that had almost lost touch, he had a thought. An idea. Before he could think he had to act. With all his strength. Strangely, there was no pain.

"Turner. Who is this man? What were you and he doing?"

A bubbling sound answered him.

"Sanchez—his mouth—"

"*Madre de Dios*—let me at him, sir. Sergeant, get a medical officer, quick. On the double."

"What's happening, Sanchez? He's bleeding all over—"

"It's his mouth, Major." Sanchez probed, then glanced up. He looked sick. "He's bitten halfway through his tongue."

Quidley slumped against the wall of the elevator, fighting nausea. He was alone; his back felt stiff, his head ached, he felt unutterably weary and disgusted with the scene he had just witnessed. No, not witnessed. Caused.

The poor bastard. Probably his great secret was something completely harmless. A crap game. A homosexual liaison with this 'Lee.' A big man like that would hold out sometimes for the most picayune reasons. For a moment, passing Norris's floor, he wondered if there could be a connection with the Shiloh leaks. But no, that was ridiculous. A common waterfront Negro?

The leak had to be one of the circle that had met right here in Port Control. Them—or someone close to them, to Norris, Sawyer, Vickery, Channing, and the four or five others that had been there. They were the only ones in Norfolk who had even heard about the Project.

So . . . how could he find out who it was?

Still no answer surfaced, and he glanced at his watch. Nine-fifteen. Well, he couldn't stand around thinking, he had more than enough to do today. He pulled a black CSA-issue notebook from his pocket and consulted it. Yes. He had to check on the arrangements for pickup of the shell sometime today. Now was a good time. He overrode the elevator's descent and sent it back to the ground floor. Roberts was there, asleep in a chair, and Quidley kicked him awake and sent him to bring the car around.

The Bentley purred west through a perfect July day. Blue, unsullied sky, the mimosa and pine on either side of Shore Drive whipping by, swamp glinting silver between the trunks. An occasional glimpse of one of the moving dunes the Cape had been famous for long before Secession, and once in a while a waving colored man or boy, tending the traps that still yielded muskrat and fox. The scenery, the smooth sound of the Rolls engine, the gay snap of the Stars and Bars all put him in a more cheerful mood. He leaned back against the cushions and thought.

It was a beautiful scene; but he knew that it covered a national malaise.

The Confederacy was in trouble. It had adapted well, he knew, after the War; the new industries built under forced draft in 1860-64 had made Northern goods and heavy industry superfluous. After 1863, too, the British had supplied iron, powder, arms, woven cloth, engines, technical advice, and investment.

At the same time, President Lee's wise Conditional Emancipation had defused the slavery issue while assuring a continuation of white dominance.

After the century's turn, and especially during the Depression, Confederate society had evolved, under the influence of such English thinkers as Bernard Shaw and Beatrice Webb, into the odd half-socialism called Dixie Socialism; voluntary, largely, for the whites; government direction and employment, for the CEs. It had worked well. Up to now.

The trouble, Quidley thought, *is all the Yankees' making.* They had never recovered from the trauma of Secession. Only Confederate-Empire military readiness had kept them from invading during the Western War, and again, in 1895, during the Cuban Acquisition. Since the World War the Entente had deterred any Yankee adventurism; even with the czar and his Russian masses behind them, the North was reluctant to tangle with the British and French Empires.

Now, apparently, it was to be different. With this weapon, and a little more time, the Union could face the Allies. He did not really think they could win. But the carnage would be awesome, and the South, once again, would be the battleground.

He set his jaw. Shiloh had to succeed. Once the Allies had the secret of the shell it would be a standoff. There would be no war. Not, he thought, that he was personally averse to war; at least, not to a gentlemanly kind of war, preferably fought mounted on a good horse, though there'd not been much use for cavalry in Flanders in 1916. A war with pennants and medals and glory and not too many casualties. But war with instruments of mass destruction . . . that made no sense at all. Not to a Southerner. To the Yankees, with their fascination for machines at the expense of all human values, well, perhaps it did.

His thoughts were interrupted as Roberts slowed the car at the gate of the Marine base at Little Creek. The sentry saluted crisply and waved them through. Quidley leaned forward. "Stop here, sergeant. I'll walk on down to the piers."

"Yes, sir, Major."

Roberts? *Impossible,* he thought, walking toward the basin where, ahead, the masts and upper works of gray ships showed. The man knew none of the details. Too, he had been thoroughly investigated long before getting his stripes. No, he was becoming paranoid. Next he would be suspecting himself. He paused at the head of Pier Two and looked down at the boat.

High-speed, shallow-draft; an adaptation, he recalled from the operation order, of the boats that had run guns and mercenaries in and out of the Yucatan before annexation in '27. It looked about sixty feet long and lay low in the oil-rainbowed water of the basin. A Navy ensign dangled lifelessly from a pole at the stern. No one was in sight. A gangway led down from the pier, and Quidley, after walking the length of the boat, strolled down it. A face appeared in a hatch amidships as his steps sounded on the deck.

"Army, eh? Help you, Lieutenant?"

"Major." Quidley looked around the deck. The sailor, a very young man with the sallow look of an engineer, hauled himself out of the hatch and stood up, wiping his hands on a rag.

"You don't salute?" said Quidley coldly.

"Navy don't salute without they got a cap on, Lieutenant."

"Major."

"Right-oh. Whatcha need, sir?"

"Is your, your captain aboard?"

"Chief Haile's over't the club. I think I've got the duty."

"I see. I'd like to look over your ship."

"Boat, sir. What for?"

"What?" Quidley felt that he had taken enough. The lack of respect, the obvious sloppiness—

"Sir, we're on special assignment in a couple of days. With the Marines. We got special gear. So I can't let just anybody look around."

"I *know* about your assignment." Quidley pulled the Shiloh op order from his briefcase and flashed the cover before the man's eyes. "I'm part of it. General Norris sent me to check your boat out. Now let's get going; I haven't got all morning."

"Okay, okay. Follow me."

Quidley tried to reflect on the rugged individuality of the Confederate enlisted man, but failed. The sailor wasted no time giving him a quick once-over of FPB-122. Most of his lecture was devoted to the engines, which interested Quidley not at all, provided that they ran. Finally he interrupted the man, who was explaining some arcane pump or other: "Where do you put your cargo?"

"Cargo? Oh, I know what you mean. We'll put it amidships, in a set of torpedo chocks."

"How fast can you go?"

"Forty knots, with a tailwind."

"What's that in miles an hour?"

"Fuck if I know, Lieutenant."

Quidley controlled himself. If he got angry with this dolt it would come down to another Army-Navy pissing contest, the last thing he needed just now. He hoped the boat's captain knew more. "One more question. I'm leaving now. Would you have your commanding officer call me at 4-4108?"

"Sure thing, Lieutenant."

"Ah—"

"Just go on up, sir. Supposed to salute the ensign when you leave, but seeing as how you're Army—"

When he got back to the car Quidley cursed Roberts out roundly for leaving the engine running.

The rest of the day went faster, and better. Around one, eating a sandwich Jeannie brought him at his desk, he suddenly had the idea he'd been waiting for all day.

There had been a military secret. It had been leaked. All right. He would make up a secret of his own, a fake one, release it to a few selected people, and see if it came back from the CBI's unknown informant. If it did, then the channel was one of the people who had the fake data. If it didn't, he could make up another and give it to those who hadn't had the first. At the very least he could claim it as a smoke screen, a confusion factor. And it would get him off the hook with Norris. He thought for a few minutes, scribbled on a sheet of paper, and he had it.

The fleet would steam east.

It was ideal. The Allied Western Atlantic Fleet, based at Norfolk and Bermuda, would never steam east. Its whole raison d'être was to deter a Yankee thrust south or north. He couldn't use it on Channing, of course; the Navy types would know it for a canard. But he could tell Sawyer—Howson—*Mays, too, don't forget the civilians*, he thought. Yes. He could start it this very afternoon, and it would look good in the report Norris wanted. Evidence of creative thought, positive action, et cetera. Maybe it would even work. He smiled. But it would take some time. He pressed the intercom.

"Yes, sir."

"Jeannie, get me Miss Hunt, at Portsmouth Military Hospital."

Minutes later she called back. "I have her on your line, sir."

"Sharon Sue?"

"Hello? Is this you, Aubrey? Well, hel-*lo!* I thought you were going to call me yesterday. Are you coming over tonight?"

60

"That's what I was calling about. I'll probably be busy tonight, Sharon."

"That Shiloh thing? How is that going, darling?"

He winced. "You shouldn't mention that on the phone, Sharon Sue. I really shouldn't even have told you about it."

"Oh, fun. What harm is little old Sharon Sue going to do? But I'm sorry. Why aren't you coming tonight? I was having Ella fix something real special, and then it was so nice last time in the garden, *you* know, I thought we could—"

He cut into the steady flow of her words. "I know, Sharon. I liked it too. But I can't. Truth is, someone's been leaking information about—that—and I've got to try to find out who."

"How exciting! Oh, Aubrey, I knew when I met you that you were just the cleverest man. That's why the general depends on you so much. But how are you going to catch them? Have you got a plan?"

"As a matter of fact—" Quidley, glowing a little inside at her praise, glanced at the intercom to be sure Jeannie was not listening in—"I do."

"Well, what is it? I'm so excited!"

"I really shouldn't say over the phone."

"Oh, go ahead." She giggled. "This is just like a mystery story, it really is, and you're the smart detective."

He opened his mouth to tell her, but just then the intercom broke in. It was his secretary. "Major, sorry to interrupt, but the General requests your presence—"

"Be right there, Jeannie."

"What, Aubrey?"

"Got to go. General Norris wants me."

"Aubrey, do try to come by tonight. I really want to see you."

"I'll try, Sharon, but I'll probably be busy. Good-bye."

"Bye, honey."

He hung up.

"Major, the general—"

"I'm *coming*."

Norris looked nearly dead as he pointed silently to a chair. Quidley noted that the little general's finger trembled, and was conscious of pity. The strain was obviously too much for the old fellow.

"Any progress, Major?"

61

"I've been busy all day, sir. Interrogated a curfew breaker. Inspected the pickup boat. Caught up on—"

"Damn it, Quidley, answer me! What are you doing about the breach of security on Shiloh!"

"Sir, I've got a plan." He went over the idea quickly. Norris nodded and looked a little less angry. "I thought we could do it with an 'information-only' message over your signature, General. Then we could send it only to the addressees we select. If they're the Railroad's source, knowingly or not—"

"How could they not know?" said Norris.

"Could be a servant, sir. Someone in their family. A friend, a chauffeur, a mistress, a personal servant—any number of ways. It could be a person that one of the people involved trusts so implicitly that they would never suspect them. But this way we can narrow things down fast, and then proceed with conventional interrogation."

Norris nodded. "All right, sounds good. Type up the message and I'll route it. What else can we do?"

"Well, sir, since the original plan's been compromised, perhaps we ought to change it."

"Now you're starting to think, Quidley! What would you recommend?"

"Oh . . . change the attack time. Move it forward. That would put the intercept farther out to sea, but if they were ready for an attack at four-thirty—and remember, sir, the leak was to the Railroad, not to the Yankees, though there might be some exchange of information there—then one at midnight might still take them off guard."

"Excellent." Norris looked considerably happier. "I'll call Sawyer and get him started on a change 1 to the op order. What else?"

"That's about all I can come up with for the present, sir, but I'll keep on it."

"Good. We're making progress."

"Will that be all, sir?"

"Yes—no, wait." Norris smiled. "Wish I were going on this—but I can't leave. We need to brief Sir Leigh on the preparations, on the security developments and our response to them. I'd like you to do so."

"Yes, sir."

"Leave tomorrow at seven, from Davis aerodrome. There's a Navy zep that makes a daily run out to the fleet. I'll have them drop you on the *Redoubtable*—that's Vickery's flagship—and then pick you up on the afternoon flight back."

"Yes, sir."

"You'll get me that message today, won't you?"

"Yes, sir."

"Dismissed, then. And, Quidley—good work. For a change."

"Thank you, sir," said Quidley. He left, oddly divided between pride and resentment.

In fact, I'll do it right now, he thought, back in his own office. He rolled one of the triplicate message blanks into his typewriter and tapped out:

//SECRET//

FM: COMDT FT DAVIS CSA
TO: SELECTED ADDRESSEES

SUBJ: FLEET MOVEMENT INFORMATION

1. RE UPCOMING OP SHILOH: COMWEST-
    LANTFLT HAS ANNOUNCED AREA OF
    OPERATION WILL BE CLEARED BY MEANS
    OF FULL FLEET REDEPLOYMENT ALONG
    LINE FIVE HUNDRED (500) MILES EAST
    OF NORMAL READY STATION. MANEUVER
    TO BE COMPLETED AT S MINUS 24.

2. NO ACTION REQUIRED/FOR INFO ONLY.

BT

Should do it, he thought. He tore off the bottom copy for his own files, pulled off the original for the general, and put the pink middle copy and the two carbon leaves into his briefcase and locked it. He buzzed Jeannie to take the original over to Norris's office and looked at his watch. Five P.M. exact. A good day's work. The situation was well in hand. He smiled to himself.

And now for the night.

Six

She lay on her back in the narrow bed and looked up at herself in the ceiling mirror. She was naked, and she looked on herself without emotion: the long, tapering legs, the tangled triangle of black damp hair, and her eyes, dark question points that stared steadily back from above her.

At length she yawned, looked at the clock on the dresser, and sat up. The House allowed a fifteen-minute break every other hour to keep its girls fresh. Now it was nine P.M., time to go back to work.

I wonder if he'll be back tonight, she thought idly, zipping back into a red satin dress, sliding her feet into red heels, refreshing her perfume from a small bottle on the dresser. The tall major, the one with the funny stuffy name. Quidley. He was right stuffy, too. She smiled to herself, a lopsided, sarcastic smile. He was a strange one, all right. All prim and proper and stuck up, and making you call him sir—even in bed, at least that first time. Then as soon as he got that gray uniform off (strange how he always folded it so carefully, never just tossed the pants over a chair like most men did), he was hard and eager as a teenager.

God, he was queer. She lay back again, fully clothed, and thought about him for a moment. Men of his general type were not totally new to her, though in some ways he stood out. *A mama's boy,* she thought. *Some old way-back family with swords on the walls and battle flags and an estate out West. Brought up at some military school in the old cavalier tradition of military glory and fancy-dress balls and pale bloodless wives and fucking the slave women in the cabins out back.*

That's all you are to him, Vyry. Just the old slave woman out back. She got up, feeling angry. *What am I wasting time thinking on that asshole for when my own man ain't been back all night.* She hoped that Turner hadn't gone and gotten himself caught. No, he was too smart for that, too fast, and too strong.

She went downstairs. The dress, a new one the House had just issued her, rustled silkily as she walked. The luxury was nice, anyway. As long, she thought, as the government forced her to be a whore it was nice to be a well-dressed one, with perfume, high heels, and even a little jewelry. There were worse assignments for CEs with political records. The behavior-research laboratories in Memphis, for example. She shuddered. No one ever came back from being sent down the river. She swept into the room, a smile fixed on her face, and looked around. Yes, sweet Jesus, there he was. He stood up as she approached his table.

"Hello, Vyry."

"Evenin', Major. You lookin' fine tonight."

"Sit down, please. I've some wine tonight—a good old port. Will you have some?"

"All right."

"You look great. Is that a new dress?"

"Yes."

"Here's something to go with it." She took the little package suspiciously and unwrapped it. Inside, under foil and three layers of tissue paper, was a long red scarf, of real silk. The label: Paris.

"Don't you like it?"

"It's nice."

"Put it on. It's beautiful. You're beautiful. You know that."

"I heard it before." Dryly. "Where's your friend? The one doesn't like us colored?"

"Sawyer? I don't know. We don't go everywhere to-gether, you know." Quidley chuckled. "He's not very well

65

bred, is he? I agree, he takes the racial thing a bit too far. Some people do. I think the races should be—well, separate, of course—but that certainly leaves room for a little friendly—"

He stopped, searching for a word, and Vyry said, "Why don't you pour the wine, Major."

"Uh, certainly. There you are. Confusion!"

She studied him as they drank. He was as smartly dressed as ever. She wondered how many uniforms the man owned, that he could wear a fresh one every day. Or maybe he changed more often—it certainly didn't look as if he had worn this one very long. His cheeks were flushed and the pale eyes sparkled. Was he drunk already? *No,* she thought. *He just got the hots for the slave woman. Wonder can he wait long enough to finish this bottle.*

"What are you thinking, Vyry?"

"Oh, nothing in partic'lar, Major."

"Finished with your wine?"

"I suppose so. You not going to leave the bottle here, are you? These women—"

"No, let's take it upstairs with us."

She hid a yawn as the elevator hummed upward. When the door was closed behind them she unzipped the dress —useless to wear anything underneath—and hung it up. By then he was undressed, too. She knew he was clean but gave him a hard honk just for luck, washed him with the little cloth, and lay back on the bed. She bucked him into position and began to grind, looking over her shoulder at the clock.

"Say, not so fast," he said, into her ear. "You weren't like this last night."

"Look, Major." She decided to have it out, uncorked him and wriggled out from underneath. "You got to get the picture here. This is a whorehouse. Now, you're a white officer, and my job is to take care of you, but let's not be gettin' the ideas I think you're getting."

A veil of hurt slid down over his eyes and she felt him grow soft against her flank. *Why . . . he really cares for me,* she thought, surprised.

"Ideas? Well, Vyry . . . I am getting to like you."

She found herself with nothing, at the moment, to say. She was surprised, yes. But there was a sense of guilt, outrage, too. As if she were a horse, a dog, something to be adopted and cherished at his whim, with no response nec-

66

essary by her . . . or rather, with her response foreordained, bred in, the automatic abject love of the inferior whose master condescended to notice her.

"What about you, Vyry? What are you thinking?"

She felt his body long and muscular against hers. He felt cool and she ran a hand over soft shockingly white freckled skin, down his neck, to his nipple, framed and protected with wiry sparse reddish hair. She felt him stir in response against her leg. "I think you're some kind of man, Major Cavalier."

He was eager again; he did not sense her sidestep, her deflection of him; his hands slid between her thighs, readied her. In spite of herself she felt a thrill of excitement. He made love differently than Turner, less roughly, almost tentatively and gently at times, till he at last lost control and she moved with him, arching her back to bring him in, in, to the deep part of her that needed a man there above all. His hands gripped her shoulder blades and she heard him moan deep in his throat. Trapped, held, penetrated, she stared at the curve of his shoulder. So unlike her strong rough longshoreman—his lovely dark shining skin, the curved ripple of hard muscle, the smell of sweaty work. This man smelled of wine, of English scent, of soap. Not of manhood.

I want my man, she cried soundlessly. *Where is he? Is he safe? And when will I lie with him again?*

Quidley's arms relaxed gradually. He raised his head and she saw sweat on his forehead, the pale eyes slightly unfocused. "Damn," he whispered. "You're—it's like a pot of warm honey. And the way you moved, there at the end. . . ."

"Uh huh," she murmured lazily. She seemed to be floating in something warm, something relaxing. Save for the odd tension around her eyes that always came for her with climax, she felt undone, completed, abandoned. It was with a sense of personal loss that she felt his penis slide limply from her. He rolled free and they lay side by side staring up at the ceiling. A fly explored their inverted images. Quidley moved his leg to lie across her thighs. She stirred. "Major—"

"Yes?"

"Hand me that cloth?"

Wordlessly he reached it over. She mopped with it and sighed and rolled over to look at the clock.

Nine-twenty. She sat up. He took the hint and got up, pulling on his trousers. She reached out to run a finger lightly along the buff stripe.

"Get up, Vyry. Let's go out."

"What'd you say?"

"Come on, we'll go for a walk. It's fine out, cool—do you good." He grinned, smoothed his moustache in the mirror. "After that little entertainment, you can't go back to work tonight."

"Like hell I can't—"

"No arguments. Up you come." He seized a wrist and pulled; she had to yield or be tumbled to the floor. "You have anything to wear besides that bed-dress? Get it on."

"Miz Rosen isn't going to like this."

"Chicken works for the Army, and that's me. I'll pay for your time, don't worry."

"That wasn't—" she started to say, but he was already dressed and gone clattering down the stairs. She shook her head slowly and reached for her shoes. God, what a queer man.

Outside—the frown erased from the madam's face by Quidley's twenty-dollar coin—a fine drizzle, a mist really, hung in the night air. It was humid but cool, and her clothes felt clammy against her still-damp skin. She shivered, pressed herself close to him. "Now where you want to walk to? I suppose you knows this is crazy."

"I don't care. Aren't you glad to get out of—there—for a while?"

"Sure I am, Major. I don't enjoy that work."

"You were assigned to it."

She nodded, silent, and he dropped the subject. "Let's walk over toward the basin," he said.

Streetlights glowed yellow at intervals along the tree-shaded old-fashioned cobblestone streets. This part of the city had not changed much since the early nineteenth century and was quiet, peaceful; they passed no one.

The basin—Smith Creek, it had once been—was now a hundred-yard-wide pool of calm water, ringed by street lamps and quiet old houses and tree-shaded benches. A rare auto purred over the new bridge, under which the tide slowly eddied. All was stilled by the mist, and the warm yellow of the lights played on the surface of the dark water. Quidley paused by a bench and wordlessly she sat down and watched his tall shadow pace back and forth by the shore, occasionally shortening as he stooped for a pebble to toss out into the water: *plook*.

What did he want with her? Some of them, the customers, asked for strange things. The House rules protected her from the real crazies, the ones who wanted to hurt. She knew how to take care of them. But this thin correct man, gentle at times, so domineering and high-horse at others . . . she felt uncertain, about him, and also . . . about herself.

At last he came back to the bench and folded himself into it beside her. His tunic collar was unbuttoned, and he let his head drop back against the bench and looked up toward the sky.

"Not a star out."

"No, Major."

He turned to look at her. His eyes seemed dark, pools of shadow, as he studied her face.

He leaned forward and kissed her gently. His lips were cold and she felt a shiver glide down her back. The trees rustled above them and somewhere a whippoorwill launched its rounded haunting cry.

"Vyry . . . what would you say if someone said . . . he loved you?"

"Wait a minute, now. Better turn that off right now, Major. No future in that for you *or* me."

He sat silent for almost a minute, and she felt his hand move to stroke her hair. "Maybe you're right," he said, voice low and thoughtful.

"Sure I is." She studied his face, then curled down suddenly, probed at his clothes, and took him into her mouth. Men were so soft there . . . when she felt his last shudder she sucked him clean, swallowed, and sat up, catching sight as she did so of his wrist: nine thirty-two. "That was real nice, Major," she said, and stood up.

"But you didn't—"

"Don't bother none about me, Major. I'll tell you straight. You one of a dozen I'll see tonight. And all white officers. I can't bust nuts with all of you. A scarf and a walk—you can't buy me with that."

There, she saw that had snapped him back. He got up, face averted, and straightened his clothing. He pointed to his neck, not looking at her. "Can you get this collar, please."

"Hold still." She hooked the high collar and patted his

cheek. "Now don't be mad at me. A women like me can't have no feelings for her customers. You know that."

"That's all I am to you? A customer?—No, wait." He gripped her shoulders and she looked up into suddenly angry eyes. "You'll answer me, bitch. I'm an officer in the Army and you'll answer me. Is that really all I am to you, a customer?"

She stared up for a long moment. Suddenly her own feelings were no longer so certain. *Was* there nothing more? Was there? "Well, you seem like a nice gentleman," she faltered. "But you know I got a man of my own at home."

"Married? Your husband, you mean?"

"N—no."

He looked down at her for a moment more before she turned her face away and whispered, "Please. Let me go, Major. I got to go back to the House. Please."

When he had taken her back he sat in the car for several minutes, listening to the first light rain pattering on the roof and rustling in the dark shrubbery in front of the House. He was engaged in an unfamiliar act. He was trying to examine his own feelings. There was no doubt about it. There was something wrong with him. With her. With them.

Black bitch. He gripped the wheel as he had gripped her shoulders. He remembered her eyes, cold at first, businesslike . . . her lips, skilled at coaxing the last drop of desire out of him. Then the fear in her eyes, and finally the confusion. *Why*, he thought, *should there be confusion . . . unless she, too, feels something for me?*

Even then it was insane. Here he was—Aubrey Quidley, fourth of the name, tenth in his class at VMI, a high-ranking officer with a responsible position in the defense of the country, mooning like a teenager about a woman who was nothing less than an out-and-out prostitute. And colored to boot. *Perhaps I need psychiatric help,* he thought fleetingly, then blotted out the thought. Couldn't afford that in his personnel jacket.

Perhaps it wasn't really that serious. Infatuation, even an affair, with a colored woman was nothing new for a Southern gentlemen. Nothing that had not been implicitly sanctioned by four hundred years of slavery and untold generations of mulatto and quadroon and octoroon. Maybe it was even normal. What was it Jeff Gaines, his old roommate at the Post, used to say . . . 'You ain't a man till you've split a black oak.' Odd how that had remained in his memory all these years when so much else had been lost.

What would his grandfather have said, the stern, remote Senior, with his chestful of medals and underneath them a lung destroyed by German gas? Surely at one time he had had human appetites, human passions. Quidley smiled at the thought of him in connubial congress with his prim, small grandmother. No. It could have happened only one time. And where had his own father put it all the years before Miss Mary? There must have been a mistress somewhere.

He started the car. It was still early and he wondered about a drink elsewhere . . . no. It would be a full day tomorrow, with the fleet visit on top of his normal duties. Well, home then. He put the car into gear and followed his headlights onto rainswept Brambleton Avenue. This early in the evening Mother might still be up. He'd seen little enough of her in the past week. Might be nice to have a quiet cup of tea with her and then turn in.

The Quidley home was a low, rambling, Elizabethan-style structure, built in the late twenties, in Ghent, less than a mile from the city center. He slowed instinctively on the drive as red flashed from a car's reflectors ahead, then braked. It was a brown Triumph, a convertible.

Sharon's car. She flicked on the interior lights as he walked up, rolled down the window, and smiled out at him. "Hello, Aubrey."

"Well, hello!" They exchanged quick kisses, cheek to cheek. He straightened in the rain. "What are you doing here? I mean, why didn't you go on in? Mother's up, I think—"

"Oh, I know, but Aubrey—I wanted to see you. Alone, you know. I waited at home, but you didn't come, you didn't call, no one answered at your office number—I was afraid something had happened. You know, Aubrey," she continued, batting her eyelashes, "I felt so close to you the other night that I really let you go a little, well, too far. Aubrey?"

"Yes, Sharon Sue?"

"You can't, after doing that to me, with me—you

71

can't just not see me. Unless you feel that you don't want to see me anymore—"

"Lord, no, Sharon Sue. I didn't mean—"

"I know you didn't. You're sweet, Aubrey, do you know that? Sweet and kind of cute, like a gray puppy. I'm sorry, that sounded like I was making fun of the uniform, didn't I? I didn't mean that."

"I know."

"Aubrey, you're standing there in the rain, you must be getting soaked. Let's get in your car."

"We can go inside—"

"Aubrey, honey, I know and dearly love your mother. She's the sweetest thing on two legs. But let's just sit in your car and be alone for a little while. All right? Please say yes."

"All right."

"Oh, good. Here, I'll get out—"

"Let me take your arm."

When she leaned against him he caught her scent, crushed jasmine, and the odor of rain in her hair. He felt the thinness of her arm through the thin fabric. It was strange . . . he had thought his desires satisfied, satiated, but now . . . he opened the door for her, and she ducked inside and tucked her skirt under her. "There. Now isn't this cozy?"

"Yes." He leaned forward, against the dash, and saw that his briefcase was cramping her legs. "Here, let me move that for you."

"No, it's all right. Aubrey . . . are you angry with me? Or something?" In the dim light her face was pale and tragic against the rain-beaded glass. "You're not coming by . . . you hardly ever call me . . . and I smell—I smell, oh, wine on your breath when you said you'd be working—"

"Oh, Sharon Sue." He stroked her shoulder clumsily, feeling like a heel, a cad, a brute. The things he'd been doing while she waited by the telephone for his call . . . she, his fiancée . . . "Look it was nothing. I just stopped by the club for a moment after work, with . . . Colonel Sawyer. He wanted to talk about this diversion. We just had a glass of wine apiece as we talked. It was nothing, Sharon Sue, believe me. Then I came right home, I was tired, it's been a long day, Norris has been on my back—"

Liar, he thought, hating himself. She was so trusting, so fragile. Yet still he felt a sneaking and not entirely unwelcome spark of pleasure within himself at his behavior. There was something of the gay blade about him after all. It was an unusual feeling for him to have about himself and he was rather surprised to find himself enjoying it.

"You really? That was all?" She pulled a tiny lace-edged square of cloth from somewhere and was dabbing at her eyes with it. "Was that really all, Aubrey?"

"Yes it was, Sharon."

"What was it you and Mr. Sawyer were discussing, then?"

"Just military matters, Sharon. Things you wouldn't under—I mean, that you wouldn't be interested in."

"I'm interested in everything you do, Aubrey. But you weren't making it up? You weren't with, another woman, tonight?"

"Oh, no, Sharon Sue. You're lady enough for me." He took her hand and pressed it warmly. "You know I love only you."

"Oh, Aubrey, I'm so glad to hear you say it, though." She sniffled and laughed and tilted the rearview mirror and examined her face. "There now, see what you've done. My mascara's all runny. I'll bet I look a mess."

"You look lovely."

"Would you mind, Aubrey—really, I've been so upset, I *could* use just a *tiny* drink—"

"Want me to get you one?"

"I'd be so grateful—I've been worrying all night, Aubrey, worrying about *us*—"

The rain was somewhat heavier and he felt its coolness soaking into the uniform as he ran for the porch. Damn. Well, the maid would have a fresh one ready when he got up. He unlocked the front door quietly and slipped inside. The light came on before he touched the switch and he looked up.

"Hello, Mother."

Mary Rae Quidley was, at fifty-three, a slim, erect, very active woman. She stood at the landing of the grand stairway and looked at her son. After a moment she raised one eyebrow in the gesture fashionable in English girls' schools in the mid-forties. "Aubrey. You're as wet as a damned dog."

"Yes, Mother. Mother, Sharon is out in the car. If I could get her a glass of something—"

"You know where the liquor cabinet is." She came down the stairs, stopping a step or two away. "But why don't you bring her in? She talks a blue streak, and that awful Tennessee whine—but she seems a nice girl. Use the parlor."

"Thanks, Mother, but—"

"Suit yourselves." She turned away. "I'm going up to bed anyway, and the people have Sunday off; you'd be alone. Bring her in. At least you'll be dry."

"Thanks, Mother."

"Good night, Aubrey."

"Good night, Mother." He looked after her for a moment as she ascended the stairs, then stepped into the parlor. Bourbon? No, Sharon was a fanatic about good bourbon; he'd take her out a brandy.

The inside light of the car was on when he stepped out onto the porch, but she turned it off as he came down the steps. "Oh, thanks, darling," she said, gulping at the drink. "What is this? Brandy? It tastes sweetish, sort of." She giggled. "Aubrey, would you—what we did before?"

"Sharon—"

"Oh, I'm sorry; did I shock you? But I liked it, Aubrey, I liked it." Her eyes were fevered in the dim light from the parlor windows. "Kiss me, Aubrey."

Her lips were sweet from the strong drink, and she clutched at him. He felt confused, a little frightened. What was it she wanted? When she began to pant he pushed her back a little. "Sharon—this is—not like you," he gasped.

"I'm sorry, Aubrey. I'm sorry. I'm sorry," she whimpered, like a scolded child. "I'm—I don't know what you'll think if I say this, but I do love you too, Aubrey, and it's hard for me to act like a lady, to wait—"

"Perhaps I'd better drive you home."

"No. I can drive." Cloth rustled in the darkness. "Aubrey—you will call me?"

"I'll call, Sharon Sue."

"You don't—dislike me now?"

"No. I love you. But I think you're tired and worried."

"I *have* been working late over't the hospital. I'll be good. I'll go now, I'll go right straight home and to bed and I'll think of you till I fall sound asleep." She pecked his cheek and waited for him to open her door. Snuggled into the little car, she looked up and smiled wanly, a tear glistening on one cheek. "Good night."

"Good-bye," said Quidley.

When she was gone he stared after her, into the dark of the driveway, the drumming of the rain loud in his ears; and for the first time he began to doubt.

Seven

There . . .

   There. . . .

   He thought . . . where? The burning light ate into him, into his brain. Sleep. Sleep. Jesus, no, there was no sleep, would be none . . . Vyry. Bo. Where are you? I am in the hands of the white man. I am in the very hell of the Book. I am my head is not here I am someone I never thought I was who am I?

   Who am I?

   "Who are you?" said the voice, echoing, making his knees hurt with the sound.

   "Turner. Turn . . . er. My name Johnny Turner." A gasp. His teeth flamed. The world spun crazily. Yes.

   Time, that elastic molasses, flowed by him like a snail raced by a bullet, the snail winning. He gaped up at the light from the bed he lay in. It was soft. He was gradually, slowly, easily melting into it, becoming one with it. Sinking in. The voice stopped, or he no longer understood it, and he slid backward and down into a pain-lit past, flickering visible by green lightning.

   Eight. He was not much at eight. He was sick a lot. He lay under the house, with the soft friendly bugs, hearing somewhere above his mother's curses. He lay staring upward and the roll of the planet turned in his pulse. His mouth was filled with sandpaper-rough noodles. Tall silver single-eyed figures pursued him. He was fevered, that he knew. The rotting bottom of the house rotated dimly above his staring eyes.

Agony. His limbs stiffened and poked out like those of a dying starfish. He screamed through fused teeth. The pain—oh, Jesus, Vyry the pain in his head in his *soul*—

"Who are you?"

What could he answer. They knew he was Johnny Turner. He was Johnny Turner. Wasn't he Johnny Turner?

"Who are you?"

Turner, I'm—

"Who are you?"

"Turner," he screamed. "Turner, Turner, Turner, Turner."

Something in his head moved. He felt it there. It was small, it was cool, and it was inside his head. Now he felt the padded cuffs on his arms and legs. He felt the pain in his swollen tongue. He felt the insinuation into his arm through which the liquids dripped. He felt the close-fitting Turner around his shaven cool head. He felt the thing inside him. Yes. What he decided. Only what he decided.

No = pain = death

Yes = love = pleasure = life

Yes, no, yes—Turner, Turner, Turner—

Something moved inside him and clicked to a new position and asked

Why were you out?

Why was I out

Why were you out?

Shotgun barrel draped over the door of the Dixie Get in nigger into the trunk don't bleed on my spare Fat pink face eager with hate

Why were you out?

Why was I out

PAIN PAIN PAIN PAIN

Why were you out?

Why was I out?

PAIN PAIN PAIN PAIN

Why were you out?

Out . . . I was out . . .

PAIN PAIN PAIN PAIN

77

Why were you out?

. . . .

PAIN PAIN PAIN PAIN PAIN PAIN PAIN
PAIN PAIN PAIN PAIN

"Turn it off," said Quidley, looking down at the staring eyes. Sanchez pressed a switch in the gray console.
Lights died. The eyes stared upward, blinking with reflex
every twenty seconds.

"How long has he been on the loop?"

"About six hours, sir."

"What did you get?"

"Very little," said the Cuban, unplugging Turner from
narcolepsis and sending glucose and saline into his body.
"Just his name. He has a barrier up for anything beyond
that."

"Barrier?"

"Yes, sir." Sanchez turned a valve and sat back, watching life drip back into the man on the cot. "He's strong.
This happens sometimes. The mind, she is so complex . . .
sometimes a man protects one thing, all the rest dies.
Dies, absolutely. No more. He will be a vegetable. But he
will not release this one thing. I have had it happen. Once
I was—"

"That's enough." Quidley watched the dark dead face.
What was this man's secret? Did he *have* a secret?

"Once there was a man—they asked me to interrogate
him—he said nothing, nothing at all—he died, saying
nothing—then later they told us he was mute—"

"I said that's enough. Wake him up," said Quidley.
"Oxygen. Adrenaline. Whatever it takes."

"Yes, sir."

Gradually life returned. The man writhed on the cot.
His eyes opened again, staring at the concrete ceiling of
the interrogation room. Muffled sounds came from deep
in his throat.

"Is he coming out?"

"*Si*, Major. He's very groggy though. The drugs and the
electricity, the effects are cumulative."

He stared down at the man. The cot had been dirtied
and his nostrils twitched as the smell came up to him.
What to do. "Sanchez. This won't work, then? He won't
talk at all?"

"This is only one technique, Major. As you know there

78

are many others." The little Cuban smiled, and brushed a hand gently over Turner's forehead.

Quidley bit his lips. He did not enjoy this, did not like inflicting pain. He hated this part of his job; it was something a regular Army officer shouldn't have to involve himself with. Let the police do it, or the CBI, the smooth types with their cold faces. This was their business by rights.

But, damn it, he was caught. He was Port Security officer, and the man had been remanded to his jurisdiction. He'd hoped for quick answers, then pack the man off for a civilian "trial," and they could do what they liked with him after that—send him to a hospital, to Memphis, to a medical reclamation depot. But it had backfired. He couldn't get rid of him now. Not with General Norris breathing down his neck for results.

Damn it. What a corner he'd gotten himself into. Not to mention this poor stubborn bastard. He came back to himself with a start, realizing that Sanchez was watching him curiously.

"I suppose . . . another technique," he said.

"Insulin shock? A psychological technique? There are many of those, many ways of inflicting pain today, Major."

"You don't use the whip no more," the man on the bed croaked, startling them both. Quidley caught the flare of hatred from the man's eyes before he looked away.

"Of course not. We don't want to hurt you, Turner. Only to have you talk with us—"

But the eyes had sunk closed again. Quidley swung on Sanchez, his decision made. "No. We won't use the . . . negative techniques. No more pain." He looked at Turner, who was breathing shallowly, asleep. "I don't think it would work on this man anyway."

"I think you're right, Major. But that narrows down what I can do with him."

Quidley clenched his fists. If only he could just get rid of him! "What do you recommend?" he asked the medic.

"We can continue the drugs, sir. But they're driving him under fast. But there's—" Sanchez looked thoughtful—"There's a new technique, one they've developed in Memphis. I was trained for it in Richmond."

"Have you the equipment here?"

"Yes, sir."

79

"Does it cause pain?"

"Just the opposite, sir."

"What do you mean?"

Sanchez bent over the sleeping Turner and placed his hands lovingly around the crown of his head. "Here. A headpiece like a helmet fits. In it are electrical coils, adjustable. With them we induce a current in the pleasure center of the brain. It is ecstasy." Under his hands Turner was motionless.

"How will that make him talk?"

"They used it first with rats, Major. Crude at first, with wires in the brain. Let them administer the pleasure by pressing a switch. Later they gave the rats a choice between freedom and the switch. They stayed. Finally they gave the rats a choice between food and the switch. They all starved after keeping the switches closed for three days straight. So you see what we do. We give him pleasure, unlimited pleasure. Then he will talk, gladly. This was actually done with a Northern spy they caught and after they traded him over the border he killed himself because he could never have the pleasure again." Sanchez' hand smoothed Turner's close-cropped head, and he looked lovingly down at him.

"Can't he hear us?"

"It doesn't matter if he can or not, Major. He will have no choice at all."

Love burned like a fire in the center of his brain. Flooding him with light. He was part of a current of joy, and it never ended.

Through it, under it, in a strange way he did not understand, he remained himself, though he did not think at all, nor feel, except for the overwhelming joy. Somehow it was connected in his deep unthinking submind with the tightness (joy) around his head. His eyes too were covered, but cobalt blue it was under them, with holy patterns. He was coming—he was coming—but it was asexual and it never ended. His genitals were gone. He didn't care. His legs, his hands, his body were gone. He didn't care. He had so much more.

This was what he had always wanted. There was nothing like this in life. Perhaps he was dead and this living current of pleasure that roared through him, turbulent, laughing, cobalt blue, was the finger of Jesus reaching down into his head. No, he knew it wasn't, knew that somehow it was *their* doing, but even then if someone gave you such pleasure unending could you hate them? He loved the whitey major with the precise voice and the pale distant eyes. He wished he were lying right here with old Johnny Turner drinking from the cup of everlasting bliss. He lay and his fingertips trembled where they protruded from the padded cuffs.

Vyry he had loved Vyry and she had never given him the tenth nor even the thousandth of what was rolling through him, burning sweet in his brain like a hot star, quivering and pulsing in his stomach and legs and fingernails. Vyry had been soft and Vyry had cared and he wished she were lying here with him and the major drinking the cobalt blue but he was here and the moment, now, stretched endlessly and thrillingly sweet, sweeter than Vyry, sweeter than jane, sweeter than the coke the sailors from South America sold at the docks. At the docks, the warehouses—Bo, Willy, he wished they were here too, all the men who had been with him.

Someone came and stood beside him. He could hear them, very faintly.

There had been a secret, hadn't there? There had been a meeting perhaps? Why had he been out after curfew? How had he hurt his leg?

And over and over again, repeated petulantly, angrily, whispered, shouted, asked soothingly, asked hypnotically, the same question:

Why won't you talk?

He lay and listened to the voice with the questions and smiled as the flood of pleasure whirled over them, submerged them, took them away like petals on a cobalt blue rush of whirling living joyous water. The questions came again and again the water rushed them away. He would have answered them, he did not care now, but to open his lips was too great an effort and the flow went on and on and his fingertips trembled gently in the padded restraints and later, much later, grew still.

Eight

Far below the ocean, blue, curved upward in a vast and restless bowl. Behind, faint in the west, a low dark line marked the Virginia coast.

Huge, streamlined, silver, the Confederate Navy aircruiser zep *Shenandoah* thundered out to sea.

Quidley, on Deck Two, stared upward at the vast bulk above him. Six 20-foot propellers, driven by huge Rolls turboprops, shimmered golden in the light of the rising sun, and their muted roar sent a slight thrill through the rail he grasped. He had seldom flown, and the sensation of speed was magnificent. As was the view below. He tore his eyes away from it to check his watch. Seven-thirty. At the zep's speed, well over a hundred miles an hour, the fleet should soon be in view.

Whether it was the experience of flying, the crisp morning air at six thousand feet, or simply a reaction from the confusion and tension of the last few days, Quidley felt wonderful. He leaned forward, looking downward through the angled glass, and smiled. Things were not so bad, and for that, he could take part of the credit. Why not?

Several hours' work after Sharon Sue had left had resulted in a thin sheaf of papers, now in the briefcase beside him on the humming deck. Norris had countersigned it, and only Vickery's approval was needed before Change

One to the Shiloh operation order would be issued. The times had all been moved up and the marine assault force had been increased. Several other little details—the results of intense cerebration on his part—had at least had the effect of making the little general happy, to the point where he had left Port Control for the first time in three days.

There were still annoyances, of course. His personal life, for one. He frowned down at the whitecapped sea and admitted that he was getting too attached to the Negro woman. He told himself this sternly and then stood motionless for several minutes recalling in detail their last time together and then imagining the next. God, but she was fantastic in bed.

He came back with a start and frowned again. And Turner was still holding out, after forty-eight hours of sleep deprivation, chemical therapy, and the other humane but necessary methods of modern interrogation. Sanchez was applying the pleasure technique now. He wondered for the hundredth time what secret the giant Negro retained with such stubbornness that in the end he might well die before he talked.

In the midst of his thoughts the beat of the engines changed and the cruiser's nose moved slowly to the left. He squinted into the sun. There, on the horizon—were those little specks ships? And beyond them, just visible over the glowing edge of the sea—something larger?

He stared, eyes watering in the glare, as the zep neared. He had read of it, seen it in films—but this was the first time he had laid eyes on the Allied Western Atlantic Fleet.

Its outlying scouts, the destroyer squadrons and fast cruiser groups, had fallen over the horizon behind before the Line came into view. He gripped the rail and his pulse pounded in excitement as the *Shenandoah* swung to fleet course and began its mooring approach. He could see for thirty miles or more, up and down the entire Line.

There were fifty of them, or more—he couldn't tell. Fifty first-line Allied dreadnoughts, Allied Joint Design heavy classes, the flags of the Empire, the Confederacy, France, Germany, and Brazil fluttering from the foretops. Spaced in perfect line ahead, the squat gray hulls barely rolled as they plowed through the quartering seas.

This was the Line. This, Quidley knew—these

hundred-thousand-ton battleships, with waffle-composite armor twenty feet thick, thirty-inch automatic guns that reached out eighty miles—these were the deterrents that had kept the peace for so long. A Union move into Canada or the South would elicit instant retaliation on New York, Philadelphia, Portland, and Boston. The new Union fleet built for the Japanese war was still in the Pacific, though some units were probably steaming back around the Horn (the Empire Canal was of course closed to Union warships). But no Northern fleet, or even a joint Russo-Union fleet, could stand against this tremendous instrument of combined Allied might.

He felt a swelling in his throat and a chill at his spine at the sight. There, below, he caught sight of the scarlet pride of the Stars and Bars passing below the zep at the masthead of the *Alabama*, one of the Confederacy's own.

"*Prepare for mooring,*" came over the airship's announcing system. "*Line and tube crews to your stations. Cargo, mail, passengers, stand by at debark station.*"

That's me, he thought. He walked aft, wondering how he would get down to the deck of the *Redoubtable,* which was now visible just ahead. Sailors herded him into a line in front of a closed door. A bearded man waited calmly in front of him. Quidley glanced nervously around, then tapped him on the shoulder. "Excuse me, sir. I haven't done this before. How do we get down?"

"Not to worry." The man removed a short pipe from his mouth and pointed forward. "Just wait about four seconds after I go, and then step through the door."

"That's all?"

"And keep a good grip on that briefcase." He tucked the pipe in again and turned round just as a light went on over the door.

"*Commence debark,*" said the announcing system.

The door slid open and the first man in line stepped through and disappeared. The line moved quickly. The bearded man stepped through and disappeared. Quidley counted to five, clutched the case to his chest—hell to pay if he lost that—and stepped forward boldly, into nothing. It was dark and he was falling and then something was squeezing him tightly, all around, something slithery and close—

He landed heels-first on a yielding surface. There was light, and hands pulling him out, into the air. Then he was standing on a metal deck and the roar of the airship's engines was loud in his ears.

"This way," a sailor shouted, and he followed him, running. Glancing back, he saw how it had been done. A long, narrow tube of fluttering fabric, like a lady's stocking, had been lowered from the hovering airship's keel to the *Redoubtable*'s stern. Down it, as he watched, moved a bulge: a person. The fabric was elastic, and its friction slowed a fatal fall to a controlled descent.

"You're Major Quidley?" A Royal Navy ensign, fresh-caught, very young. He saluted back gravely and nodded. "Follow me please, sir. The admiral's waiting on the flag bridge."

He followed the boy through seemingly endless corridors, bright with shined metal, lined with machinery of vague purpose, and crowded with sounds and smells utterly foreign to him. At one point they waited for an elevator. He was a little weary when the officer opened a last door for him and said, "Sir Leigh is the one—"

"Yes, I know him. Thank you."

"Nice to see you again, Major," said Vickery, extending his hand. "The trip out, pleasant, eh?"

"It was—quite an experience. I'd never—come down that way before."

"Never been dropped, eh? Can't say I'm too fond of it myself. Still it gets you down quick. That the material?" He gestured at the briefcase.

"Yes, sir." Quidley started to open it but the admiral waved it shut.

"Not just yet. In a moment we'll go back to my cabin and sit down with it." The old man squinted out at the sea. "Damned fine sight, aren't they, Major."

"Inspiring, sir." He searched for words. "Really thrilling. The glory of the Alliance, I'd say."

"Glory? Yes—and its greatest weapon," said Vickery thoughtfully. "A quarter of a million officer and other ranks—and an investment of something like twenty billions of pounds sterling." He stared out at the line of gray dreadnoughts. "To think," he said softly, "if this new weapon is as powerful as the Yankees say, it could annihilate a fleet like this in the space of an hour or two."

Quidley was silent, and after a moment the admiral shook his head and turned from the sight. "Follow me, please, Major," he said.

The sea cabin was large, plush, finished in mahogany-hued metal. A single painting, a rather amateurish architectural study of a Viennese square, adorned the bulkhead. Vickery waved at a deep chair. "Drink, Major?"

"It's rather early, sir."

"Nonsense. Rum?"

"If you insist, sir."

Vickery poured it himself, neat, from a wicker-wrapped pottery jug. Quidley tasted it cautiously and found himself enjoying it; liquid tradition. Sir Leigh sat heavily opposite him. "Very well, Major. You may report now."

"Yes, sir." Quidley quickly outlined the progress of Norris's preparations for Shiloh, and explained about the CBI report of a leak. "Because of that, sir, here are our recommendations for changes to the operation order."

Vickery studied the papers for several minutes. Keen old eyes flickered in Quidley's direction. "This misleading message you mention, Major—"

"Yes, sir." He dug into his briefcase again. It was there, the pink copy, still with a carbon leaf fluttering from it. "I'll summarize it, sir. It's a canard, of course. to the effect that your Fleet is moving east some five hundred miles."

Vickery's eyes narrowed. "For what purpose?"

"Well . . . simply to find out who is leaking information, sir."

Vickery stared at him. "Major . . . do you really understand what forces you're dealing with? Really?"

"Well . . . I know about the fleet, yes, sir."

"You do!" Vickery stared for a moment longer, then heaved himself up and began pacing about the cabin. "You do! I've no doubt that you're an intell—well, a conscientious officer, Major Quidley, but still you're Army, and not even Royal Army at that. Do you really understand what a Fleet movement like that might mean?"

"Sir—"

"Look, Major." Vickery stopped beside a world globe and beckoned Quidley over. "This is the Empire and its allies." He traced a wash of red, from Europe, through Africa, to the Confederacy.

"Yes, sir."

"And this—" His finger moved along a wash of blue. The Union, Western Canada, Alaska, Northern China,

Imperial Russia. "And now Japan as well, since the Yankees seem to be absorbing that island nation."

Quidley felt fear in his stomach. If he had miscalculated at this level—

"We live upon a delicately balanced planet," said Vickery, not unkindly. "At times I think that it was inevitable; that no matter what happened in history, it was a natural consequence of progress that two superpowers should emerge at the end of the industrial era. Well, they have—the Northern Bloc and the Empire Alliance. Of which the Confederacy is an indispensable part."

"Yes, Sir Leigh."

"Now," the admiral went on, spinning the globe lazily, "do you know why there has been only an 'almost' war between the two sides for these past thirty years?"

"Because together we've been too strong for them."

"Only partially correct. It's because we've had that strength ready, on station, in a palpable and visible form," said Vickery. He rapped his fist against the bulkhead and steel rang. "Because of the Allied Fleet."

Quidley nodded.

"But now, Major, you propose single-handedly to remove this deterrent from the consideration of Philadelphia."

"Sir, it's a false message—"

"And what if you're right and the traitor is among you? What if your plan succeeds and this message reaches the North? They believe that the door is wide open for them to move. A false message is fine, but to use this one—I find it difficult to believe. General Norris approved this?"

"Yes, sir, he did." Quidley wiped his hands on his trousers; under the tight gray tunic he was sweating. "He read it and approved."

"He's either insane or a traitor. This could bring about war on its own. Did you ever consider that little detail?"

Quidley stammered.

"And with this new shell of theirs, a war now could mean—my God, man, you're threatening the security of the entire civilized world." Vickery held the message for a moment more and then tore it up twice. He dropped it into a slot in the bulkhead and Quidley heard the whine of a shredder.

"There, that's done." The admiral shrugged and managed a smile. "Don't look so glum, Major. No harm done, after all. But you'll have to find the source some other way."

Quidley nodded, relieved. "Sir. Then—we'll operate under the original operation order?"

"No, the change in timing was a good idea. Let me note that down. Tell you what, I'll go over your Change One with my staff and get it back to Norris later with our recommendations."

"Yes, sir."

"Another tot?"

"Thanks, no, sir."

"Going to catch the afternoon zep back?"

"Yes, sir."

"I'll try to have my comments ready by then. You met my adjutant on the way up, didn't you? I'll have him give you the shilling tour, take lunch in the wardroom. Oh, and there's a shoot in the afternoon, as well. You were coastal artillery, weren't you? You'll want to see that. Could you stop back about 1600?"

"Very kind of you, Admiral." Quidley rose, hearing the note of dismissal in Sir Leigh's voice, and shook hands. The adjutant was waiting outside the door.

For the next few hours he followed the boy (whose name turned out to be, almost unbelievably, Cecil Hopton-Feeblebunnies) through the vast warship. It was a floating city of men, an endlessly complex engine of industrial war, the culmination of human ingenuity and coordination. The size and wonder of the steel monster in whose guts he moved like a worm, a microorganism, began to numb his senses. Ten times larger than the primitive dreadnoughts Jellicoe and von Scheer had maneuvered in 1916, in the closing days of the World War, each modern line-of-battle ship took seven years to build and strained the resources of its sponsor government. Launched, their crews trained to rigid Atlantic Alliance standards, the ships took their places in the Line, steaming endlessly up and down the North American coast from the Antilles to Nova Scotia. For thirty years now there had been a Line there, the cost of peace, of the policy (first formulated by Winston Churchill in 1937) of " 'containment' " of the expansionist Yankees and their no less aggressive Russian allies.

Only now . . . that ring of guns and steel might be broken. If Shiloh did not succeed.

Hopton-Feeblebunnies broke into his musing with an invitation to lunch. Quidley nodded abstractedly. The meal was very British, he thought—plain food and plenty of it—and there was a good port afterward. There was time for a nap on one of the wardroom couches (the adjutant had some abstruse kind of coding work to do), and then he found himself being shaken awake. It was Vickery himself, carrying a set of binoculars. "Ready, Major? Spot of shooting scheduled. Come on up."

On the open wing of the flag bridge Quidley slipped a pair of the glasses about his own neck, and glanced apprehensively down over the edge of the breast-high splinter shield. Far below was the flat steel surface of a forward turret, fully as big, it seemed, as a polo field. From one side of it, extending out over the deep blue foam-streaked sea, were six vast tubes, so huge that he was hard put to recognize these tapering bulbous-snouted pillars as cannon. They moved slowly, elevating and dropping as the *Redoubtable* rolled ponderously. He turned, to find Vickery close behind him. "Impressive, eh?"

"They certainly are. These are the—"

"Thirty-inchers. Cecil here will now give the figures." He smiled at his adjutant, who blushed but began spouting numbers. Armor-piercing shells weighed fifteen thousand pounds, exited the barrel at five thousand feet per second, carried out to sixty thousand yards free ballistic and one hundred sixty thousand with rocket assist. The armor-piercing round could penetrate sixteen feet of waffle armor, while the heaviest Yankee ship, the USS *Pacific Canada*, carried but fifteen; the high-explosive round had a destructive radius of two hundred yards. He was deep into the complexity of the automatic loading mechanisms when Vickery, smiling, waved him into silence. He looked over the rail and signaled to someone below, then turned to Quidley. "Believe they're ready to let fly. Might want to hold your ears, Major."

He had his hands halfway up when the world erupted around him. The shock smashed at his face, sucked the air from his lungs, and sent him spinning against the rail. A brown cloud of burned powder, mixed with scraps of dirty papery material, blotted out sun and sea. His feet smarted from the jolt of the deck. Vickery, he saw, had retreated inside the enclosed portion of the bridge; but intoxicated with the guns, Quidley resolved to stay outside. Hopton-Feeblebunnies flashed him an excited, boy-ish smile. Quidley looked over the edge of the shield just in time to catch the second salvo. When, dazzled, blinded, and slightly punchy, he raised his binoculars, the cluster of tiny specks was still visible high above the sea. As he watched, they winked out; then, dragging seconds later, six thin lines of white appeared, miles off and low on the jagged horizon.

"The rockets," the boy shouted. Quidley nodded. Coastal batteries had them too; each shell carried an en-gine that added speed at the top of its flight, where the air was thin. Some English scientific type—Clarke?—sug-gested that a large enough engine in a lightweight shell could escape gravity completely and circle the earth forever. Crazy idea, he thought, watching the white lines curve downward and out of sight. What would be the use of firing a shell that never came down?

Two salvoes later, when his eyes were becoming un-focused, he finally retired to the shelter of the flag bridge.

"Damned impressive, Admiral. I'd hate to be a Yankee captain facing the Line!"

"That's the idea," said Vickery. "And so there won't be war . . . unless." Their eyes met and Quidley under-stood.

Shiloh had to succeed.

An hour later, Vickery's rewritten documents in his briefcase, he stood again on Deck Two of the *Shenan-doah*, watching the Line dwindle astern. Large as they were, they seemed at last only toys, dwarfed by the im-mensity and dispassion of the sea.

For just a moment, standing far above the waves, he had a sense of both the power and the fragility of men. The Line, the concentrated might of half the world, was now a distant scatter of dark pinpoints, trailing white wakes. With the feeling came a sense, too, of his own part, small though it was, in the vast counterpoise of peo-ples and ideas that men on both sides called the Almost War. Aubrey Quidley was a tiny pivot in the immense ticking shell of Earth. But he could be an important pivot. By doing his duty—as Quidleys had ever done, *Audemus jura nostra defendere*—he could defend and preserve the cause of freedom, of leadership by the natural elite, of the rights of property, safety, and duty. God himself favored the Allied side. They alone held Him in proper reverence as the source of their dominion over the less-advanced peoples. As those peoples—the Indian, the colored, the Asiatic—themselves recognized.

He nodded. The cause was just. But from somewhere the dark tortured face of Turner took form, blood welling from between clenched lips, eyes hot with pain and hatred. He caught himself and gripped the rail as the sea below began to spin lazily around him, countermarching with slow dignity as if he were above the axis of the slowly rotating Earth . . . he bit at his lips. A slight dizziness, no more than that. Possibly he was airsick, possibly the slow roll of the ship had done it. Perhaps a touch of concussion from the guns. It would pass. . . .

Nine

Her hands shook as she fitted the key to the lock. It would not go in. She cursed viciously with the mother oaths that were common coin among the women at the House and when it went in, twisted it hard and pushed the door open.

"Johnny?"

There was no answer. She could tell by the dead air in the apartment that no one had been in it since she had left to go to work. It was now five in the morning and she was tired and her thighs, her cunt, ached and burned; the last customer had been heavy, savage, and so drunken that he had labored over her for almost an hour without his spasm.

She sat down suddenly on the tatty sofa and put her face in her hands. Where was he? Had he run out on her? His wound was still unhealed, he shouldn't be out on the streets. And what if he were picked up! Fear made her hug herself and rock back and forth, staring at the bottle he had left, two days before, empty, with two used cups—

Two used cups. For the first time she noticed it. Someone else had been here with him. They had a drink. Sometime later he had left. Who might it have been? Only his Railroad friends knew he was staying with her. Only Bo, Willie, the other men at the docks.

She felt weak; her body longed for a lonely bed. She

looked at the window. The first gray light of dawn showed through the cracked square of glass.

She would go out, after him.

The little electric heater set a cup of water bubbling in seconds. The CE issue coffee powder made an insipid brew, but she poured the last few drops of the corn into it and drank it off. It sent warmth through her.

Johnny, my man, where are you?

The street was empty. She had no curfew worries; the Night Worker notation on her pass took care of that. But where to look first? *Willie's*, she thought. *His place the closest.*

Willie lived upstairs in one of the cheap brick two-story cribs that lined Church Street. His woman, China, a dried-up old creature with twinkling dark eyes and a reputation as a root doctor, answered her rap. "What you want this time a' the morning? You that Lewis girl, ain't you?"

"Yes'm. Please, is Willie in? Ask him if he knows where my man Johnny is."

The woman laughed—cackled, rather—and closed the door. Something thumped and then Willie opened it and came out and stood on the narrow landing in his under-wear. He was grossly fat, but his expresion was good-humored. "Hello, Vyry. What you wantin'?"

"Johnny. He hasn't been back for two days. Where is he?"

"Johnny? I see him th'other night at the"—Willie seemed to catch himself—"the other night. Friday night it was."

"Was he all right? Where did he go after?"

"Yes, he seemed right lively, though his leg was hurt a little. I didn't see him none after I left. I thought he would go right on back to your place. Didn't he never arrive?"

"No. He hasn't been back since then."

"Git my clothes, China," said Willie. "I help you look, Vyry. Don't know just where—but there'll be two of us out. You tried Finnick's?"

"No."

"I'll go over there. Maybe you best try the hospital, the po-lice—"

"You think he might have—"

"Might have got rolled comin' home late. Or the pa-trollers pick him up, in which case he either at the station waitin' on trial, or down at the hospital."

"Oh, Lord."

"Les' go, girl."

The dawn was strong in the east now. She was glad of that; Willie would be legal. The police? The hospital? She had walked several blocks before she thought of phoning. She passed several booths for whites, but had to walk considerably farther before she found one for colored that wasn't broken.

There was no John Turner in the colored ward at Norfolk General. She cursed and dropped coins and dialed the police. The dispatcher hung up at the sound of her voice.

No time now to curse being black in a white world. She hurried west through the streets. White men, up early, stared at her through the glass of automobiles as they passed. To hell what they thought, she said to herself.

Johnny, Johnny.

She was almost running when someone gripped her roughly, almost throwing her down, and she looked up into the solid, suspicious face of a cop.

"What's going on, sister?" Small, hostile eyes. A large stomach, a hairy hand resting on a holster. "Late for work?" He laughed.

"I'm going to the station."

"The station? Why?"

"My man—he's not come home."

"That's risky business, little darlin'." The man's hand held her arm insistently. "Maybe it'd be best if you was to just wait for him to come back. If'n he don't in a couple of days—well, you're a pretty young Negress. Might fancy you myself—"

"Let me go."

She heard him laughing behind her as she fled. Down Fenchurch, toward the marbled heart of town. Past the old brick colonial homes on Freemason, past the old Norfolk Academy, past the new domed convention center, fire-blackened from the riots; past the new tall buildings of the banks and the government. Till at last, panting, she stopped at the corner of Granby and City Hall Avenue, and looked up at the police building. It was an immense monolith in red brick and red mortar and blank black narrow windows. A decorative tiled moat surrounded it. Over the narrow bridge at the entrance arched a stark square of orange steel, flanked by the flags of Virginia and of the Confederacy, that of Virginia deep blue, of the Confederacy scarlet. . . .

She had never been inside the building. No CE would . . . voluntarily. She forced herself forward. As she reached for the door it opened automatically. A guard in the foyer looked up. A receptionist stopped talking to a man in a business suit. The guard came up swiftly. "What do you want?"

Vyry feared the eyes—the flat hostile eyes with no sympathy, no human feeling at all. But she had to find Johnny. "I'm—I'm looking for someone."

"Who?"

"My man. His name is John Turner."

"He a prisoner here?"

"I don't know. I called, but they hung up on me."

"What makes you think he's here?"

"He hasn't been home . . . and he don't have a night pass."

"Oh." The guard's eyes seemed to soften a bit. "Come over here . . . Marie, she wants to know if a—"

"Turner, John Turner."

"Has been picked up. Last night."

"Or night before. He been gone two days now."

"Wait." The receptionist picked up a phone. Her face curled as she watched Vyry, as if a bad smell had invaded the foyer. "No? Thank you, then. No—just some nigger run away from home. Thanks, Les. Bye-bye." She looked past Vyry to the guard. "Nobody in custody by that name."

"Sure?"

"I said no." The woman glared at Vyry and then at the guard. "Are you going to let her—"

"Come on, let's go," said the guard.

"But—"

"He's not here. You'll have to go."

Near the door she twisted free from his hand. "Where else can he be, officer? Where can I look?"

"Have you tried the colored ward at the hospital?"

"He's not there."

"Well—he might have took off." The guard looked unhappy; he, at least, Vyry felt, seemed to see her as a human being and not as a black skin, a CE, something to insult and get rid of as soon as possible. "You know, men do that sometimes. Get tired of a woman, take off—don't come back."

"Johnny wouldn't do that."

"Well then." The guard shifted from foot to foot. "There's one other place you might try."

"Where!"

"If you aren't afraid. That's patrol headquarters. But that . . . well, they can be pretty rough down there. On you."

"Oh."

"If you could wait an hour, I'll be off then. I might could go down with you."

She looked up in surprise. "That's right nice of you, officer. But I can't wait no hour."

"Fred," said the man in the business suit.

"Good luck, then," whispered the guard.

The door opened for her. *Door can't tell if I white or colored,* she thought. *Just opens for any person. Must have been made up North.* The air outside felt close and muggy after the air conditioning of the station.

Every CE knew where the Citizens' Patrol headquarters was. Since the riot the armed patrollers, all white and primarily working-class, had been combing the city after curfew. It was ten blocks away, near half a mile, and she began to walk again, through streets that were beginning to fill with people on their way to work.

And as she walked, pictures began to form in her mind.

Johnny had not been like most CEs. He had dared to hate and, in some ways, dared to show it. She felt cold as she remembered some of the things he had told her about, things he and the other waterfront men had done to outgoing cargoes. Sugar in the tanks of outgoing General Johnstons from Tredegar. Optics cleverly cracked or knocked awry, ruining weapons worth thousands of dollars. Sand in bearings, tools thrust through turbine blades, buckets of salt water in radio sets, warehouses of tobacco and cotton going up in fires of unexplained origin.

What if the patrollers had caught him in the act of destroying something? Of committing some crime against state (white) property? Every CE in the South knew the summary justice of the patrollers and of their even more radical faction, the mystery-shrouded Kuklos League. She herself had seen a lynching in Charleston when she was small. A little white girl had disappeared. An old Negro,

96

half-crippled, had admitted seeing her; searched, his person yielded a tiny ring, which the frantic mother swore was her child's. He had been hung from the quaint old antebellum balcony of the Dock Street Theatre. The little girl had turned up the next day, unhurt. The ring, Vyry had been told by a playmate (the old man's niece), had belonged to his childhood sweetheart, who had died of influenza in 1919.

And it was still the same. The white-led police had fired at Turner regardless of the crowd beyond. The patrollers still rode at night with shotguns and powers of summary arrest. Nor did they stop at that; Turner had told her of the broken bodies that drifted down the Elizabeth in the mornings, bodies the longshoremen were forbidden to touch.

This was their "conditional emancipation."

And yet, she thought as she hurried through the streets, under the proud new buildings and gay bunting of the New South, she could not blame nor hate the whites as whites. There were good ones, like the guard, people who tried to help within the constraints of an iron society. There were even some in positions of power who might be reached—like the major, Quidley, who fancied himself in love with her. But there were others of unqualified evil, though for them there was an excuse—government policy.

In the end, she thought, perhaps it comes down to what the government makes them do. If the CEs were in charge, would it be any different, really? *I hope it would,* she thought, looking away from a passing truck as the driver shouted an obscenity at her. *At least we've known what it is to suffer. That alone has made us wise.*

Music drifted around her and she slowed as she reached the end of Granby Street. Here the downtown area degenerated into a slum of low, grimy buildings; night clubs, pornographic bookstores, drug shops, liquor stores, low movie houses, and dozens and dozens of bars. On weekend evenings they were filled with sailors from Sewell's Point out for a drink and a lay. This morning, early on a Monday, they served a different clientele: the patrollers, who sought refreshment in whiskey after a long night on the streets.

"Hey, you!"

"Hey, baby!"

"Oh, brown sugar, c'mon suck on this!"

Patrol headquarters was just ahead, at the corner of Granby and Brambleton. She looked straight ahead and walked on. The men behind her nudged one another. Some of them, carrying bottles, began to drift after her; she could hear their footsteps and their drunken laughter, and walked faster. For a moment she thought of turning back. No, not back—they were behind her, closer now, calling and giggling—but to the right, walking (running?) down Olney toward the wider streets where people would be walking and driving . . . *But I can't. They might have Johnny in this place.*

"Hey, sugar, what you doin' down here?"

The smell of liquor flowed over her. She pulled away from the hands, and her sleeve tore with a minute ripping sound. The headquarters building, barred flag in front, the men lounging there looking her way, was less than a block away. To its left was a bar, the Gibraltar she saw, and then the clutter of boxes and cans that marked the mouth of an alley.

"Slow down, bitch! We want to talk to *you.*" The voices were angry now, fierce with lust. More hands. She twisted and lashed out with her purse. It was almost torn from her hand as it hit someone with a solid thud. A man cursed; they fell back for a moment. "Jesus, she's a fighty one," said someone. "Where you goin', baby?"

"To headquarters."

"You goin' to *headquarters?*"

"I got business there."

Perhaps it was the sharpness of her tone (actually born of fear) that made them hesitate, but she walked faster and in a moment was inside the building. More air conditioning, like a cold blow in the face. A row of startled white faces—all men—startled, then instantly hostile. A game of pool in a corner stopped dead, the players turning with cues in hand to see the cause of the sudden hush. No one spoke as she crossed to a gray-uniformed man at a desk. He stared at her as she approached.

"Morning, Officer. Is you with the patrol?"

"Yes."

He seemed, if not friendly, at least not openly hostile. Tall even in the creaky wooden chair, blond hair, blue eyes, young. She took a breath in relief—but then she saw that it was not an Army gray that he was wearing, but

98

a darker color. And then she saw the white armband with the flaming-cross symbol.

And the three red letters: KKL.

"What can I do for you?" he said.

The men watched, all silent. Cigar smoke drifted lazily in layers. Vyry put her fingers lightly on the desk; they trembled. "I'm looking for a man. My man, sir. His name is Johnny Turner. He hasn't been home for two days. I wonder if the patrol picked him up."

"I'm afraid we can't help you," said the blond man.

"He isn't here?"

"It isn't that," he said, looking at her steadily. "But do you really think we keep records on every nigger we kill?"

There was a murmur of laughter in the room. Vyry stared.

"Take your hands off my desk," said the man.

"I thought—"

"Shut up." He stared at her as if deciding what to do. As he did so another man, fat, dressed in work pants and a dirty, short-sleeved white shirt, came over from the pool table and bent to whisper in the blond man's ear.

"I see. Thanks, Billy." He swung back to Vyry, and now his voice was threatening. "Here's what *I* want to know. What gave you the idea that you can come in here for an accounting from us? Who told you that?"

She didn't know how to answer. "Who are you, anyway? Where do you work?" he said, picking up a pencil.

"Elvira Lewis, sir. I work at the CSAB on Bute Street."

"Oh, yeah." He wrote, and looked up with a dreadful smile. "Well, *Miss* Lewis, maybe they won't want you there much longer."

She knew to keep her mouth shut and to look at the floor. After a moment he laughed. "Get out."

Some of the men nearest the door had left before her. A knot of them stood outside, waiting. They closed on her as soon as she stepped out, taking her purse first, tearing the strap off. She screamed.

"Shut her up."

"What for? Let her scream. Ain't nobody going to come after her."

"Sergeant might hear."

"She just seen him. He ain't protecting no niggers."

Close around her, the men held her arms. One rifled

99

through her purse, throwing things to the bricks. "Pretty fancy stuff she carryin'."

"What's that?"

"Perfume, by God! And look here! Gold earrings! Confiscate *them* right now."

"Those are my things. I need them for work," she gasped.

Laughter. "What kind of work you do, bitch?"

"I'm an—entertainer."

"Lessee her card. Shit, boys, look at this. She's a whore over't that Army club!"

"No shit?"

"High-class officer tail, huh?" The hands eased off her for a moment. "Say, honey—whyn't you show us some of what them Army officers get. We'll let you keep your joolry."

"No. I don't do outside work. Get your hands off me."

"Maybe she wants money."

"Maybe she don't get the picture yet."

Looking up, she saw the alley ahead. Step by step they were forcing her into it. Once inside, she knew what would follow. Rape—by all of them, and painful. Already she saw the gleam of a knife.

". . . Fix her face, sergeant says," someone said.

Maybe they won't want you there much longer.

She panicked. Crying, kicking, she was pulled toward the alley. A hand felt for her mouth and she bit, hard; a high womanlike scream. A man doubled as her shoe found his groin. Something hit her from behind, hard, in the kidneys, and she went limp at the sudden flash of pain. Her feet dragged on the pavements. She stopped struggling. She was beaten.

"What's going on here?"

The men stopped. "Sir?" said someone.

"I said, what's going on? I heard a scream."

She staggered, trying to stand. Men stepped away from her. The high, annoyed voice—it seemed that she had heard it before—

"Vyry!" said Quidley. "What in heaven's name is happening?"

She leaned against him and gasped something out. He stared down and then his hand moved to his holster and the men drew back.

"Who's in charge here?"

100

"Sir." The blond sergeant had come out on the walk.

"Baylor—are these your people?"

"These are Citizens' Patrol, yes, sir. Can I help you? Is the lady a friend of yours?"

Quidley stared at him for a long moment. Then his hand came up from his holster to stroke her hair. Baylor, watching, grew a shade paler. "I believe she fell, sir. My men were probably helping her up."

"Get in the car, Vyry," said Quidley. "Roberts! Put her in back!"

"Yes, sir, Major."

She sank, numb, into the soft rear seat of the big gray car. The pain in her back lit odd flashes in front of her eyes. She saw the driver turn in his seat, glance toward the building, and slip a small bottle from inside his uniform and hold it out toward her. "Can you use a quick one, sister?" he said.

"Thanks." She took a long swallow and handed it back. Roberts made the bottle disappear as Quidley's voice drew closer.

"Yes, sir," the sergeant, Baylor, was saying.

"Find out. And see that they're disciplined. Taken off patrol. You hear me? And do it right now."

"Yes, Major." The blond man came to attention and saluted, but slowly, just short of a contemptuous slowness. Quidley leaned out the window of the Bentley and poked him in the chest with a stiff finger.

"I've had my eye on you, Sergeant Baylor. On you and all your Kuklos League thugs. You'd better lie low—you hear?"

"Sir," said Baylor, his face white with anger. "You won't talk to me like that when—"

"What what?" Quidley waited, but the man shut his lips firmly. The men around waited, silent, and at last he sat back in the car and said, "Roberts, let's go. I've had enough of this trash. Anywhere, just drive. And draw the blinds."

He turned to Vyry as the Bentley began to move, and took off his cap; the interior grew dark as the car curtains unrolled. He wiped sweat from his face with his handkerchief. "Vy—what in heaven's name were you doing *there*? If I hadn't shown up—"

"I know, Major. I know what they wanted to do."

"But why? What an insane place to be for—"

101

"For a nigger. That's right."

Quidley winced. "I didn't use that word, Vyry, nor do most educated people now. But you are—colored—and those Citizens' Patrol people aren't properly supervised. That Baylor. . . . The whole Kuklos bunch ought to be outlawed."

She glanced at him and felt herself softening a bit. Queer and stuck up and strange and not really very likable . . . but he had rescued her.

Perhaps *he* knew where Johnny was.

"Did they hurt you?" he said.

"Stole my purse and hit me a couple of times. I guess I'm feeling better now, Major. I was scared. Scared I was going to die back there in that alley."

He pulled her over to him and kissed her. "You're all right now. But you still haven't told me what you were doing there in the first place."

In a rush of words she told him about her man—how he had vanished, her fear, her search that morning. He frowned at first, when she said 'my man,' but then listened carefully. When she was done he said, "I have access to patrol records, of course. And to those of the police, too. Perhaps I can find out for you where he is."

"Oh, if you would—"

"His name Lewis, too? What's his first name?"

"No, it's not Lewis. We're not married. Yet. His name is Johnny Turner. He works on the waterfront."

"Turner!"

"Yes. You—you act as if you know something."

Quidley leaned forward. "Roberts. To the fort."

"Major . . . *what's the matter?*"

"I know where he is," said Quidley, but the way he said it made her feel suddenly faint. She lay back against the fabric of the seat, waiting for him to say more.

"He was picked up Friday night after curfew, crossing the fence at a government installation. Patrollers brought him to me. We've been holding him.

"Vyry, he refused to talk to us."

"Oh, no," she whispered.

"Vyry—"

"I want to see him."

"He's not in very good shape, I'm afraid."

"If he's dead, I'll kill you, Major. I will."

"He's alive, Vyry. But don't talk like that. Not to me.

It was his own fault. My duty was to investigate, to get answers. Why was he climbing the fence at that warehouse area? Do you know?"

She stared at her hands, seeing only now that several of her fingernails were broken. The terrible thing was that she *did* know. It had to have been a Railroad meeting. Why else would Willie have been so evasive? Why else would Johnny have left her apartment, with the police after him and a bullet wound still unhealed?

She looked up at Quidley. For the first time she realized his power. This gray-clad man, so careful with his trousers, so oddly proud—he had the power to release her Johnny.

Or to kill him.

"He hasn't told you anything?"

"He's said nothing under interrogation but his name. We're using a new technique, but so far—"

"No. He wouldn't ever tell," said Vyry.

"Tell what?" Quidley leaned forward, pale eyes fixed on her face. "What was he doing?"

"He was stealing food."

"Food!"

"That's right, Major."

"But why . . . ?" He spread his hands helplessly. "Why shouldn't he confess that?"

"Major—do you know what happens to CEs they catch stealing?"

"Vaguely. Jail?"

"Not for Johnny. You see, he kill a man once. Beat him to death with his hands. That's why he's a longshoreman now. Transferred and reassigned—like me, Major, like me. But if he ever gets caught again for a crime. . . ."

Quidley nodded. "Reconditioning," he said. "But what he's getting now is as bad."

"Except that I'm left out of it." Vyry nodded, eyes locked with his. "They'd take me too. For knowing about it and not reporting him. They'd take me too. This way it's only him.

"That's why he'll never talk to you, Major."

"My God." Quidley stripped off his gloves and slapped them nervously against his palm. "But look—he was hurt, his leg was torn up when he was brought in. How did that happen?"

"Who bring him in, Major?"

"Citizens' Patrol."

"That's how. You seen them po' buckra back there. Them trash shot him, or cut him—then told him if he talks, they'll come back and kill him. They would, too."

"Hm," said Quidley. *It's a duel,* Vyry thought, watching him as he struggled to make up his mind. *A duel— and Johnny's life is the prize.*

"And if he'd had any food, anything valuable on him when they caught him—"

"They'd have taken it." Quidley sighed. "What a world we live in."

She snuggled closer to him. "Major Cavalier—I'm sure glad you happened by."

"This man. Just what is he to you? Your lover?"

"Well—he was."

"Was?"

"Till you come along." This was it—this was it. But even as she said it she was not sure how much of it was a lie and how much was the truth. "I owe you a lot, Major. I know I do. Helping me, helping Johnny—"

"How have I helped him?"

"You'll let him go. Won't you? Now that you know?"

Quidley sighed again, then nodded. "Yes, I suppose I will, Vyry. For another person I might not. But your story rings true, and I feel I know you well enough to trust you." He smiled. "I think I'm giving in to you . . . but somehow it doesn't matter. And Turner obviously is not dangerous."

"Sir, we here," Roberts said.

"Park in back of port control."

"Yes, sir."

The Bentley turned, slowed, and rolled to a stop. A moment later Roberts opened the door for Quidley. "Come up with us, Sergeant," he said. "Walk with her. Behind me."

"Yes, sir."

"Where's your damned cap, man?"

"Sorry, sir. Right here, sir."

"Come on." He strode into the rear entrance. Mercifully, there was no one he knew in the lobby. They said nothing in the elevator as it dropped downward.

"Stay here," said Quidley. Vyry, standing in the antiseptic-smelling corridor, began to tremble. From the rooms beyond she heard, "Sanchez! Where the devil—"

and then a low murmur of conversation. At last the major returned, his face set. "He's not in very good shape," he said.

"I'll take care of him."

"I hope so. That new treatment—when we turned it off, the result wasn't quite what we expected."

Vyry pressed her hands to her mouth. A white-sheeted figure was being rolled into the corridor on a table. It looked odd, as if something lumpy and deformed lay beneath it. But then she saw that yes, it was Johnny, lying on his side, knees drawn up, arms crossed.

She bit her fists to keep from screaming. His eyes . . . they were open under the shaven skull, but they were empty. Empty and unfocused as a newborn child's, as the eyes of an imbecile, of a dead animal.

"Catatonia," said a small, swarthy man, steering the trolley to a halt. "I'm sorry, Major. When the pleasure stopped I gave him the choice: talk, or have it shut off for good.

"He did neither. Instead, he just . . . withdrew. He's completely and unreachably insane."

Ten

When the jitney he'd called had come and gone and Vyry was gone and the thing that had been Turner gone with her, he had dismissed Sanchez and Roberts and walked slowly up four flights of stairs to the ground floor of the building. Now he stared at himself in the mirror of the officer's rest room and tried to keep from throwing up again. He was telling himself that it had been an accident but his stomach did not believe him, for it knew that he had done it, he had done it to Turner. And to her.

When his mouth filled with saliva again he bent to the basin. As he ran the water he heard the voices of men arriving for work outside in the lobby and he looked at his watch.

It was time to be in his office; he was already late. Norris would have him on the carpet again, overlooking the fact that he'd been working all weekend long. *Well, damn the little bantam, I'll take my time,* he said silently to the ruthless mirror.

"General Norris has been looking for you," said Jeannie, as soon as he came through the door.

"He wants to see me now?"

"No. Half an hour ago. Better go right down. There's something on the front of your uniform there."

"Never mind," he said, heading for the door.

106

"Major Quidley. You wanted to see me, sir."

"Where the hell have you been, Quidley?" He opened his mouth to explain, but Norris cut him off. "You got that change out to the op order yet?"

"Sir, our plan was disapproved."

"What! By whom?"

"Sir Leigh, General."

Norris closed his mouth and sat down. "Oh. Why?"

Quidley explained. When he came to Sir Leigh's comments about Norris he felt particular pleasure in repeating them word for word. ". . . insane, or a traitor, he said, sir."

"What! No, don't repeat it. Damn it, Quidley, this was *your* idea!"

"Yes, sir. But you approved it."

"I did no such thing."

"You signed it, sir."

Norris went from red to purple and Quidley decided to back off. After all, the man (though below him socially) was his commanding officer. "But there's no harm done, sir. He tore the message up before my eyes."

"He did, eh?" Norris suddenly pulled out a drawer; Quidley almost reached for his sidearm. The silver-haired little general tossed another gray-and-black CBI folder on the desk. "Read that, Quidley, and then tell me there's no harm done."

He did, and swallowed. According to the CBI, the complete text of the moving-east message had been passed upward within the convoluted network of the Underground Railroad.

"Major Quidley," said Norris, with great dignity, "I shall now ask you to explain why you should not be interrogated. Only you, I, and Admiral Sir Vickery have ever seen that bogus message of yours. By God, we *are* narrowing that leak down, aren't we! That's the best idea I've had in weeks."

"I didn't pass it on," said Quidley.

"And I didn't!" screamed Norris, slamming his desk. "Quidley, it's you, me, or Vickery! And don't try to tell me it's me!"

"Yes, sir. I won't."

"Who have you told about this message, Quidley? Who did you tell about Shiloh?"

"No one, sir."

"No one at all? No one that you thought was above suspicion? Do you talk in your sleep, did your mother overhear you? Think, man!"

"I didn't tell anyone about the message, sir."

Norris stared at him, at the report, then back at Quidley. "Major," he said at last, softly, "there's just one thing stopping me from court-martialing you now. Today. No, two. One—whatever your faults, you're of an old Confederate family and I'll give you this—you're a loyal and honest Southerner. Two—you're just not smart enough to be a foreign agent."

"Sir—"

"I warn you, don't anger me further," said Norris softly.

Quidley waited. Norris turned his chair to look out the window, his method, his subordinates knew, of forcing himself to relax. "All right, then. No matter what, we've got to go ahead with Shiloh; the Allies need that shell. Vickery disapproved our plan, eh?"

"Yes, sir." Quidley hoisted up his briefcase. "But he had his staff make some changes. I have the amended plan here."

Norris took it and began leafing through it. "I'll probably have some last-minute changes myself, although we've got to get this out—it's tonight, isn't it?"

"Tomorrow morning, sir."

"I'd better hurry, then. Let's have a final briefing meeting at five today, too—put the changes out verbally." He looked toward the door. "Dismissed."

"If I may ask about that, sir—"

"You may not. Obviously the only way to keep something secret around here is to keep it to myself. Accordingly, I'm not saying a word until five o'clock. Be there."

"Yes, sir." Quidley saluted smartly. Norris stared at him and sighed.

"You know, Quidley, you're like a collie," he said. "Exquisite . . . but dumb. All the brains are bred out of them. No, don't bother to call me out. Even in this country, that's a little quixotic, isn't it?"

"I resent your personal remarks strongly, sir."

"Get out. Before you go—whatever became of that curfew violator you were examining? Herter?"

"Turner, sir. Ah, it was—petty theft."

"Turn him over to the police?"

108

"He's been disposed of, sir."

"Right." Norris, to his intense relief, bent to his desk and did not pursue the subject. A moment later he looked up. "You still here?"

"No, sir." He saluted again, executed an about-face, and left. In the elevator, alone, he took the Leech & Rigdon out and aimed it at the wall and fantasized pumping seven rounds into Norris's weasely little face. A collie! Maligning such a beautiful dog! But what had that to do with him? He buttoned the holster down as the door slid open and wondered if he were being too hard on the man. Perhaps old Norris was losing interest, losing his grip.

Ten A.M. He sat at his desk in thought. After a time he shuffled through some papers. Jeannie brought him in a co-cola and that seemed to settle his stomach. He sat at the desk and looked out at the Bay and brooded over the affair of the message.

He'd typed it himself, on his own Twain here in the office. A triplicate message form. One had gone in his file. He rose and checked; it was still there, and only he had the combination to the cabinet. The original Jeannie had taken down to Norris. The intermediate pink copy he had put in his own briefcase. He snapped open the case and took the slip of pink paper with the flimsy carbon sheet attached and stared at it. Gradually his eyes widened.

The middle copy. Hadn't there been *two* carbons attached when he slipped it into the case?

He pressed his forehead with his hands and then pulled cigarettes from the desk and lit one. There *had* been two carbons. He looked at the remaining one. The typed message, in reversed letters, was clearly visible on it.

Where had he gone that day? From the office he'd gone to the officer's mess for dinner with Sawyer. Then they had parted and he'd gone to the house on Bute Street. The briefcase he had kept with him even in the room with Vyry. After that, home, where Sharon Sue had been waiting outside. The next day he'd looked in on Turner and then taken the zep out to the Fleet. He remembered now that when he'd taken the message out to show Vickery there had been only one leaf attached. Sometime in between someone had opened his briefcase and taken the other.

A horrible feeling of doom, of treachery, was beginning

to pervade him. He stubbed out the cigarette. It was un-bearable.

It had to be Vyry.

There had been plenty of chances for her to take it now that he thought about it. When he'd been in the bath-room. When they'd been walking he had left the briefcase in her room. An accomplice could easily (well, not *easily*, but it was certainly possible) have finessed the rudimentary lock and taken the document. *Why* hadn't he been more careful!

Vyry. He saw it all now. She must be Railroad. Hadn't she said something about being R&R'd for carrying Rail-road literature? Why hadn't he *thought?* Instead he had allowed himself to fall in love with her. Norris was right: He was a fool.

He jumped to his feet. There was only one way to sal-vage his career, but there was not a second to lose. He snatched at his phone. "Guard Section—this is Quidley, Port Security. Emergency One. Scout car and squad of troops at the main gate. On the double!"

He ran out. Sawyer was in the corridor, just stepping out of the elevator. He looked up in surprise as Quidley stormed down the hall. "Good Lord— You sure look in a hurry. What's up? That colored gal of yours got a hank-erin'?"

"You armed? Good, come on. Earl, you were right."

"What about? Where we going?" Sawyer stared at him as the elevator purred downward.

"Going to the House."

"A li'l early, but long's we're back by five—"

"It's that woman. She's stolen classified material from me and passed it on to the Railroad."

Sawyer whistled.

They ran through the lobby. Roberts ran for the Bentley with the two officers on his heels. "To the gate, quick," Quidley shouted.

As they neared the main gate he noted with satisfac-tion that his telephone message was getting results. Two big half-tracked Tredegar armored trucks were idling on the berm, emitting blue clouds of diesel haze, and armed troops were scrambling aboard. As Roberts braked for the gate a squad of motorcycle MPs arrived. Quidley leaned from the window and shouted to the driver of the lead half-track, "Follow me!"

The sound of engines built to an ear-splitting roar as Roberts rolled onto the highway. He glanced back. "Major, sir—where we goin'?"

"CSAB. Bute Street. You know where it is."

"Yes, sir, where I been takin' you . . . but all these soldiers, the girls not goin' to—"

"Damn it man, step on it! And put your cap on!"

"Yes, sir!"

Two army cycles swept by them and settled into position ahead of the staff car, switching on their sirens. Looking back, Quidley could see the Tredegars closing up. Men in the semienclosed top turret were charging the machine guns. A light armored unit, by the silhouette a General Early, was emerging from the main gate as he lost sight of it. He turned forward again.

"You can move right smart when you want to," said Sawyer, and Quidley caught the trace of admiration in his tone.

"Have to, sir. Only just realized that it had to be her. We've got to get her and any accomplices before they disappear."

"Right."

The Bentley swayed as Roberts sent it hurtling over the Lafayette River Bridge. Colored folk, crabbing from the narrow sidewalks, leaped for safety as the motorcade screamed by, sirens wailing, engines roaring, flags flapping crisply. Quidley reached for the Bentley's radio. "All units, this is Quidley. Our objective is the CSAB, Bute Street. Woman to be apprehended; possibly others. May be dangerous. I want a cordon thrown up on the lines York—Duke—Botetourt Streets. I'll go in alone."

Acknowledgments crackled and he signed off. "How did you find out?" said Sawyer.

"Process of elimination. Only three people could have had access to the material in question. Two were obviously above suspicion. That left her. I should have seen it before, Earl, but . . ." He looked at Sawyer unhappily. "I thought that she—that I—"

"You loved her?"

"I thought I did."

"Listen to an older man, boy," said the colonel, putting his beefy hand on Quidley's shoulder. "Don't *evuh* get mixed up with the colored, Major. We got to keep a pure race in this country or there just won't be nothing left in

111

a hundred years. Mixin' your blood with theirs . . . that'll lead to no good end. My folks have always held with that down Mississippi, and I sincerely believe in it now."

Quidley was only half-listening. He felt sweat starting under his armpits. If she were Railroad, she was probably part of the Town Point shooting incident. That group had been armed. If there were others with her, all armed . . .

"Slow down," he said as Roberts looked back for guidance. "I want to roll in slowly, as if for a visit." He reached for the mike again. "All units—cut those damned sirens!"

He held Roberts on a side street until the troop leaders reported their men in position. When the word came he checked his pistol and stepped out into the street.

"I'm comin' with you, Aubrey."

"Better stay here, Earl. If they're armed—"

"Then you'll need someone backin' you up." Sawyer patted his own gun. "Le's go, Quid."

When Chicken opened the door she looked surprised. "Why, gentlemen, you're here in midday! We have special rates till three. Who—"

"Vyry Lewis. Is she here?" said Quidley,

"Vyry. She's the one you're sweet on, isn't she? And the colonel?" Mrs. Rosen smiled. "He likes the white meat, doesn't he? Come on in."

Quidley, sweating, nodded to Sawyer to close the door. He took Chicken's pale plump arm. "Look, Mrs. Rosen, there's been trouble. I'm sure you're not mixed up in it, but we've got to arrest Lewis. Take us up to her room."

"Oh, but she's not here. It's trouble you say? Oh! I never knew anything, you understand—but no, Vyry's not up there. She's not been in at all today. I don't know why."

"Better search," said Sawyer.

Quidley nodded. "Come with us," he said to the madam. Looking nervous, she followed them up to the second floor. Quidley heard creaking, coital moans, through the thin walls. He paused outside the door to Vyry's room and listened. He put his hand on the knob and twisted it.

There was no one in the room. His nostrils caught a faint familiar scent of her. He turned, to find himself staring down the cavernous muzzle of Sawyer's drawn and cocked .455.

"Earl—you're pointing that thing—"

"Sorry, Aubrey." Sawyer let down the hammer and holstered the pistol and stepped back into the hall. "Looks like we done missed her."

"Where does she live?" Quidley asked Mrs. Rosen.

"I think—it's a West Main address—yes, I remember, 1228 Church Street."

"Come on," said Quidley.

"She'll be gone," said Sawyer. "She got wise to you, Aubrey. That's why she ain't in today. There won't be nobody at her apartment either."

"Got to check," said Quidley, but he knew Sawyer was probably right. Still, she might have left some clue, some piece of evidence by which they might track her. Anything to take him off the hook with Norris. "Call me at Port Security, 4-4108, immediately if she comes in," he said to the madam. "Earl, let's go."

The column proceeded east at a lower speed; the streets were narrower in this part of town, and he didn't envy soldiers riding in half-tracks over cobblestones. As the buildings grew more dilapidated the faces that turned to follow them became more and more those of CEs. "Nice neighborhood," said Sawyer. "You come calling on her here?"

"No."

"There's 1201."

"Roberts, stop here."

The 1200 block was a patient queue of flaking brick two-story tenements. Colored women and many children stared from low concrete stoops at the big gray car and the two officers. When the half-tracks rumbled up they all disappeared indoors.

"There it is," said Sawyer.

They climbed rickety stairs, gummy with dirt, hot, and humming with flies, and were confronted at the top by a torn screen door. It was ajar. Sawyer took out his pistol again and Quidley did the same. The buzzing of the flies seemed very loud. He pulled the screen open and stepped inside.

"Vyry?"

They went through the three rooms quickly, guns drawn. Quidley swallowed. He had never been in a CE's home before. He had no idea such squalor existed in a modern city.

113

"Look here," Sawyer said from the bedroom. "Bloodstains on this sheet. And looks like these rags was used for bandages."

"Turner," said Quidley.

"What?"

But he didn't explain. Only now was he thinking: *He's Railroad too. He was wounded by the police Wednesday. I had him in my hands—and she talked me out of him.*

Lies, all lies. He kicked viciously at a little pine nightstand. What a fool he'd played. He had been manipulated, used, and then discarded.

"She's gone, Aubrey. Is they any other place we can look?"

"No."

"Call the boys off?"

"Yes. Send them back." He took a deep breath, fighting his disappointment and anger.

"Burn it?"

"What, Earl?"

The other man had his lighter out and was kicking the sheets to the floor. "Burn the building. Hell, the whole block. Teach them to harbor Railroad terrorists."

"No. No, that's not necessary, Earl." He looked slowly around the apartment. "I didn't know they had to live like this."

"Had to?" Sawyer looked at the lighter, then shrugged and pocketed it. "It's natural for them, Major. They don't need no better, they don't want no better. My people down Mississip, they're not your rich aristocrat types. They lived cheek by jowl with nigras for generations. They're just a little better'n animals."

The day before, Quidley thought, *I would have sneered at this man as a cracker, as a typical redneck who never outgrew his poor-white upbringing.* But now he was not so sure. Of this . . . of himself . . . of anything.

From the street outside came the racket of departing motorcycles. "Come on, Quid," said Sawyer. "We'd best get back."

At five precisely Norris entered, bouncing in the way short men sometimes do. Quidley saw him first. "Atten—hut!"

"Seats, please, gentlemen."

The general looked around the table. "Channing—

Sawyer—a new face, you'd be Captain McLaws of the *Shenandoah,* correct? Thank you for coming over on such short notice, sir—Quidley—Chief Haile—all the rest, yes. Good of you all to come." He paused dramatically. "Since there are only a few of us, I'm going to just spread things out on the table here. Now," he glared around, "This is all secret. All secret. Do you understand this? None of you will discuss it with *anyone* but his immediate subordinates until the moment comes to act."

Quidley nodded with the others. Norris continued. "I've been informed that the *President McClellan* sailed from New Jersey on the twentieth, on schedule. Our original timetable should then be good."

"It is," said Channing. "She was sighted this morning by one of our submersibles, off the DelMarVa peninsula."

"We can assume then that the Yankees haven't got wind yet of our intentions. That's just the way we want it. Captain McLaws, will you and the *Macon* be ready tonight?"

"We're ready now. Fueled and armed. The marine boarding crew is reporting aboard now."

"Excellent." Norris looked at Quidley. "Because of certain breakdowns of security on the original Shiloh plan, changes have become necessary. I've decided, in consultation with Sir Leigh, Commander Channing, and Admiral Dennis, to make the assault by air.

"Yes, by zep. Don't look so surprised, gentlemen. Granted, it's never been done before, but that gives us an overwhelming advantage: surprise. The Yankees are not an imaginative people; they need time to react.

"They won't have it. The *Macon* and the *Shenandoah* will leave their masts at midnight. *Shenandoah* will carry a Confederate Marine boarding party. They have been briefed and exercised in secret. The zeps' course will take them out to sea and then due north, to a position, at two A.M., about ten miles northeast of the *President McClellan.*

"Boarding will be a split-second operation. Prime objective for three men, armed with grenades and submachine guns, will be the radio room. Five will head for the bridge, three for the belowdecks cargo areas, two for the engine spaces. All will be in blackface."

"Will that be necessary?" said Channing. "If, after all, there must be no survivors—"

"We have to face the possibility of failure. If the unforeseen occurs, the disguise may help us with the terrorist cover story."

"I see."

"Swift and decisive action will be essential," Norris resumed. "Surprise must be total. There must be no chance for organized resistance. Now, the Marines will handle this on the tactical level. But I have decided to include an Army officer, though this was not in the original plan. Major Quidley."

"Ah . . . me, sir?"

"You. I want someone charging, brave, a 'follow-me' type of leader. Not necessarily a brilliant officer"—Norris's little eyes crinkled—"but the kind that has inspired and stiffened our glorious Army throughout its history. I consider the Major a prime example of this type of officer."

He understood. The general was being kind, in his way. He was offering him a way out. If the operation succeeded —or if he was killed gloriously in action—the affair of the message would be forgotten. If the attack failed . . . then it wouldn't be worth it for Aubrey Lee Quidley to come back.

"Is there a specific assignment for me, sir?"

"Definitely. You've ordnance experience—you know as much as any of us do about fuzing and arming. I want you to make for the shell as soon as you land. Let the grunts take the ship. You get to the shell, guard it till all is secure, check it out—there's a small chance it could be a dummy, or our intelligence could be wrong. Prepare it for offload. Treat it like your own child, Major; get it into the boat, stay with it, guard it with your life all the way to Georgia. Plain enough?"

"Yes, General. Ah—thank you."

"Gentlemen, there's little else. The plan otherwise goes as printed. I will issue nothing written concerning the aerial attack. There is time, right up till two A.M., for the Yankee ship to turn north, go to battle stations, and make the operation impossible. *You must keep this secret.*

"Now—any questions?"

As they filed out Quidley felt Sawyer's hand on his shoulder. "Congrats, Aubrey. Norris really trusts you."

"Um."

"This could be a real coup for you, y'know. The President is very interested in this project; could mean a colonelcy for you. I envy you, you prissy son of a dog!"

Quidley grinned reluctantly. Sawyer in good humor was beginning to amuse rather than annoy him.

"What about a little snort to celebrate? I've got some stuff in my desk that will—"

"Thanks, Earl, but I've got a lot to do to get ready for tonight. The airships leave at midnight, and my going along is news to me—I'm not prepared at all."

"Thought you looked a little surprised." Sawyer lowered his voice, though they were now alone in the room. "Look—this here Lewis affair—you might could wipe that all out with Norris tomorrow. If he doesn't report it, you're off the hook. Just wanted you to know I won't mention it up at the Castle."

"I appreciate it, Earl," said Quidley, though a court-martial seemed a remote danger compared to dropping from an airship in the dark onto the deck of the enemy. "Well, look—I'll be seeing you after the operation."

"Sure, Aubrey. Good luck then."

He plunged into his preparations as soon as he reached his office. He had to review and study the op order, seeing it now from the point of view of a participant rather than a planner. He had to memorize the plans for three decks of the President class of U.S. Navy combat freighters. Had to review everything he could gather concerning a nuclear shell, how it might work, how it might be fuzed and armed. Had to check out from supply a Geiger counter, flashlight, battle helmet, tools. And on top of that had to find time to make some personal arrangements.

In case he didn't come back.

Because this operation would be dangerous. It was one thing to drop to the deck of the *Redoubtable*, a friendly ship, in daylight; quite another to do it at night, over a small ship, possibly in heavy seas. And once aboard there would be human enemies. Most of the *President McClellan's* crew had probably seen action in the Pacific; they'd know what guns were for. Blackface wouldn't fool them for more than second or two. Enough time, he hoped, for him to get off a shot.

At ten he closed up shop. He was tired, exquisitely so. The scene with Vyry, the race downtown, the long day itself . . . only driving home did he realize he hadn't eaten since breakfast. He parked and let himself in quietly and went upstairs.

There was no time left for sleeping, though. A half-hour's drive back to the airfield, plus the usual Army last-minute hurry-up-and-wait, would consume all his time. There were, though, a very few things that he had to do; and they had to be done at home.

First, the documents: his will, a letter for his mother and one for Sharon. He left them on his bed.

Second: a fresh uniform. He bathed and dressed himself carefully from the skin out. Fresh, new underclothes. A new standard-weight cadet gray dress uniform, high-collared, badges of rank worked in sparkling new gilt. It fit tightly, broke cleanly just above his glossy dress boots. The Sam Browne—old, but still presentable; Post issue, the belt and holster he'd worn at VMI on the day the colors had been paraded before the graduating cadets and he had been saluted for the first time as an officer of the Confederate Army. Into it he slide the .455 Leech & Rigdon, oiled and loaded with fresh cartridges.

His spurs? No, that was silly. Besides, they might tear the fabric tube. Dressed, he went softly downstairs to the great hallway.

There they were. The lights were soft above their portraits, but he knew them. He had spent his childhood under fine stern features of the men above him on the walls.

Claude Quidley. The family's founder, who had arrived in Raleigh penniless but had ended owning four hundred acres of land and eighty-two human beings.

Jason Quidley: the first Army man in the line. He'd grown to manhood before the War of Secession, establishing the family fortunes in cotton and tobacco. A fine, bearded face, still rough with the strength of a farmer.

Colonel Jarrett Quidley. Claude's grandson—and the fastest-rising young officer in the newly formed Confederate Army, until he was killed at Gettysburg by Union canister during the terrible last charge that broke the Union lines. A dark, brooding visage, heavy with doom.

Then the next portrait, larger than the rest: the family's great hero. The painter had sketched a pale, long face, with the gray eyes of a dreamer—or of a fanatic. General Aubrey Quidley had commanded the turning movement through the Painted Desert—horses and men dropping at every step from heat and inadequate supplies but kept

118

moving by the fierce will of one man—that had staved off disaster in 1888 and kept Arizona and southern California for the Confederacy.

The second of the great name had been his grandfather, the Senior. Shown upright in a tinted photograph, he had commanded a regiment in the Great War. Quidley remembered the day he died, of pneumonia brought on by the gas he had inhaled twenty years before at Passchendaele. And then, last of the portraits, his own father. Aubrey Quidley III had died young, at forty-six. All his life long he had served country, Army, honor. His great sorrow had been (he remembered his father well, his pacing before the fireplace, his gentle regrets over brandy with guests) never to have served his country in war. It was a testimony, he used to say, to the power of the Allies. Yet still. . . .

Aubrey Lee Quidley IV stood in the shadowed hallway and looked into the stern, lofty faces of those who had preceded him.

Country. Army. Honor.

There was one more thing he had to take with him, and it hung here, on the wall beneath the portrait of Jarrett Quidley. He reached up, careful to be silent, and brought it down reverently.

It was a sword. Crudely made by twentieth-century standards, but not without its own kind of grace, it was heavy, long, and slightly curved; he had in his childhood admired the elaborate etchings on the blade, intertwined cotton and tobacco leaves, with a large "C. S." On the throat of the blade, scarred with use and worn with age, yet still visible, were the initials, "K.G.& K., Columbia, S.C."

And on the opposite side of the blade, his own great-great-grandfather's name.

It was a precious relic and he held it for a long time before he decided: yes. He slid it back into the long brass-mounted scabbard and snapped it onto his belt.

Thus, I pledge, he thought, staring up at the dim line of his ancestors, *that I will be true to you and to our country. I will not give way to fear. I will fight for the right and for the Confederate States of America.*

He drew the saber with a hissing swish and presented it.

I will never give in.

Eleven

"My Lord, oh, my *Lord*," said Willie, staring first at Vyry, and then back at the man who lay curled sightlessly in the back of the jitney. "What they do to him, girl? What did they *do*?"

Vyry felt the anger in her again as she too looked down at what was left of Johnny Turner. Her man . . . his arms about her at night, his roughness in loving her . . . *it's not all over,* she thought, drawing a shuddering breath. *I'll bring him back. I got to.*

"Will you help me with him, Willie?"

"Sure, girl, sure. But where you goin' to take him? Back to your place?"

"No, can't do that." She had to trust the fat comical-looking man; had to trust him, as Johnny had trusted him because they were both Railroad. "We can't go back there. The—man—who did this knows where I live. Or can find out. I had to tell a hell of a tale to get Johnny back and sooner or later he going to wise up and come after me."

"I don't see how you done it at all," said Willie. "It was the patrollers caught him, wasn't it?"

"Yes."

"Oh, man." Willie stared at the blanket-covered form. "If Johnny talked, we in deep shit."

120

"He didn't say a word. They told me. But sooner or later they going to figure out he was at Town Point and then they'll come after him—and me. You've got to hide us, Willie. He's your friend!"

"He sure is. Hey, man," he rapped on the door to get the white driver's attention. "Would you mind drivin' on down this street, take a couple of rights? Be an extra five in it for you."

They lifted him from the jitney when it stopped, waited, and then began the long carry. Together they tried to lug Johnny Turner up the narrow stairs. As his legs dragged he seemed to stir, opening his eyes, but when Vyry called his name and smoothed his shaven head he did not respond.

China grasped it all at a glance. "Git him in here on the bed," she said, running for blankets. "Where does he hurt? Say, Willie, that your friend the Turner boy, ain't it?"

"Yeah," said Willie. "Where does he hurt? He's hurt in the mind, mama. Where it don't show."

Vyry straightened his limbs and slipped a pillow under his head.

"Ah seen men like that before," said the old woman. She pulled one of Turner's eyelids up and peered under it. "He's gone away to the spirit world. Seen chil'ren do that, seen it happen to a woman once. Say they could help her, but she never come back from down the river."

"This is different," said Vyry. "They did it to him, but I'm going to bring him back. He's going to get well. You hear?"

China shook her head and her eyes gleamed. "You have faith, chile. You is got that sure enough."

The first thing he needs is food, Vyry thought. The next—stimulants? He had to be shocked out of this strange state. A doctor? No white doctor would come into West Main—and there were no colored doctors the length and breadth of the South, only quacks, root doctors, granny women like Willie's wife China. She could give him medicine, there was a black market in that on the streets—but what kind? Amphetamines? Narcotics? Coke, penicillin, sulfa? She blinked back tears. She just didn't know.

China was back, bent under the weight of a tattered, ancient book, interleaved with scraps of paper and rag

121

and dropping small dried leaves as she flopped it open. She scrabbled through the brown-inked pages, muttering to herself.

Just before dark that night there was a series of soft taps on the door. Three. Two. One. Vyry jerked awake —she had been dozing by the bed—and went to open it, leaving the chain on.

"I'm Leo," said the thin, almost white young man. "You must be Vyry Lewis."

She watched him through the door.

"Can I come in?"

"What for?"

"Johnny knows me."

"Come in." She unhooked the chain and let him in. Leo's eyes widened as he saw a washed-out, haggard-looking Turner, slumped in one of Willie's broken-down armchairs.

"Turner. They tell me you were captured but got out."

The dark eyes shifted to him at the sound, but otherwise Turner didn't move. Leo looked at Vyry. "What's wrong?"

"He's a long ways away," she said. Her own shoulders slumped; she was exhausted. First, there had been the hours-long argument with China, and her reluctant acquiescence in allowing the old woman to use her remedies. Then—after forcing the nauseating infusion down his throat—she and Willie had begun to walk him up and down the room. Up and down, hour after hour, stopping only for China to feed him more of the drug. Walking, slapping him, they had at long last brought some remote spark of recognition back to eyes that seemed to have looked into hell. "But I think he's coming back a little. What do you want with him?"

Leo crossed the room and squatted by the chair. "Turner. Turner, it's me, Leo. Did you tell them?" He waited. "Johnny, did you talk?"

"He can't talk to you."

"He can if he wants to. Turner, remember Shiloh?"

The distant eyes drifted downwards from the ceiling to meet Leo's. Vyry, watching, felt a chill. They were not the eyes of Johnny Turner but the eyes of someone else, someone . . . not quite sane.

He nodded. Leo smiled. "He understands!"

He put his hand on Turner's knee. "Listen, man. We have to know what happened where you were. Most important, did you tell them we knew about Shiloh?"

After almost a minute Turner's head moved slowly left, then right. "He didn't," said the octoroon gleefully. "Oh, this is a fine man. They couldn't break him. I don't know what they did to him, but they couldn't break him. The Railroad is proud of you, Johnny."

So that's who he is, thought Vyry. A Railroad man. That same Railroad that had tempted her man out of a sickbed, then seen him caught, and then had not interfered.

He was talking swiftly to Turner, almost bubbling with relief. "You'll see, Johnny, we'll make them pay for what they did to you. Shiloh! We'll do it, we will. I'll take over for you. We've got a boat picked—"

"No," said Turner.

"His mouth seems to be hurtin' him," said Vyry swiftly. "You best leave. I got to get him some soup, then he's going to bed for tonight."

"I thought he said something."

"T'say . . . no," murmured Turner. He stared down at one arm. It trembled, then lay still. Then it trembled again, and slowly lifted from the arm of the chair. The fingers moved, and became a fist.

"He's coming around," said Leo.

"China!" called Vyry. "China, come quick!"

The old woman came in, a pan in her hand, took a look, and nodded. She went back into the kitchen. A sound of frying began.

Turner closed his eyes and shuddered. It was more like a convulsion, his vast bunched arms and chest tensing in a long spasm that moved downward, rippling over his body. Vyry wiped away the sweat that formed over the staring eyes.

"What . . . day."

"Tuesday, Johnny. Twenty-second."

". . . Men?"

"They're getting ready now. We got guns and Finnick's picked out a boat. We'll be going out at midnight."

". . . Going."

"What did he say?"

"I don't know," said Vyry. She felt relief that he was speaking but also a kind of horror. He had not looked at

123

her once, had not even recognized that she was in the room.

"I . . . going," said Turner, with an effort.

"No, Johnny. I'll take care of it all. I was supposed to lead anyway. We'll do it, your men and I. You rest, and—" he stopped speaking as Turner's hand fell on his arm.

"I'm going . . . Leo."

"Damn you, Turner—that hurts—aah!" The thin man curled like a dying spider as the hand tightened on his upper arm. "Let me go! Vyry—can't you—"

"I never could tell Johnny Turner anything," she said.

"Turner—all right, damn you, ease off—you'll go!" Leo rubbed his arm as he stood up. He threw her a furious look. "He's in no condition," he said.

"I know that."

"You're strong, but you need rest. You look like hell. You need—"

"Need to," said Turner, his mouth moving slowly and with obvious pain, "Need to pay . . . them off."

"Leo? Come over here." Vyry moved toward the bedroom, a tiny niche that Willie's part-time profession of trash collector had filled with a hideous pile of dirty, broken furniture, heaps of rags, and discarded mattresses. "Mister, he's going to go. I know when he's got his mind set on something. I don't want him to go and you don't neither but he is and if we try to stop him there only be trouble."

"Look, Vyry, I'm responsible to the Road for the success or failure of this job, and it's an important one. I don't mind taking him, but I don't know—the way he is —well, I just don't want to have to worry. What if he went crazy all of a sudden?"

"I don't even know where you're going," she whispered. "Guns—boats . . . can you tell me?"

The bedroom was quiet and he looked at her, and in the next room Vyry could hear China clashing pots and pans.

"All right," said Leo. "I will."

In low quick sentences he told her. She shook her head in astonishment and started to speak but from the other room they heard a heavy tread that she recognized as Johnny's, yet slower and . . . more deliberate, somehow.

She lowered her voice. "Leo, I think I can handle that

124

man. If he gets out of control. If he goes, I got to go, too."

"Why not take every CE in Norfolk? I can't take a woman. Not one that looks like you. Those boys will be fighting over you the minute you step in the boat."

"Not if Johnny's with me they won't. Leo, I've *got* to go if he goes. You know I do."

Finally he nodded. "I don't like it, but—all right, woman."

Turner came in. He walked a little unsteadily. He stared through them. Vyry put her hand to her mouth. His look frightened her. Again she found herself thinking, *This is not the man I knew. This is something else . . . something held together, controlled, only by his own powerful will.*

Had Quidley burned everything else out of him in the humming quiet of the cellar? Everything but will, everything but—*hate?*

"Johnny, I'm leaving," said Leo, moving around him toward the door.

"Where's the boat?" said Turner.

"Finnick's picked one out at the yacht club. White man hires him spare time to keep it running, keep it cleaned up. We'll meet just before curfew at the main gate to Smith's. I've got things arranged from there." Leo reached the door. "So long," he said, and vanished.

"Oh, Johnny." She covered the two steps between them and threw herself against him, reaching her face up to his. "Johnny—"

Something was wrong. His arms did not come up for her in the old crushing hug that made her fear for her ribs. The hardness that should have been growing against her belly as she clung to him was not there. And he did not even look down at her face. Slowly she let her hands slip from around him and backed away, almost tripping over the stack of mattresses. "Johnny . . . what's wrong?"

"I can't . . . tell you," he said.

"Something they did? Does it still hurt? Johnny . . ." She could hardly speak with fear and hurt—"Johnny, please, try to tell me!"

There was something wrong with his head.
There was something missing.
He knew who she was. He knew the syllables of her

name. Vyry Lewis. But there was something missing. He did not feel anything for her.

It was hard to look at things. Something back behind his mind, where he had once been, had been replaced by the emptiness. And she moved him no longer.

What was she asking now? Her voice came from far away, from a place he would never go again.

What did they do to me?

First there had been the pain. He remembered the pain. His lips moved without his knowledge, forming again and again one syllable: no. No. Nonono.

But then there had been something else. After the pain. He couldn't quite pin it down. When he tried to remember what had happened then something in his mind seemed to turn and snap open just as he was about to come to that memory and

went off

went on

went off

He flickered. He saw the woman standing in front of him and then he saw the brilliance of the sun inside his brain. It was the sun because it was bright but it was so blue. Then it too flickered and his mind reeled with the unimaginableness of . . . nothing.

There was nothing in his mind. He was not Johnny Turner any longer. Someone named that had lived here but now he was empty as the bleached crab shells where the old men threw them along the piers. There was only one thing left to him; only one desire; only one compulsion, when all else had gone. It was the memory of a face, pale, thin, with a small auburn moustache. And one overmastering emotion:

Hatred.

At nine that night, leading him by the hand like a child, Vyry Lewis moved out into the street.

There was only a memory of the late afternoon sun left, and where the buildings that lined the narrow streets of the Colored Area cast their shadows it was already dark. The white glare of electric lights and the softer, ruddier glow of kerosene lighted parts of their path, where people had left their shades undrawn. There were few people out on the street, but she could sense the teeming life that surrounded them; could hear it in the distant coughing of a sick child, the curses of a couple fighting, the muted jazz that spilled from an open door of a joint. It was reassuring, this music, this presence of unseen thousands of her own kind, but at the same time it was lonely. The saxophone wailed behind them and was lost, echoing between the crumbling buildings and rusting fire escapes heaped with garbage.

"Johnny, you all right?"

He was big, dark, menacing beside her. A teenage gang fell silent as its members saw him; they eddied around them, giving him distance. A long time passed before he answered. "Yeah. I'm all right. What time's it, girl?"

"Not much after nine. We got time."

"Don't want to be late."

Down the east-west streets at times came the throb of engines and the probing white fingers of headlights. When they came too near she pushed him toward an alley, behind reeking trash piles, and shielded him with her own body till the patrollers were past. It was not quite curfew yet. But she knew instinctively that now they were after the two of them. By name. By description.

". . . Further."

"No, Johnny, it's not far now. Stay on the dark side of the street."

Like moving shadows they slid through the downtown streets. Thronged in the daytime by office workers, the tall buildings and the wide streets and the stores were abandoned at night to fear. Traffic lights clicked and changed, sending their flashes of red and green and orange down empty avenues. A police car rolled by as they crouched behind the squat marble wings of the Secession Monument. THAT THESE NOBLE SONS OF VIRGINIA SOIL GAVE THEIR LIVES TO PURCHASE FREEDOM FOR ALL TIME. "Now run with me, Johnny," she whispered, and they raced through dead streets down to the river.

"Down that way," said Turner.

A block away from it she stopped, drawing him into a shadowed corner again. At the R R Smith gatehouse brilliant lights flooded the street, and men—white men— walked slowly about with guns.

"Johnny! Vyry!"

She turned at the hoarse whisper. In the alley behind the building were several dark figures and a large rectangular silhouette.

"It's us. Hey, Johnny! You come back!"

They slapped him, touched fists, punched him good-humoredly. As they reached the large object, Vyry saw that it was a standard green flatbed pickup with the city of Norfolk seal on its side. A city roads truck. Of the men, she recognized Bo, Willie, Leo, a couple of the others; there were seven in all. Leo pulled out a flashlight and consulted his watch.

"Might as well get on with it," he said. "Climb in, boys."

One by one the men hoisted themselves into the bed of the pickup. "You too," said Leo to her. "Get in next to the cab, so there'll be men all around you. Here, put on this hard hat."

When they were all in the light-skinned man closed the gate. "Listen now," he said in the same hoarse whisper. "All these roads trucks have the Labor Transport option for when they take the gangs out. There should be a chain back there somewhere."

"Here 'tis," came Willie's voice. "Lemme do this. I did time on the roads once." There was the rattle of a chain on sheet metal. "Here, Johnny. Put this cuff round your leg and pass the loose end of the chain through that there padeye on the bed. Good."

"Listen now," said Leo again. "You're a road gang just coming off for the night. You let me talk if we get stopped, I got the accent down pretty well. If I can't talk them out of it—" he pulled up the lid of a tool box and revealed, gleaming within, the shining barrels and smooth dark wood of six Tredegar submachine guns. "They're loaded. But use them only if they're about to use a radio. Otherwise there are picks and crowbars in that box, too.

"It's about fifteen minutes' drive to the yacht club. You'll be bouncing around in that bed a little, they didn't design it for comfort, but it's all for the Cause."

"Amen," someone said, half sarcastically.

"Johnny Turner come back," Leo went on. "Patrollers picked him up, but he didn't say a word. Vyry got him out, I don't know how, but she did it and she's coming with us tonight, too."

"Let's get movin', man," said Johnny Turner.

"All right." Leo stared up at the chained men for a moment more and then walked round to the cab. A moment longer and the motor ground, the truck lurched, and they slid out into the open street. Leo turned left, directly toward the brightly lit gate.

"Damn," someone in the back—a thin silhouette, Bo Finnick?—whispered. "Hey, if this Leo wants to turn us in, brothers—"

But the truck rolled steadily past the gate. One guard, shotgun butt resting on his thigh in a stance as old as the South, raised his hand to them. Leo waved back. They were past.

The chains rattled on the metal of the truck bed as they swung onto Brambleton Avenue and picked up speed. One or two private cars passed them, the white faces of their drivers glowing in the truck's headlights.

"This goin' to be easy."

"That Leo's a smart man. A city truck."

"Won't nobody look twice at a road truck full of darkies."

Leo leaned out of the window and shouted something.

"What he say?"

"Says he wants a song."

"Song! . . . Kind of song."

"Willie, what they sing out on the road gangs?"

"Lot like we sing down the docks. How 'bout 'Fifty Dollars'?"

" 'Fifty Dollars.' "

"Sing 'Fifty Dollars,' he says."

Over the sound of the engine, the harsh rattling of the chain, the curses as Leo failed to see a pothole in time, the words of the song rose in a sad refrain to a tune that had been old before there had been a Confederacy.

"If I had me a fifty doll'r,
    Fifty dollar *all* in gold,
    Buy me-*ee* a ticket back to home,
    Buy me a ticket home.

"Look where the train done gone, oh Lord,
    Look where that train done gone.
    Gone on to Richmond, gone to Tredegar,
    Gone never to return."

Behind them: lights. It was an older make of car. "Sixty-eight Dixie," someone said.

"*Sing, damn it!*" Leo cried back against the wind.

129

"Do that John Turner one," said Willie, and they looked round at Johnny. It was half a joke with them, a song they'd made up on the waterfront to the tune of 'John Henry,' a song they sang half in praise and half to get under Johnny's skin a little. But now he stared sightlessly and did not shut them up with a roar the way he always did, and so they sang on, just to be singing.

"John Turner was a little baby,
  You could hold him in the palm a your hand,
  Well, the first word they heard that little baby say,
  He said, "I wanna be a longshorin' man, Lord, Lord,
  I wanna be a longshorin' man.

The car was close now, just behind them, its headlights picking out their tired faces in cruelly sharp shadows and glares. The men leaned back into the sides of the truck and looked at each other in the white light and lay their heads back and sang it out,

"John Turner tol' his mother,
  'You better cook my breakfast soon,
  A dozen freighters come in las' night,
  I'm gonna get 'em loaded by noon, Lord, Lord,
  I'm gonna get 'em loaded by noon.'"

. . . And in the middle of it the car pulled into the right lane and streaked by them with a throaty roar.

"Muffler's shot," said someone.

"Them patrollers should be shot," said Willie.

Besides her she felt Johnny tense. "What is it?" she said.

"Those the ones picked me up," he said. "Open that toolbox, Willie, and give me one a them guns."

"No, Johnny—"

"Hell, Johnny, let 'em go. You'll give us all away."

She felt him sink back against the cab, mumbling something.

"That Johnny Turner, he a real bad man."

"He a real guinea nigger, all right."

"Hell, you knowed that. Remember down pier ten once, he—"

She searched his dark profile as the streetlights

130

whipped by. Yes. Her Johnny was bad. But he had sense, he had caution. Who was this man beside her?

"Got a new one," Willie shouted. "Listen, you black sons of bitches! New one, remember it!"

> "John Turner tol' the President,
> He said, 'A man ain't nothin' but a man,
> And before I'll let you drive me down,
> I'll die with a gun in my hand, Lord, Lord,
> I'll die with a gun in my hand.' "

The truck slowed. The men sat up in back. Tension flickered among them. The truck slowed some more and then turned left.

"We 'bout there?"

"Yeah," said Finnick. "Let's get these chains off." At the rattle of metal Leo leaned out and looked back.

"Keep it quiet back there now—some of these boats, the people live aboard them."

"Where's your yacht, Finnick?"

"Fifth from the right. I filled her up this morning and ran up the engine. She ready to fly."

The pier, a long wooden structure smelling of old fish and fresh creosote, seemed deserted, brightly lit but empty, though music and laughter came from the clubhouse farther up the river's shore. Leo braked the truck quietly near a gate that cut the road off from the pier and got out. "Finnick? Where's Bo?"

"Here I am."

"Say you know the watchman?"

"Sure do."

"Colored?"

"Like a bucket a tar."

"Can you make a deal with him?"

"I'll try. Stay here."

From the truck they could all see the conversation, though the words were too muffled to catch. The watchman, a middle-aged, very dark man, finally nodded. Finnick held out something; the man took it and looked about, then went into a small gatehouse and closed the door. When he came out again he nodded once to Bo and turned his back on him. Finnick removed a cosh from his pocket and struck him, caught the man as he folded, and dragged him behind the shed, out of sight of the road.

"Let's go," hissed Leo. "Fifth on the right, man?"

"That's it," said Finnick, looking at the cosh and then putting it back in his pocket.

They moved stealthily along the pier. One of the larger boats, not far away, was strung with festive-looking lights, and they heard the voices of women and the cheerful clatter of a piano.

"Here," came Finnick's hoarse whisper.

It was a tuna boat, not a yacht, but that was just as good and perhaps better. Vyry followed Johnny, jumping quietly down from the pier.

"Bo?" Leo's voice.

"Here."

"Start her up. The rest of you better get out of sight till we get out on the river. Does that door there open?"

But Finnick looked past him, to where Johnny, immense, quiet, stood in the stern. "Johnny?"

"Start her up," said Turner. "One of you guys go forward, cast her off. Then stand by starboard side with that boat hook, fend us off from that sailboat. I'll cast off here." His big body became suddenly catlike as he sprang up on the counter and flipped lines free.

With a burbling rumble, the engines started.

"Where to, Johnny?"

"Put her out in the stream, Bo." Turner came forward into the boat's little cabin, a vast dark presence that automatically took over from the now-silent Leo.

"Right, Johnny."

The lights of the pier and the yacht club fell away astern. The gay sounds of the piano grew faint. Rich noxious diesel fumes blew forward over them from the exhausts. "Bring her round to the right. Aim more toward Tanner Point there. Then we got a sharp left to get out into the 'Lizabeth."

"Right. Johnny . . . it's good to have you with us, man."

The other men nodded, agreed, reached out to touch him, their dark talisman. Vyry stood close to him, feeling with a shiver how his silent immobility was reassuring and frightening at the same time.

"Johnny?" she whispered, touching his arm.

He grunted.

"Are you feeling more—more like yourself?"

He didn't answer, and she thought *Please Lord, let him*

come back to the way he was. I don't care about any
shell, I don't care about the Railroad. Just give me my
man back the way he used to be.

"Come on right and speed her up now," said Johnny
Turner, his voice loud, cold, and harsh in the freshening
wind of the night.

Twelve

For Jerry Higgins it had so far been an uneventful and even a rather pleasant voyage.

Captain Higgins sipped tentatively at the pottery mug in his hand. The coffee was blazing hot, black, and thick. Just the way he liked it. He carried it out on the wing of the *President McClellan's* bridge and leaned against the rail.

Though it was late, he felt no desire to turn in. Fair weather, mild two- to four-foot seas, and good fixes all the way down the coast had allowed him to put in a full night's sleep. Larsson—a muscular, bullet-headed Minnesotan, of little imagination but much dependability—had the conn, and could be trusted with the conduct of the ship. Higgins was left to himself to stare out into the intermittently starry night and to meditate.

To think about the land, for example—that land just beyond the horizon to the west. Only the loom of a few lights marked it against the darkness of the sea. *That now,* he thought, *is enemy land. That is Virginia.*

The enemy. In a way it was nice to have an enemy who, at the moment at least, was not shooting at you. Peace, he loved it. Higgins scratched reflectively at his six-inch stump, all that a Jap armor-piercing shell had left of his right arm. Well, he had his memories, anyway.

134

And, by God, he'd come out of it lucky. The last year of the war, close to the home islands—that had been hell. A bloody hell of close-in naval engagements, ship to ship with the well-trained, well-armed Nip fleet. It had not been entirely certain near the end who would win. Or might not have been . . . except for Dolly.

What an innocent nickname for it, he thought. But he recalled too his relief at hearing Admiral Moorer's voice over the Fleet Common band, announcing the destruction of Yokohama and the Emperor's surrender.

Peace. It was great.

And now the chances for a long peace seemed better than ever. With the Union holding, alone, the ultimate weapon, the aggressive maneuvers of the Empire off the coast would mean little now. Once the weapon down below, and others like it, were in place, peace would be guaranteed for years to come.

A slight murmur nagged at his ear amid the sounds of his ship. Engines, pumps, the hundreds of small whirring motors and ventilators and the all-pervading subsonic note of the single big screw—over, or through, all of them he thought for a moment that he heard airship engines. He peered astern. The stars back there, to the north, were bright and clear. A few scattered clouds made dark patches among them. No, nothing there. He thought for a moment of stepping inside and getting the night glasses and searching the sky and the horizon as he would have done the year before.

But on second thought he decided not to. It was probably one of the commercial flights, maybe the London-Richmond run. But there was no reason to be alarmed.

After all, it was peacetime.

Aubrey Lee Quidley's mouth was dry.

It was a fantastic sight. Below, ahead, through the slanted window of the zep, two white lights rode low on the sea. Around them was nothing, the dark wide silent circle of the sea, a pit of darkness so complete that he had to swallow and look off to the right, to the scattered lights of the sleeping peninsula, to reassure himself that they were not falling. And above it all were the soft brilliant summer stars, marred only by high clouds and an oval patch of darkness that rode to their left: the *Macon*, pac-

135

ing the *Shenandoah* in its now-silent drift downwind toward the ship.

"All prepared?" he said to the young Marine captain, Mitchell, who stood beside him in the darkened gondola.

"Yes, sir. Men are in assault order. The descent tube is trailed—"

"About ten more minutes, gentlemen," said the aircruiser's captain, McLaws. "Wind's not as strong as we expected. We're drifting down on them from their port side at about two knots."

"What's that in miles an hour?"

"Say two and a quarter. About walking pace."

"We'd better get back to the debark station," said Mitchell.

Quidley blundered along after him. The dirigible's corridors were narrow and lit only by the dimmest of red lights: the slightest gleam from the sky might alert the enemy. *Enemy*, he repeated to himself, savoring the word. Yes, tonight they really were the enemy.

He thought of Jarrett Quidley and the first Aubrey. He too would face the Yankee, the hereditary enemy, tonight. The damned Yankee. But not for war, though there might be fighting tonight. No, the purpose was peace. To maintain the balance.

Because the Yankees could not be trusted. If the balance were not maintained they would abuse their power; they would interfere in Canada, in the South. So the Confederacy and Allies needed that shell. That was all and that was enough. Here, they were in front of the door. He took a deep breath. "I'm going down first, sir," the captain was saying.

"Right, I'll go second, Mitchell."

"No shooting unless you have to, boys. Use the knives," Mitchell said to his men. Quidley turned to survey them as the dozen or so men murmured agreement. It was a weird scene: They were packed together back-to-front in the narrow corridor, in dark unmarked blue denims like those sailors wore, but bulging in odd places with equipment and weapons. Their faces were carefully blackened, and in the dim red light all he could see was their eyes.

". . . uniform," Mitchell was saying.

"What's that?"

"I was surprised to see you here in uniform, sir. Our orders were not to—"

"I know, Captain. How much longer?"

The young marine had his mouth open to answer when the buzzer sounded. He turned as the door hissed open, looked once at his men, and jumped. Quidley looked at his departing back, stepped forward, and heard someone behind him shout; but it was too late, he was already falling.

The slide was a hundred times worse this time. He was able to think: *Oh, God; what if we're not over the ship?* Then he landed, hard, on the marine captain's head, and rolled. The fall smashed him into something jagged and very hard in the dark, and he tasted blood inside his mouth and knew that he had jumped too soon. He shook his head to clear it and found himself lying against a piece of machinery on the stern of the ship. Above him loomed the black silent bulk of the airship. Lord—how could the Yankees not see her? The surprise must be complete.

"Sir—Captain Mitchell's been knocked out."

"Leave him here. Execute your orders," he whispered. "Go. Peters, Laverette, Carter—take your men. Get going." There was a quick scuffle of departing feet, and he was suddenly crouched alone in the dark on a hostile ship.

The shell. He had to get down to the hold. That was his job. He stood up and ran forward, holding his sword up to keep the scabbard from clanking, looking for a door to the interior of the ship. Behind him he heard Mitchell stir and moan softly but there was no time to turn back.

Higgins flirted the empty cup, sending the grounds overboard into the blackness of the sea, and caught the flash of green as the drops caught the glow of the running lights on the way down. Running lights. Peacetime. He remembered ramming his destroyer darkened through the Strait of Malacca at thirty knots, hundred-yard interval between him and the next ship ahead and astern, and smiled and turned and went inside the bridge. It was relatively bright and he was dazzled for a moment.

"I'm going below, Mr. Larsson."

"Aye, sir."

The President-class ships were wartime construction,

and not designed for comfort. Higgins preferred to use the outside ladders when the weather was nice; they were not as cramped as those inside, and easier for him to handle with one arm. He hummed softly to himself as he reached the main deck and walked aft, stepping carefully because it was very dark and he was still a bit dazzled.

Midway back he stopped. The outline of a man stood before him. "Evening," he said.

"Good evening," said the outline. Higgins had moved outboard to pass, when his mind stopped him and said: *that was a southern accent.*

"Who is that?" he said, hesitating in the darkness. The sea whispered unseen along the hull beneath him. His eyes were beginning to adapt and he could see that the man was wearing some sort of uniform—not a sailor—it was a *gray* uniform, and beyond him, over his ship, loomed an enormous *shadow*—

It all came together then and his one remaining arm went for the worn Colt he had carried on his hip through long years of war, but there was nothing there for *it was peacetime.*

And the outline moved too and the last thing Jerry Higgins saw was the bright silent flash of the stars on

A sword . . .

Quidley waited, crouched, his heart pounding in his ears, but the man did not make a sound; only moved once as he lay, and then was still. He stepped over him and moved forward.

There, to his right—a gleam of reddish light. A door. He stepped through and found himself in a deserted corridor. A ladder led downward to his left. He went down it, step by step, his sword at the ready, but found no one. *The crew must be asleep,* he thought; his watch said, 2:41. There was another ladder at the bottom of this one and he went down it, too.

Should be the right deck, the hold deck. Now he should go aft. He found himself confused, though, as to which way that was; the double turn of the ladder had thrown him off.

The sound of a scuffle, muffled thuds, drew him. By the time he saw the marines it was over and the Yankee—a cook, judging by the stained apron he wore—was lying on the deck. He nodded to the marines. "You the party headed for the hold?"

"Yes, sir."

"Where is it?"

"Should be back in this direction, sir."

No one else interrupted them on the way. The three marines followed him, carrying their knives in their hands.

"This should be it," Quidley whispered.

It was a watertight door, dogged and padlocked, with a heavy chain. One of the marines took out a flat package and molded it around the lock and looked at him for orders.

"Let's wait a couple of minutes more. Give the others time."

"Yes, sir."

He watched the seconds tick by on his watch. The second hand, normally so swift, seemed to creep listlessly round the dial. The marines paid out wire and retreated around a corner of the passageway. After three minutes had passed he could stand it no longer and he walked back to join them. They looked inquiringly at him with eyes startlingly wide in their blackened faces and he nodded.

The explosion rang loudly in the confined space, and Quidley ducked as pieces of the lock and chain ricocheted from the metal walls. Gray pungent smoke eddied in the air. He walked forward to the door. It was bent inward and he fumbled with the dogging handles and swung it open and motioned the marines through.

Inside it was dark. He groped around the door for a light switch and found something and snapped it on.

It was the hold, all right. They were in a large room, high-ceilinged, with scuffed and splintered wooden walls. There was wood underfoot, too, bolted down with what looked like brass. Of course—to prevent sparks. It was the ammunition hold. Quidley sheathed his sword and touched one of the marines on the arm. The man jumped. "Guard the door," he said. "They'll be down to investigate the explosion."

Quidley looked next at the room's contents, stalking along between high piles of wooden and metal cases, all clamped to the hold's floor with carefully rigged nylon straps. Most of it seemed to be conventional ammunition, smaller stuff, four- and six-inch for Monroe's antiairship batteries. There were some replacement rocket motors for the thirty-inch coastal battery shells. But none of the shells themselves.

Then he saw it, clamped down solidly by itself in a corner: a heavy wooden crate, some ten feet long and four feet on a side. The numbers and letters stenciled on its side meant nothing to him, but there was nothing else in the hold big enough to hold a full-sized shell. He put his hand on the box gently, feeling the roughness of the unfinished wood. This had to be it. He didn't even want to consider the possibility that what he sought might not be aboard. *What would we do, what would Norris do then?* he thought. Apologize? Give the ship back? No, it would have to be sunk, just as planned. A complete and useless waste.

"Need some help with that, sir?"

"Yes. Find a crowbar, or a hammer."

"This do, sir? Our squad was issued them."

The tool was like a short pick, but made of some metal lighter than iron. Sparkless, no doubt. Good planning. He took it and began disassembling the crate, starting on one of the corners. Boards shrieked and came apart reluctantly. He paused, sweating, after several minutes' work, and looked back toward the door. "Anyone coming?"

"Nothing, Major."

Perhaps the other squads had already taken the bridge and the engine room. Maybe it was all over, without fighting. He remembered the man he had sabered in the dark. "Hear anything?" he said again.

"Dead quiet, sir . . . *wait.*" The man at the door raised his knife as running steps came from the corridor.

"It's the captain!"

The young marine officer, Mitchell, slid through the door. A trickle of blood ran down from his scalp, darkening the collar of his shirt, but he looked alert and anxious. He saw Quidley and smiled. "See you made it, sir. Good. Is that it?"

"How are things going elsewhere?" said Quidley, turning back to the crate and levering another board loose.

"I think we've got them under control, sir. We have the bridge secured. The engines are under our orders. There's some skirmishing going on up forward, where the crew sleeps, but they haven't the weapons to hold us for long. They weren't prepared for boarding, sir; neither warned nor armed. They weren't expecting us at all."

Quidley nodded. Something green was beginning to show in the hole he was making in the crate.

"It's 2:55, sir. About an hour and a half till the offload. Can I help?"

"Yes, you take a turn. This crate is damned hard to get open."

"Seems to be a catch up here," said Mitchell, examining the box. He raised the tool and struck two carefully aimed blows. The top of the crate creaked. He walked to the other end and hit it again. The top popped up and he motioned to one of the marines and they lifted it off. Quidley felt a bit annoyed. Why hadn't he seen that? He bent forward to look inside.

The shell was dull green and immense, filling the bottom of the crate. It looked like a small whale, drab and curving and bluntly pointed at one end and tapered at the other. Two thick bourrelets of yellow metal ringed it three-quarters of the way back from the nose.

Quidley was interested in other things. Three other things. One and two were the two stout padeyes that bulged up from the top of the shell (before firing, he recalled from his artillery days, they were screwed out and replaced with blind plugs). They would need those to lift the shell out of the hold and into the boat. Three was the fuzing cavity, which would, he reasoned, be either in the nose or the base. No, the nose was smooth. At the base of the shell he found it. A threaded hole, leading deep into the thing. It was empty. There was nothing else in the crate. He looked up to see Mitchell watching him with concern.

"Something wrong, sir?"

"Fuze is missing," said Quidley.

"Not there?"

"No."

"Do we need it?"

"Yes."

Another marine came in. He looked exhausted and his blackened face was smeared, and he was carrying a Tredegar. "All them Yankees quit fightin' up front," he said in a nasal North Florida accent.

"SIR?" A booming voice, amplified, startling them all. "THIS IS SARNT CAULFIELD FROM THE, UH, THE

141

TOP PART OF THIS SHIP, HERE. NEED SOME-BODY UP HERE RIGHT AWAY. SIR."

"I'll go," said Mitchell. "Caulfield's probably wondering which way to aim the pointy end."

"Just a minute, Mitchell. The fuze. Where can it be?"

The marine hesitated. "Well, sir—if it's important, maybe the commanding officer wanted to keep it."

"I'm coming up with you. You men"—he motioned to the others—"guard it. Try to find out how to get those doors in the ceiling open."

The *President McClellan*'s bridge was brightly lighted now. A dark fluid covered part of the floor, glistening wetly; there was the smell of blood and gunpowder in the air. "One of the ship's officers—big blond guy," said Caulfield.

"Where is he?"

"Over the side."

"Anyone else killed up here?" said Quidley.

"He was the only one resisted, sir."

"Are we on course?" Quidley asked one of the Yankee sailors, a dark-moustached young man wearing lieutenant's stripes.

"For where?"

"Fort Monroe, you idiot. Where you were going."

"This is the same course we've been on since midnight," said the lieutenant. Quidley felt sweat spring under his uniform. He had no idea where they were on this dark sea, or where they were headed. The lieutenant seemed to take courage from his expression. "Look here," he said, "this is an act of war. This is piracy. And murder. Mr. Larsson was—"

"Mr. Larsson—you mean the man who was killed—was resisting foolishly, sir. I advise you not to repeat his mistake, and to cooperate with us."

"Why should I?"

Quidley waved grandly at the black behind the windows. "Do you know where we are?"

"No. I was asleep below when I heard—"

"Then I advise you to find out. For the safety of the ship and *all* aboard her." *Not badly put,* he thought. *Who said I had no imagination, no brains.* He wished Norris could see him now.

The lieutenant stared at him for a moment longer, his scowl fading into uncertainty; then, suddenly, he moved to the chart table, then stared out the window to the right. "Wilson, mark your head," he said, harshly.

"One-seven-zero, sir," said the sailor at the wheel, a bit too quickly.

"Has that been our course since the—the incident?"

"Except for a minute or two, when I got scared, yes sir."

"We want to stay on course for Fort Monroe," said Quidley.

"Monroe! They'll—" He fell silent, glancing meaningfully at the helmsman. "All right. I'll get you there."

Quidley looked at Mitchell. "Where is the ship's captain?"

"Wilson, wasn't Captain Higgins up here last watch?"

"Yes, sir—he went back aft just before these people came."

Quidley remembered the man he had met in the dark. "I know where he is. Lieutenant—detail a man to show us to his cabin."

"Detail him yourself," said the Yankee, glaring down at the chart under his hands.

He picked out the most craven-looking man on the bridge, a short pasty-faced fellow who was trying to squeeze himself out of sight in a corner. "Let's go, you."

On the way he stopped to search Higgins's body. The jingle of keys rewarded a few seconds' work. He looked down at the now-cold body. So that had been the captain. Lucky he'd got him first, but . . . he remembered the crunch of the heavy saber into bone and shuddered. "Now take me to his cabin," he said.

The cabin was small, bare painted metal, no decoration at all. He quickly found the safe, at the head of the narrow bunk. The fifth key fit it. Three code books, which he flipped through and then stuffed under his sword belt, a worn Colt pistol, and, far back in the safe, a long, cylindrical metal case. He drew it out carefully and unscrewed the cap. A metallic gleam inside . . . pins, to interlock inside the shell casing. Yes, this was it. He tossed the gun back in the safe, locked it, and motioned the quivering seaman out ahead of him. On the way back up to the bridge he threw the keys over the side.

The next hour was fairly busy. With the help of the marines, and the gunpoint advice of some of the crew, he got the shell uncrated and moved under the hold doors overhead with a bomb dolly. He forced the crew to rig the freighter's boom for offload, watching them carefully for any attempt at sabotage. It was after four when he said, "Open the hold doors."

It was 4:10 when the shell dangled halfway up, swaying slightly, but with the effect of great mass, as the ship rolled. Looking up at it, he felt the first drops of rain from the black square of the open doors. "Hold it there," he shouted, and to the marines on deck, "See that they do."

"These bluebellies won't try anything, Major," said one, the North Floridan.

"Don't get overconfident." He wiped his brow. It was warm in the hold and in all the activity he had left his helmet somewhere. That didn't matter. Now—now he faced the trickiest part of the operation. He headed for the bridge.

"See anything?" he asked Mitchell, who sat by the wheel, watching the Yankees.

"Not yet."

They stared out into the dark line of the sea. During his work in the hold the ship had changed course and now he recognized the familiar low headland of Virginia Beach off to the left. It was still very dark and would be for some hours yet.

"We should see it soon," said Mitchell.

The Yankee lieutenant looked at them. He pointed ahead. "Is that what you're looking for?"

Quidley reached for a pair of binoculars and focused them. Yes. Low in the water, a mile or so ahead, rode two lights: red over red. Below them, with the glasses, he could make out the motionless black-against-black of the hull of a small boat.

"That's it," he said.

Thirteen

She lay crumpled in one of the fishing chairs, her eyes closed, listening. She did not feel well. The fumes made her head spin, and the rocking motion as the boat entered the more open waters of the Roads threatened to upset her stomach.

She lay in the dark and wondered whether they would all be dead by morning.

Up forward, in the stolen tuna boat's little wheelhouse, she could hear the men talking. An almost white-sounding voice she identified as Leo's was explaining how he intended to approach the Navy boat that waited somewhere ahead. "She'll be standing still, maybe even anchored, waiting for the ship to arrive. They won't be expecting us. We'll come right up to them—"

"That won't work." Turner's voice.

"Why not?"

"They got guns too. We run up on 'em and they shoot us out the water before we ever get a chance to use these."

"What do you want to do, Turner?"

"Let me go."

Vyry sat up. What was he saying? She got up quietly and went forward and crouched to hear better.

"Bo, you got the wheel. Which way did you say the tide's runnin'?"

145

Finnick took a moment to reply. "I'd say she startin' to ebb, Johnny. We seem to be goin' a bit faster than this boat usually goes."

"Then here's what we do. Willie, you boys, listen here."

"Yo, Johnny. Go on, we're listening."

"We got maybe eight more miles to go. So we get there about three. That's early for a fishing boat going out but not too early. If we goes right on by out the channel they think we a fishing boat. Specially if they get a good look at us."

"I see that," said Leo. "But if we go by, how—"

"Shut up and listen, man. Put me over the side on the way by. Upstream. Tide going out. I'll swim, come right down on 'em. You say they'll be lit up?"

"Yes, two red lights."

"No trouble, then."

"Yes, there *is* trouble."

At the sound of her voice all the shadows turned. The little wheelhouse was jammed with men. In the dim light from the binnacle they gaped at her. "You men listen. Johnny can't go alone. Not in the water. Not after all they done to him."

"You shut up, woman."

But she didn't shut up. "You can't let him do it, Leo. Willie. Bo, you're his friends. It's like killing him—"

Turner moved then, pushing his way past men who moved quickly aside. "What you sayin', woman?"

"Johnny, you can't—"

"Get out of here. What're you doing on this boat anyways?"

He would hurt her now, she knew. Even . . . before, he did not allow her to contradict him, to give him sass. More than once she had carried bruises to the House, not only from his lovemaking, but from his punishments for being "uppity" to him. It was part of their love—part of what she was now so afraid of losing. So she lifted her head and turned to take it. "Johnny—"

The slap rocked her back, and the night suddenly danced with light. Before she could recover he hit her again, in the stomach, and she caught her breath and sank to her knees on the rough deck while he stood over her not speaking.

He's a violent man, a rough man, she told herself silently, struggling to breathe. *But he grew up that way. He works on the docks. He had to be hard to go through prison and what the Man done to him.*

It's not his fault, she thought, and dragged herself up. He waited till she stood, then hit her again, in the face. She fell back against the side of the boat, half out of it. Couldn't hit back—that made him angry. And pleading, crying, was not in Vyry Lewis. *But,* she thought, *He never hit me so* hard *before*—

She gasped as his fists crashed into her again. These were not slaps, not punishment. He was hitting her hard, hitting to hurt—"Johnny!" she screamed. She felt his arms go around her, and started to relax, to lean into them for the kiss, for the apology, but felt herself lifted —lifted high, like a child's broken toy, about to be *thrown away*—

Then there were other men there, other hands, hands that pulled at Turner and at her just as she swung outward.

"Damn, Johnny, put her down!"

"That's Vyry, Turner, Vyry!"

Slowly, she felt herself being lowered. In the dark she couldn't see his face. Someone pulled her away. It was Willie. "Hey, Vy—come on away from him. He done gone crazy. I don't think he knew it was you there for a minute."

The fright was almost too great for her, and she felt herself shaking. He had meant to throw her into the water. If the other men hadn't come, he would have. "Willie, that's not Johnny," she whispered.

"It don't hardly seem so." There was fear in the fat man's voice too, fear he did not bother to disguise. "They done something bad to him, all right. I thought China done brought him back. But maybe not."

Leo was with Turner now, talking soothingly to him, coaxing him back into the wheelhouse again. Gradually, the men drifted back there, and Vyry was left alone there on the stern with Willie as the lights of Willoughby Spit moved by, cold and hard and brilliant. When she caught her breath and the trembling eased off she felt her face. Bruises, yes, but no cuts. There was some pain when she breathed, but it was all right.

The pain in her heart was worse.

"Willie."

"Yeah, Vy."

"Will they . . . do that? Let Johnny go in the water alone?"

"Sounds like the only way, to me. He's right, Vy, we can't just run up alongside."

"How much longer do we have?"

"A while. This a pretty lively boat, but Finnick, he taking his time." The fat man took her hand. "Now look, Vy, don't go getting no ideas. About stopping him, I mean. Or stoppin' us. This snatch is more important than one man, even Johnny Turner. And if any one man can take over that boat . . . he the one."

"I know," she whispered.

But inside, she feared that her Johnny was already dead.

"I need a good knife."

"Take my work blade, Johnny," said Finnick.

They were close to shore, the low-lying shore of Virginia Beach, and it was very dark. Misty, too, with a slight fog, the precursor of summer rain, making the distant lights dissolve into fuzzy patches of glow. For several minutes now they had watched the two red lights ahead grow closer as they moved down upon them. Turner, stripped, was a vague blur standing at the rail. The engines muttered and burbled softly.

"This close enough, Turner?"

"Yeah."

"Here's what we'll do, then. After you're in the water we'll get moving again. Go on out past them. Run the motors loud to cover any noise you make. Go on half a mile down the channel, then stop and wait. How will we know if you need us?"

"If you hear shooting, I need you. If I do it without shooting—I'll blink them red lights."

"You're sure now," said Leo. "I'm not asking you to do this. Nor is the Road."

"Shut up. I'm doin' it myself. Now get going." There was a low splash, and the shape at the rail was gone.

"Man, I hope he makes it," said Willie softly.

Finnick waited for a long minute, and then pushed one throttle forward, the other back. The engines roared and the boat began to swing, but he spun the wheel quickly, and it moved sluggishly forward, engines frothing up foam around the hull.

The red lights drew nearer through the fog, and time ticked by.

They were still five or six hundred yards away from the low shape of the Confederate patrol boat, when the first signs of activity appeared. Vyry, staring out at it till her eyes hurt, saw lights wink on and begin moving about. "Get down," she heard Finnick say. "Not you, Leo. You the man with the white face here."

Across the water a new light came on, yellow at first, quickly brightening to become a brilliant shaft that swung back and forth across the smooth dark water. Vyry stared off to the right. Johnny was out there now, swimming for his life. What if that light caught him? As if in answer the searchlight beam came up, found them, so blinding that even with her eyes closed she saw red. "Wave, man," Finnick hissed to Leo. "Let 'em see you. Wave."

Leo stood up and waved slowly. The light lingered on him and then moved forward, throwing stark shadows off the fishing gear and the tall tuna tower, picking out the civilian registration number on the bow. Then, as if satisfied, it went out, dying to a dull red spark and then to darkness. "We're abreast of her," said Finnick softly. "This as close as we're going to get. Maybe three hundred yards. If we hear any ruckus over there—"

"Yes. Better hand those guns out." Leo motioned to the men around him. He sounded more confident than he had all night as he explained the use of guns to men who had never held one in their lives. Willie cradled the short heavy Tredegar lovingly. "You and me, baby," he crooned to it. "Goin' to talk with the Man. Going to have a little argument with whitey!"

"Vyry?"

"I'm not going to shoot one of those. Don't give me one," she said shortly. All her attention was on the other boat now. As they moved slowly past it, heading now out to sea, the lights on the deck went out. The men crouched tensely, watching with her.

"Now it up to Johnny."

"Yeah."

"Goin' cut them white fuckahs up. One by one. Never know who done it."

"Wish I was with him."

149

"Whyn't you go?"

"Shit, you know I can't swim, man. I 'most drown taking a bath."

She touched her face where it was sore. Please the Lord Johnny would come back all right. And maybe this was what he needed. To get revenge. To get his own back after what Quidley had done to him.

She hoped it was so.

The boat moved on. Leo and Finnick conferred in whispers in the wheelhouse. "Think he's there yet?"

"How the hell would I know?"

"Let's turn around. It's been too long."

"Only ten minutes. Man go pretty slow in the water. He prob'ly just gettin' there, Leo." But Finnick throttled back and again they drifted with the slow tide, pushing them silently outward toward the sea.

"What's that?" said Willie.

At first it was a light, moving in from the northeast, low above the water. Then the roar of engines reached them. It was flying low, and very fast. It was headed straight for them.

"Airship!" said Leo. He caught Finnick's movement as the little man stepped away from the wheel in time to slap the barrel down. "Don't fire, you idiot!"

The roaring grew into a hellish sound, vibrating the boat under their feet. The black bulk of the zeppelin came into view above the cabin lights, swelling to fill the sky as it passed over them. They caught a glimpse of portholes, running lights, of the long reddish tongues of fire licking from the exhausts—and then it was gone, dwindling toward the coast to the south.

"Shee-it," said Willie reverently. "Never seen one of them so close up."

And Vyry, who had alone of all of them kept her eyes fixed on the other boat, said, "Look."

The red lights had gone out.

"Let's go," snapped Leo. Finnick was already moving, spinning the wheel hard to starboard, slamming both throttles ahead. The boat lifted and began to pound as it gained speed, roaring in a tight circle back toward where the lights had been. "Go on in close," the Railroad man shouted. "Get those guns ready."

Steel barrels thudded on the gunwales as the men aligned themselves and slapped in magazines and charged

150

the weapons. "Don't shoot till I give the word," Leo reminded them.

"Jus' a few shots, give them white boys somethin' to worry about besides Johnny—"

"No. You might hit him."

"For God's sake, don't shoot," said Vyry, watching the dark hull materialize from the gray mist ahead as they drew closer.

The red lights came on. Then off, then on again. "Damn, I think he might have . . ." breathed Finnick, from the wheel. "I'll run her right alongside."

"If he has . . ." said Leo, and let the sentence trail off, as Finnick had. A hundred yards separated them from the other boat. The men aimed their weapons. Finnick leaned forward over the throttles, eased them back. Fifty yards. Thirty yards. Then twenty.

"Johnny!"

"Come on."

It was his voice. Vyry let herself breathe out, and a golden wave of joy washed over her. He was alive. She could see him, a shadow moving about that other deck. There was a splash, and something bobbed to the surface and drifted away on the tide. She could not see what it was.

The two boats came together with a slight jar. Finnick held them together with his engines as they scrambled over and up to the slightly higher deck of the patrol boat. Vyry followed them, and found the deck of the other boat slippery, running with something sticky and dark in the red light . . . a burst of gunfire made her start, and a moment later Finnick, the last one off, jumped up to the deck. "Where's Johnny?" he said.

"Here, Bo."

The two men embraced clumsily. Finnick laid down his gun. "I blew the bottom out of her, she'll go quick . . . damn, man. How'd you get them all?"

Turner bent and picked up another body. The arms dangled; a lanky, pale-faced boy. He held it for a moment and then pitched it overboard. "Just one at a time, Bo. They didn't expect me. Here." He held out a dark-smeared hand. "Here's your blade back."

There was a moment of awed silence among the men gathered around him. But Vyry put her hands to her face in horror. The men were white; white military, part of the machine that had oppressed and twisted her life, men perhaps who had used her for their lust, yet lying there about the deck, dead, they seemed not white, not military, but only *men*—

Turner moved about the boat, pitching corpses overboard. As if to wash the deck clean, it began to rain, fat drops pattering *splat* around them. "Good," said Leo, looking upward. "Rain will help. Johnny, Finnick—can you run this boat?"

"Long's she's got a motor, either of us can run it," said Bo.

"Try to get it started, then." Leo checked his watch. "We're a little early . . . got about an hour yet till the rendezvous. Willie, I want you to keep watching in that direction." He pointed to the east. "If you see a light, a ship—call me." He looked around the boat, then walked to where Turner was standing, looking into the sea. "Johnny."

Turner grunted.

"The Railroad will be grateful for this. That was a heroic act."

Turner stared at him.

"I mean it. In your shape—you'd better lie down, get some rest, you know?"

"No," said Turner.

Vyry lost Leo's reply as she walked toward the bow. This boat was much longer than the other, and she felt that she had to get away and think. The blood. The bodies. She was happy that Johnny was unhurt and at the same time horrified at what he had done. Killing had been abstract to her before. Now it was real, real as the stickiness under her shoes, the smell in her nostrils, the bobbing shapeless bundles that the current whirled away into the night.

But they're white, she told herself.

The feeling would not go away. She felt dirty. She felt as if she had done and seen things that she would never be able to forgive herself for. Had it been necessary to kill them all? Couldn't he have—oh, tied them up, or knocked them out? Her mind said that was insane, that he had had to kill them because he was one and they were many and one groan would have doomed him, and her mind told her that they were white, that they were the evil. But she looked down at the dark blood swirling

152

and dissolving in the rainwater and she knew that it was wrong.

And Johnny had done it.

The engines fired, rumbled, then began to run. They were louder, higher-pitched, obviously far more powerful than those in the little tuna boat. She looked around for it. It was already gone. Sunk. The engines fell back to an idle and she saw Finnick and Leo watching her through the low windshield. "Who's that up forward?" Finnick called.

"Me. Vyry."

"Come on back here."

She walked back to them. Leo looked at her. "You'd better go below," he said, not unkindly. "Fewer black faces up here when the ship comes, the better. And maybe you can find a place to lie down."

She studied his face in the reddish light. A youthful face, pale but with the colored blood still there in lips and nose if you looked close, if you knew. A face that meant well. But the face, too, of a man who could sacrifice others—the white sailors, Turner, perhaps all of them—for his cause. From the hatch that led below she heard Turner's deep voice.

"I'll go when you say. But I'd like to stay up here for a while longer. Please? In the fresh air."

Leo nodded. She walked to the stern and let herself sink onto a coil of rope and raised her face to the rain.

"Now what, man?" said Finnick.

"We wait," said Leo. "Hour—hour and a half if they're late—and the ship will show." He pointed to where Willie, Tredegar cradled lovingly in his chubby arms, stared into the rainswept night. "Soon as he reports it, everybody below but you and me. You find a hat, pull it down low. They'll set the shell down in those things over there—"

"Chocks?"

"Chocks, yeah. Then we get out of here."

"Sounds simple."

"The Road likes simple plans. Less to go wrong."

"Man, didn't Johnny do the job, though," Finnick said, admiration in his voice.

"Yes, he did," said Leo, but he sounded worried. "Bo, tell me—I only met him once. Does he seem different to you? As if he doesn't really care what happens to him?"

Finnick stood by the wheel for a moment, then drew his knife nervously and sank it deep into the wood. "I know, man. You're right. He *is* different now. He's—well, Johnny always been a bad nigger, you know, you don't get to be foreman on the docks unless you can take down any man works for you. He done it to me a few times. But he done it because he had to, not because he wanted to. But now—you're right, he's actin' crazy." He twisted the knife in the wood, leaving an ugly, splintered gouge, and grinned at Leo. "Or maybe—for the first time, he's sane."

They stared at each other. "Sane?" said Leo.

Bo Finnick held up the knife. It gleamed in the red light. "Yeah. That shell, man. How many you mean to kill with that? What Turner done ain't nothin' next to you. Are you sane? I want to use this blade on a white man myself. Am I sane?" He stared at Leo, and his eyes narrowed. "Shit, man, they ain't a nigger in this Southland knows what sane is. They're only Toms, or killers like you and me, and Johnny. That's what whitey done to us. You're right, Leo. We don't waste no more pity on them than they ever done on us. I say kill 'em all. Revolt."

"We can't revolt," said Leo. "There's been plenty of people wanted to, but the Road's always stopped it. We can't. We're outnumbered, and they've got the Army, the police—all the guns. It would be a massacre. It would be just what the Kuklos League is waiting for."

Finnick pointed out, into the darkness. "Well, we're going to have those guns soon. Something a lot more powerful than guns." He leaned forward to lay his hand on Leo's shoulder. "And Mister Railroad Man—*you better use it.*"

Fourteen

"Goddamn this rain," said Quidley, looking down at the *President McClellan's* wide cargo deck.

Four brilliant floods turned the falling raindrops into silvery tracers that winked out as they disappeared into the darkness of the opened hold. Around the smooth massiveness of the suspended shell danced a mist of spattering water that glowed in the light in a multicolored halo. It turned slowly, dangling at the end of a thread of steel from the after-cargo boom.

"It'll make it hard on the men in the pickup boat," said Mitchell, who stood beside him on the after portion of the bridge, looking down. "To wrestle all that weight around on their little deck—"

"They'll have to manage." Quidley cursed petulantly as a cold trickle found its way inside his collar. It was raining harder, fat heavy drops, surprisingly cold for July. "Where the devil did they get to?"

"Coming around back of us, sir." The marine pointed, and Quidley turned. Yes, he saw them now. Two red lights, shimmering in the rain, and under them a dark shape against the darker sea. They were quite close now. But he wanted them right alongside before he risked swinging the shell out. If that cable broke . . . he cupped his hands. What had been the name of that FPB fellow —oh, yes.

"Haile!"

An answer drifted back, barely audible above the sound of rain and engines. "Heah."

"Come alongside!"

"Right."

He watched as the FPB neared, neared . . . a grating sound came up to him as, below him, the two hulls kissed. Quidley walked to the edge, careful of his step on the wet deck, and looked down. The boat looked a lot smaller from up here than it had alongside the pier at Little Creek. But it was the same craft, low, rakish, built for speed. He noted the chocks ready amidships. But something was wrong. There were only two men on deck.

"Hello there," he called down. "You all ready to take cargo?"

A pale face turned up to him, pale in the white glare of the cargo deck floodlights. The other man—the one at the wheel—had his hat pulled down against the rain and did not look up. "Send it down," he heard, faintly.

"Where's the rest of your men?"

". . . rain," he heard faintly.

"Better get them on deck," he bawled. He turned to Mitchell. "Let's get things moving, man. We've only an hour till dawn."

"Sarnt Caulfield! Get that shell swung on out. Watch those sailors—"

"Yessir. Swing that out, you. Any tricks, the lot of you get it." The sergeant waved his submachine gun meaningfully.

A motor began to whine and the shell rose a few more feet, then began to rotate outward. It passed low over the rail, brushing one of the lines; the wire cable vibrated like a plucked string. Quidley bit at his lips. If it went in the water . . . he felt inside his tunic for the fuze. He felt vaguely that he should keep it dry, though he knew that was nonsense.

The winch motor whined again, in a different note, and the shell, water streaming from its gray-green bulk, began to descend. He leaned out to watch.

There were several more men visible on the boat now, standing with heads bent against the rain. The shell moved downward, stopped, swung ponderously—"You there, pull on that rope," Caulfield shouted—righted itself, roughly parallel to the line of the chocks, and then

156

resumed its downward creep. It was coming down too close to the boat's stern, but before Quidley could say anything the man at the wheel below reversed his engines and moved the craft a few feet backward. He relaxed. They knew what they were doing.

The motor changed pitch again, climbing the scale, and the men below, gathered around the shell, shoved in unison. The wire went slack.

"There, it's safe," Quidley breathed.

He watched as the men below, bracing themselves on the slippery, rolling deck, tossed restraining straps over the shell and made them fast. "Good work," he shouted, leaning far out over the rail. "Damned nice work, boys."

And stopped. One of them had glanced up at his voice. He was black.

No, he corrected himself. He felt a wave of relief. He wasn't black; he was in blackface, just like his own marines. He looked at Mitchell, beside him. The makeup was running badly in the rain, but at a distance, yes, he could be mistaken for colored. Quidley shook his head. For a moment there he had not known what to think.

The end of the cable, free now, whined up; the boom was being swung inboard again. The engines of the craft below roared and he realized they didn't know about him. "Hey!" he shouted. "Hey! you in the boat! Wait!"

The one man without makeup looked upward. Quidley was reaching for the heavy steel hook as it came up on the cable. It was cold, rain-wet, greasy, but he could hold on for a minute or thereabouts, he was sure.

"Wait for me," he bawled.

The man below hesitated, then nodded. He said something to the one at the wheel. Quidley called to Mitchell, "I'm accompanying it on, as per orders. You're clear on what to do from here on?"

"Yes, sir, Major. Take her back out. Destroyer'll pick us up off the Cape. Then"—he motioned at the knot of sailors who stood, wet and silent, ringed by the armed marines—"proceed as was planned."

"Ah, right." Quidley looked hastily away from the Yankees. Their faces showed their fear too plainly. Not one would survive the sinking of their vessel. But this was war. Almost. And for that almost, these men had to die.

As I might, too, he thought. But still he was grateful

that he would not be the one to carry it out. He swallowed and looked over the side. The man below waved impatiently and Quidley gripped the hook, tight, and swung himself over the rail and free of the ship.

The cable, unwinding, spun him round, and he heard the winch whine again. The floods made bright red trails across his eyes and the rain lashed at him with redoubled force. He felt its moisture creep under his locked fingers, and under his weight they began to slip apart on the uncaring smooth metal of the hook. He saw the hull, tilted over him, water running down the rusty flaking paint.

"Get him," said someone below, and he felt hands on him and a moment later the blessed firmness of the boat's deck under his boots.

Then things seemed to happen very quickly. The hook was torn from his hands and several more people laid hold of his arms and legs, pulling at his holster, at his clothes, at his sword. The engines roared, very loud, and he felt the boat tilt into a tight turn away from the *President McClellan*. "I'm all right now," he said. "I'm all right!"

"Are you?"

Something in the voice made him blink and try to see in the sudden dark as they left the floodlights behind. Even the red lights at the patrol boat's masthead had gone out, and he couldn't see—couldn't see—

"Who is it? Anybody knows him?"

Quidley felt a chill. The voice was low and indistinct above the hammer of engines, yet there was something . . . he tried to shake off the unseen hands, but instead they tightened their grip.

"Yeah. I know him."

Could it be . . . did he know that voice, that deep tone? *No,* his mind cried out. But now he recognized where he was, what manner of men he was among.

They were colored. He shivered. He could not comprehend it. The boat—the shell—no, it couldn't be—
"Search him," said the first voice.

"*Then give him to me,*" said the second.

It was a familiar voice, that second one, the deep one, but not one that he could place, just yet. "Look," he said. "I'm Major Quidley. What's happening here? Who are you all? Where—"

He didn't get to finish. A blow to his stomach doubled him over, gagging.

"Finnick, where you headin'?"

"In through Lynnhaven Inlet, I guess."

"Half an hour, or so. Let's get whitey below."

"What are you doing with that man?"

"Shut up, Leo." The oddly familiar voice again. "This man my meat. This the man did me over."

No one spoke after that. Quidley stifled a moan. He felt hands unbuttoning his tunic.

"He got something here."

"Gun?"

"No . . . here, feel it."

"Who got a light?"

A flashlight came on, showing the metallic cylinder of the fuze. By its light he could see the faces around him, and his heart sank. They were all colored. Even the man he had taken for the captain. Close up he could see the hair, the lips . . . octoroon, probably. Not one white man.

He was in the hands of the Railroad.

"Just a piece of pipe," said someone, sounding disappointed. The flashlight went out. Before he could think further he was jerked up and shoved roughly forward. A hatch opened—the same one, he recalled, that he'd seen on his first visit, and how welcome the sight of that carelessly disrespectful machinist's mate would be to him now —and he was shoved stumbling down a ladder and into the small cabin below. It was dimly lit and he looked swiftly around. A mess table, couple of chairs, a rack of tools on the bulkhead. There was blood on the floor. Fresh blood. The hands behind him shoved him again and he fell against the wall and turned, at bay.

It was Turner.

Turner stood there, drenched with rain and with a darker stain on his sleeves. Turner, his scarred face twisted with rage. Turner, towering, the top of his shaven head brushing the low ceiling of the cabin. Turner, his powerful hands clenched, stridiing toward him. Quidley reached for pistol or sword. Gone, taken in the dark. He lifted his hands.

The first blow knocked them aside like a child's and crashed into his chest. He felt himself stagger. He saw the second one coming but it was like lightning striking his shoulder, too fast to dodge, too powerful to block.

He never saw the third. It burst from nowhere into the side of his head, sending him down to the floor in a burst of dancing light. Then he felt himself being hauled up. He balanced shakily, bringing his hands up again. "Turner—no more—"

The man said nothing. From the fixed mad look in his eyes Quidley doubted he heard. Turner closed again, shook him violently, then all but picked him up and threw him again into the wall.

He means to kill me, Quidley thought fuzzily. He tried to get up but couldn't and felt himself being dragged up again. The strength of the man was unbelievable; he felt like a child, like a doll, in his hands. From somewhere in his reeling mind the thought came: *He wants revenge. He wants to kill me.*

And maybe I deserve it, for what I did to him.

Again he was shaken, and thrown against the wall. Dazed, he raised his hands weakly. There was very little more left in him. He watched as Turner closed him again.

"Hey, Johnny. Johnny!"

The big man paused and looked toward the hatchway. He blinked, looked confused, as if awakened too suddenly. "What—what you want, Bo?" he said.

"We're passin' the inlet. Where to now?"

"Ask Leo."

"Right."

The hatch slid closed again. Quidley licked his lips, tasting the salt sting of blood, open cuts. Turner stared at the hatchway for a moment after it closed, then walked in a little circle around the room. When he saw Quidley he looked surprised.

"Who're you? What you doing here?"

Quidley lifted his head warily. What was the man doing? He'd been about to kill him, and now he seemed taken aback to find him here. Well, he had no choice but to play it out. He tried to steady his voice. "I came with the—with the shell. What are you going to do with it?"

"Richmond," said Turner absently. "You take it off that Yankee freighter, man?"

"Yes," said Quidley aloud, but his mind was repeating:

Richmond!

"You kill people to do it? You kill any Yankees?"

160

A shape in the starlight, a quick movement, as if reaching for a weapon—"Yes. I had to kill one."

Turner grunted, lowered his head, and continued his circular prowl of the room. Quidley lay in the corner and sweated and watched, wondering: *What is going on inside his head?*

There was an emptiness inside his head.

There was something missing—someone he had once been. Something flowing—deep blue?—a random memory, chance hints and half remembrances, tantalizing him, yet—the thing itself he could not recapture. He walked and paced and felt air whistle in and out of him, in and out, and looked at the white man lying piss-frightened against the corner of the room and *could not remember.*

The pain he knew. Oh, yes; and he knew who this thin prissy man in gray was. Had known the instant he'd heard his voice and looked up, not thinking, to see his long stiff silhouette above them on the deck of the freighter, dark against the lights. He'd known it was Quidley. Quidley he remembered, and Sanchez—but Sanchez did it all under orders. So it was Quidley, and the pain. Oh, yes, that he knew.

And that, remembering that, had sent him out of control, battering that pale ginger-moustached proud face, feeling that stiffly held body solid under his fists. Good to hear the crunch of bone against bone. Good to feel him buckle and fall, good to see him bleed.

But now, puzzled, he paused. He was fairly sure that he knew where he was and who. He was now Johnny Turner, yes. He was on Railroad work; even now Finnick, topside, was steering this boat he was on into Lynnhaven to offload a special cargo bound direct through for Richmond. That he knew, yes.

But there was something missing.

He stared at the white man. He saw the thin lips move hesitantly, and heard him speak.

"Turner—"

And at the sound of his voice something moved and *snapped*—from where did he remember that—

The sun, inside his head—

Turning and quietly faultlessly inside him snapping shut and then the *flow*—

161

Quidley saw the eyes change from bafflement to rage. It was instantaneous, like a switch closing, changing the man from human to animal. He looked around the cabin wildly, looking for something to defend himself with—a stick—anything—and, behind him, his searching hand found the rack of tools and his fingers closed around a wrench. He brought it around. Too short, really, only five or six inches, and too light. But there was time for nothing else, and Turner's hands were at his throat. He strained to keep his head down, but the powerful arms forced his chin up, his head back, back. He felt the thumbs slide under his chin and against his throat and in panic he struck with the tool, struck hard, as hard as he could. Now, again. He felt Turner stagger. He mustered his strength and struck again and felt one hand leave his throat and felt his own arm gripped and forced back, the wrist encircled by a hand that felt like steel.

The tool clattered to the floor. He was choking. The hand came back to his neck—

"Johnny!"

He heard the voice only faintly. He was sinking into a red-shot haze. He felt other hands—felt something soft against his body—but there was no more air and he was submerged in a darkness that was somehow welcoming—

She had been told to stay out of sight below; a woman on deck, no matter what her color, would have aroused instant suspicion. She had stayed in the small berthing compartment forward, sitting on one of the bunks. There she had listened to the scrape of metal and the rattle of chain from above and heard the shouting and the sudden roar of engines. She had stayed there, sitting quietly, willing herself not to think. Not to think of Johnny and what he had become. Not to think of the men he had killed. Not to think of what he, and Leo, planned for the largest city of the Confederacy.

Sitting there she had heard, but ignored, the sounds coming through the thin bulkhead from the next compartment. Ignored the sound of blows, and then the sound of voices. But then she had heard Johnny cry out in pain, and she was up and through the door in a moment.

She saw it all at a glance. He was struggling with someone. His broad back was to her, but she saw his arm tighten on the other man's and saw a metal object fall free and clank hollowly on the deck. She had to help him. She snatched it up and raised it to strike—

She froze. It was Quidley.

"Johnny!"

He didn't seem to hear, and she saw that he couldn't. He was in that frenzy again—that killing frenzy—

She had no thoughts at that moment of loyalty or love. She only knew that she had to stop what was happening. Had to call Johnny back, back to life, back to himself. To her. She hammered at his wrists with the wrench, clawed with her nails. Inch by inch, she wriggled herself between them.

"Johnny . . . Johnny-Jo . . . please, stop! Stop it!"

She felt him tense. Had the name, the pet name only they shared, only she used at the moment of passion— had that called him back? *"Johnny-Jo,"* she whispered again.

His lips formed a syllable. *Vy?*

"Yes, it's me. Let him go, Johnny. He hurt you, but . . . he saved my life, too. You didn't know that, but you got to count that in." She spoke softly, quickly, pressing herself against him. *My man,* she thought. *Mine. If his mind don't remember maybe his flesh will.* "C'mon, Johnny-Jo. Come on with me. Come on." Relentlessly she pressed forward into him, her softness a wedge between the two men, her body melting into Turner's, moving him back, forcing him off balance.

At last he had to step back, and he did. She felt his hands come down around her and felt the body behind her fold and slump to the floor as he released it.

She smiled up into his eyes. He looked puzzled, little-boyish, as if he were trying to remember something hard. She traced the rough line of his jaw with her lips, feeling the roughness of old scars, the thick bristle of his un-shaven chin, the heaviness of his jaw just under the skin. His familiar smell, heavy, masculine.

Her man. He was not back yet. He had been a long way away. But he would come back. He would. She knew that now. If she stayed by him, called him back to himself whenever the strange moods returned, he would recover. She drew his puzzled face down toward hers and lifted her lips for a kiss.

"Hey, Turner." It was Leo, halfway down the ladder

163

from above. "We're almost there. Need to get your men ready to move this mother."

She felt his arms, which had begun to tighten around her, loosen and then slip away. He raised his head, looked at Leo, and moved back another step. He looked back at her, his face still lost and wondering, and then turned and went quickly up the ladder. She stared after him.

Something, a sound, made her turn around. It was Quidley. As she watched he moved again, stirring, though his eyes were still closed. Blue bruises were beginning to appear on his face and on the side of his head. She slid the hatchway closed behind Turner and then went back to kneel beside the white officer.

If she was sure of her love for Johnny, it was less easy to define how she felt about this man. He lay quiet and her eyes sharpened themselves on his face.

For what he had done to Johnny she should use the long House fingernails to tear out his eyes. For all that the South—and he was one of the rulers, yes, right here —had done to her people, he deserved death.

Yet . . . it was not so easy. She remembered his strangeness in her bed, his odd gentleness. The fact that he'd cared for her, or had thought he had. And after all he'd saved her, too, saved her from rape and worse at the hands of those Kuklos patrollers. And he'd given her back Johnny. Just because she'd asked him to.

So what did she *feel?* Kneeling beside him, unsure as to whether to help or to destroy him, she had to examine her own heart.

But before she could think further there was another step on the ladder and she got up hastily. It was only Willie, chubby Willie, puffing with the effort of squeezing through the hatchway. In one fat hand, incongruously, he carried a Tredegar. Looped over his shoulder was a coil of light line.

"Vyry. Got to tie him up."

"I'll help."

"I can do it. Oh—say, can you find some cloth? Maybe a piece of rag? Got to blindfold whitey here so he don't see where we are, who we are, Leo says."

"Let me look around." The compartment offered nothing to a quick search. She unwrapped the red scarf. "Here. Use this."

164

"That pretty thing? You don't want to use that. Might not get it back." Willie winked.

"He gave it to me," she said. *Paris*. "Now he can have it back." She held it out.

Willie was rolling Quidley's unresisting body over, looping the yellow line skillfully around the long white wrists. She could see fine ginger hairs curling around the knots that Willie pulled tight. Suddenly, the cabin was too small for her, too stuffy. She needed air. From above came the sound of voices, and she went to the ladder and looked upward. The hatchway-framed sky was just flushing with the first gray of a rainy dawn, and she breathed the fresh wind gratefully.

Fifteen

"Can I come up now?"

"Yeah, Vy, come on up."

She recognized Finnick's voice; and his feet, in the heavy government-worker issue steel-toed work shoes, were the first things that she saw as she poked her head out of the hatch and into the waxing dawn.

They were just offshore. Barely a hundred yards away lay the land, thickly covered with dense-looking woods. The heavy rain of the night had turned to slow, steady drizzle, falling endlessly from a low thunder-gray sky. She pulled herself the rest of the way up. On the open deck behind her she saw the men busy around a great gray-greenish shape, as big, it seemed to her, as a small automobile, but squatter, heavier, egg-pregnant with its own purpose. It lay there in its cradle with the men toiling around and under it like a queen ant tolerating its workers.

"Get them timbers under her."

Turner's voice this time: no longer puzzled, nor angry, but resonant with command. She saw him now moving among the others, in his own element, lending his back and arms to tug a beam into place, flipping a line into a tight knot with a fluid motion of his wrists. Almost she thought it was the old Turner. Almost, until he happened to glance toward her, and she saw his eyes, flat, cold, and empty.

Willie came on deck. "All right below?" Finnick asked him.

"Yeah. He tied up good."

"Bo, we're ready, I guess," said Turner. He raked the shrubbed shore with his gaze. "Leo?"

The Railroad man was leaning against the shell, breathing hard; Vyry could see that he was unused to heavy work. He dragged an arm across that disquietingly pale forehead. "Yes, Turner?"

"Where's your goddamned truck, man?"

The octoroon pointed to a little bay, indenting the coastline some few hundred yards away. "It all looks different from out here, but the place is over there. The estate. The truck is on a dirt road, not far from the water."

"We can't hump this mother very far," said Turner, kicking the shell contemptuously. "And rain makes mud. That truck of yours—it got four-wheel drive?"

"No. Just a regular commercial Southern Motors delivery truck. But with the best set of tires the Road could steal."

"If we could run her right up on that bank—" Turner pointed to the little bay, where, as they drifted closer, Vyry could see an edge of trim green lawn descending to the muddy tide line. "You'll have to get the truck right up close's you can to us. Bo, get her nose to, let him off."

The boat shuddered suddenly as Finnick nosed her closer. "She shallow draf'," said Turner, looking over the side. "Run her right on in, Bo."

When they grounded, Leo swung over the side into mud, ankle-deep, gluey, and dark brown. She could hear the sucking sounds his shoes made as he struggled toward the grassy verge. When he disappeared into the trees they waited. Finnick, hands on the wheel, glanced anxiously around the empty water behind them. Willie searched the sky. Then, faintly, came the sound of a truck engine starting.

"Let's get her well in, now, Bo. Every foot goin' to save us a gallon of sweat. Run out a bit, get up some speed, and get her on in."

"Might not get her off, Johnny."

167

"Take that chance. Anyway she'll float a lot higher without this thing in her."

Finnick maneuvered free, playing with screws and rudder like an organist, then waited offshore till the truck came into view, backing slowly, jerkily, down the lawn; then aimed the bow like an arrow and punched the throttles. "Hold tight and bend those knees!" he shouted back.

Vyry crouched as the boat gathered speed. She expected a crashing impact, but instead all that happened was that the nose tipped up and the boat seemed to come to rest with a slithery gentleness. As the engines throbbed at last to quiet she leaned out. The bow overhung grass, but the shell, halfway back along the length of the boat, was right at the muddy verge.

"Rollers there, under her. Them timbers braced proper? Bo, you the smallest, I puttin' yo on the holding-back rope." Men moved swiftly into position as Turner cracked out orders. "Take a couple turns with that; it gets away, likely to crush somebody."

"How heavy you figure it?" said Wash, cinching tight a broad leather belt around his waist.

"Can't tell. Ton—maybe more."

"Thass too heavy," said someone. The men looked at Turner.

"I can't make it no lighter for you," said Turner. He looked at the mud and at the forty yards still separating the back of the truck from the boat's side. "And they ain't nobody to help. And no way to winch her, and no winch if there was. So we sweat it over, that's all. And there ain't a better bunch of men to do it in the South."

The men shifted and looked at each other and the shell. Turner gave them no chance to speak. "Let's go now. Free up them straps. Sammy, Ben, lower that carryin'-frame right down there in the mud. Good. Now, get behind her—*hunh!*"

A little chorus of grunts came from the men as they leaned into the round heaviness of the shell. To get it up over the waist-high gunwale of the patrol boat, Vyry saw, Johnny had laid heavy long timbers in a sort of ramp, up which, as the men shoved, the shell now began to roll. The timbers pointed skyward outside of the gunwale, over the mud, and she wondered why—they seemed far too long.

"Ready, *hunh.*"

"*Hunh*," Wash, Ben, Willie, Nose, Turner grunted as they heaved. The shell hesitated, rolled a quarter-turn, hesitated, rolled a quarter-turn. The wet timber creaked. "Bo, keep 'at line taut. No slack," said Turner, his own big shoulders bunched intimately against the curving dripping metal.

"Ready-and-a-*hunh*."

"*Hunh*."

The grunts grew higher in pitch, took on a rhythm as the men shoved, gathered themselves, shoved. The shell rolled, paused, rolled. The brass bands gleamed gold-dull. The shell rolled.

"Turner—"

Leo, standing in the mud below. Turner didn't answer. Vyry called down, "Leo, stand over by the truck. Don't stand under there."

The Railroad man retreated and stood by the idling truck, hands in his pockets, watching, looking worried. JAMES G. GILL COMPANY / GOURMET TEAS AND COFFEES / GILLS HOTEL SPECIAL loomed behind him, lettered on the side of the truck.

"Hol' it." She looked back at Turner. The shell was poised menacingly almost at the gunwale. "Ben, can you reach to slip a keeper under it?"

"Yeah . . . there."

"Ease off." The men stood back, wearily eyeing the thing. It seemed undecided, ready to roll either backward or forward, ready to recoil back on them or to plunge forward, downward, and bury itself in the waiting mud. Finnick frowned, looking at that mud.

"Johnny, tide's comin' in."

"Shit. You boys ready?"

The men breathed, flexed their arms, nodded. Turner pointed. "She's almost there. I want three of you behind her at first. Bo, you keep ahold of your rope, but get ready to shift to the other side when she come over the rail. Wash, Nose, want you down there, ready to take her as she come down. Watch your hands."

They moved into position obediently, their faces wet with drizzle and their first sweat, serious with their concentration. She heard Nose murmur, "Comin' down always worse than goin' up."

"Okay, boys. Three on the ass-end—shove!"

169

The gray-green cylinder seemed for a moment to resist them.

"Shove, you bastards!"

. . . They turned, almost imperceptibly. One of the men groaned, caught himself, and shut up.

"There she come," said Finnick, soft. The little man leaped suddenly for the rail, whipping his momentarily slack rope to a cleat on the other side of the boat. The men grappled sweating with wet slick metal, balanced gently, and then its center of gravity shifted ever so slightly on the gunwale.

"Stand clear below!" shouted Turner. "Them beam ends—"

She caught her breath at the sight. Delicately, gracefully, the long heavy timbers he had used for ramps were shifting, the boat ends coming up, the outboard ends coming down, rolling gently and with a weird squeal about their fulcrum under the breathlessly poised shell. The men waiting in the mud below reached up, guiding the ends as they came down, as the shell shifted again, beginning the yield to gravity, the downward roll. Finnick's line tautened. He doubled and tripled its coils about the cleat and set himself, back cat-arched, against the weight. The shell moved. The rope became lean and straight and drops of brown water oozed out from it and pattered on the deck.

"I got it," said Finnick, between clenched teeth.

"Sammy, you guys move round to the downhill side. Bo, you give it to us a couple of inches at a time."

"Yo."

Fascinated, she felt the tension in her own muscles. The ends of the beams were gone, burrowing themselves deep into the sucking mud. The advancing tide sent little wavelets over the one nearest the water.

"Gimme slack, Bo!"

"Yo."

"Hold that. Wash, careful your footin', you going to go ass over teacups—"

"Teacups shit! He got his foot on mine!"

"Slack, Bo."

"Yo."

She looked east. Perhaps twenty minutes had passed since Finnick grounded the boat. The sky was growing lighter by the minute and the drizzle seemed to be easing off.

Soon, she thought, *they'll be after us. They'll know. When this boat don't show up where it supposed to be they'll start to look.* Airships, like the one that had passed over them on the journey out, would fly low, searching the miles of river and inlet and swamp that envined the Tidewater. The police, the soldiers, the patrollers—for this they would all be called out. There would be searches everywhere. Searches. . . .

She remembered bodies floating silent in the decaying Elizabeth at dawn.

"Little more, Bo."

"H' she come."

The men holding the shell back from its downward urge were breathing well now, short wheezing explosive pants of effort. They grappled with the shell, hugging it, wrapping their arms into it, pressing their bodies into the slowly descending terrible weight as if to force themselves into it. An almost sexual striving with its terrific potency of mass. Their feet trampled the mud, seeking better footing to take the weight they transferred through their straining bodies. She saw Johnny, his blue shirt torn where it crossed his chest so that the massive neck and blood-swollen hairy-bristled pectorals showed, gleaming, and his neck was taut, and his legs set like concrete posts, deep in the mire.

"Slack—"

"Comin' to the end, Johnny. Got maybe four feet left."

"Awright. We 'most there. Ben, I'll hold it, you shove that cradle over thisaway. Yeah. Now, let her down—little more, Bo—"

The shell rolled, stopped, rolled. The cradle of wooden beams, crudely but strongly lashed together with mooring rope, took the weight of it and began immediately to sink into the mud.

"Get on the handles now. We'll need you all. Hey, Leo!"

"Yes."

"You can't back that truck no closer?"

"Got to stay on the grass. If I get the rear wheels near that mud—"

"Okay, come on over here. Gonna work your half-white ass for a change." The men laughed, stretched for a moment, wiped sweat.

"You want me on it, Johnny?" she called down. He

171

looked up at the sound of her voice and she felt her heart leap up as he met her eyes. The work—he seemed so much better, so much more sure of himself, at his work. He seemed to lose whatever it was that puzzled him in it.

"No, Vy. Don't need no women to do my longshorin'. Leastways, not yet."

That, too, drew a laugh, and even a smile from Leo. She smiled, too.

"Lots of handholds here. Space yourselves out, like. Get a good grip."

Ranging themselves along the sides of the thing, they reminded her now of pallbearers, the carriers of a mighty corpse.

"Couple deep breaths—ready, now—"

"Hunh." They grunted together, hoisted viciously together, backs straight, thrusting with muscle-pillared legs. The cylinder tilted, the cradle sucked up from the mud reluctantly, with little smacking sounds like parting kisses.

"Hunh." And they moved forward a step, in unison, like marching soldiers, like Hebrews struggling with the Pharaoh's granite. Arms rope-taut, necks corded with effort. The thing surged forward, swaying.

"Hunh." A second step. She gripped the rail till pain came to her fingers. Their bodies were drawn down with the effort. It was too much for them, she could see that, too much even for these brawny men.

But not for Johnny Turner. The biggest of them, he seemed to be taking the weight of the whole base of the shell, alone. She could see his agony in the rigid upward angle of his head. But he held on—held on—

"Hunh." Another swaying step. For the men in front the grassy verge was only a few feet away. Another step, and then another. The front tilted, dipped, and dragged along through the mud. Leo's side. The thin man, boylike among the massive longshoremen, jerked himself upright and she heard his breath whistle, a long-drawn-out inspiration of anguish.

It happened, then, as she watched. A *hunh,* in chorus. The front dipped again, dragged, and Leo went down. As he dropped to the ground the cradle fell too on that side and the shell rolled, moving with the casual deliberation of great mass, and its nose slid a little to the right and blotted out his upper body.

When she reached them, losing a shoe in the mud but

172

not caring, they'd set the cradle down. Finnick was kneeling by the Railroad man, with the others gathering around him. They looked down in complete silence. "Let me through," she said, pushing between Ben and Nose's broad backs. They gave way, and she could see what had happened.

The middle of the shell, its widest point, had stayed on the cradle. The dip as Leo fell had caused it to pivot, the rounded nose of it swinging to the right. This now lay across the thin man, who lay face downward, motionless, on the wet grass. His left arm, shoulder, and upper chest were out of sight under the shell, and its weight pressed into the curve of his neck and cheek. Finnick had half-turned his head to the right and had scooped out the soft sod so that he was able to breathe, shallowly, quickly. His face was old paper and his eyes were shut. She couldn't tell if he was conscious or not. She looked up at Turner. "Johnny, we've got to get it off him before we can help him."

He was staring at Leo, his face strange. The distant look was in his eyes again, nor had he heard her. *Lord, not again,* she thought. "Bo, Willie, we've got to get it off him."

"Gimme a hand," Finnick cried, putting his own shoulder to the shell's bulk. The others stepped into place. "Now—*shove.*"

The shell pivoted, hesitated, and settled into place again on the cradle. Vyry's eyes widened at the sight of the arm. Visibly flattened, it had been pressed down into the soft soil, and the shoulder was oddly angled. Leo had not reacted to the removal of the weight. He must be out, perhaps in shock.

"That arm gonna go," she heard Willie whisper.

"That's not what worries me." She pointed to the shoulder, and then her finger moved downward. "It's his chest. And his heart. That was layin' right across his back."

She bent down to listen at his mouth. No; no trace of bubbling, no trace of blood. But that didn't mean it might not start when they tried to move him.

But they had to move him, and right now. Already the dawn was brighter, and the outlines of a large house were becoming visible at the top of the long sloping lawn.

"Come on, Johnny." It was Finnick, almost pleading.

"We got to get movin'. We get caught out here by one them airships and we all gonna be dead."

"Yeah." Turner seemed to come back from somewhere, and shook his head. "Take hold again, boys."

They bent again for handholds, their eyes shifting now to the goal, the open maw of the truck, only ten more paces and then up.

"*Hunh.*"

Behind them, she felt for Leo's pulse. She was no nurse, but it felt weaker than it should. She touched the sleeve of the left arm and swallowed. It was becoming sodden with blood, and she could feel the pulpiness of crushed tissue beneath.

A tourniquet—that was the only thing she could think of. But even as she pulled his belt free from the muddy trousers, she was thinking, *then what? Then where do we take him?*

To Richmond with them; they had to. Locked in his mind were the names of the Railroad men there and the place where they would meet them and the plans of what they would do; the details of how they would act to convert the tremendous destructive power of the shell into political leverage. And also only he could drive the truck—in daylight, at least. She could drive, most of the CEs could after a fashion, but it was illegal, and any police or patrollers would stop a black man or woman in a car on sight. She set the belt in place and tightened it until the slow ooze of blood slackened.

Turn him over? No, she decided to wait and see if he came to before doing anything more. She looked up, toward the truck, in time to see the last stage of the shell's journey.

United in an ecstasy of straining effort, their bodies trembling-rigid, Johnny Turner's men were lifting the shell straight up. Their hands, knotted on the cradle, moved slowly, so slowly as to seem almost stationary, as if they were arm-wrestling with gravity. Up. So slowly—past their knees, to their waists— a collective gasp, a shift, bending lower under it now—Turner himself with his broad back and shoulders under the base of it, with its small black cavitied eye staring back at her—then up again, even more slowly, as the men cried out softly and the nose of it came level with the truck's bed—

174

They grunted and heaved together and slid the cradle a foot forward into the truck. That end supported, Willie and Ben, the two front men, could come around behind Turner and the others and heave it forward. It slid slowly into the truck, the men grunting explosively, the mud-lubricated wood of the cradle scraping on the metal bed. Foot by foot it disappeared into the truck like a strange reversal of birth. Then it was inside and the men stood back and looked at one another and some fell to their knees on the grass and were sick. Turner stretched himself and leaned against the truck, swaying, for a moment; then reached up and banged shut the doors and snapped shut the padlock that was there.

Under her hands, Leo moaned. She bent and stroked the wet forehead. "Leo, it's Vyry. Can you hear me, man?"

"Ahh . . ." He moaned. His eyes flicked open, unfocused. "Vy? . . . oh, *damn*."

"Do you feel like you can move?"

"I can't feel my arm." His smooth pale forehead was dotted with sweat, and all trace of his boyishness was gone.

"It don't look too pretty. I put a tourniquet on it, stop the bleeding." She looked toward the truck. "Leo, we got to take you with us. Can you try to get up? I'll help."

"Uh, I'll try." He gathered himself for a moment and then struggled up. The left arm dangled and he looked down at it with an odd blank disbelief. "It's broken. Shouldn't we set it?"

She thought it was far beyond setting but didn't know how to say it. There was a steady dripping from the tips of the finger, and a dark stain spread on the mud.

"Vyry? You all right?"

She tried to smile. "Yes, Leo. I'm just worried about you."

"Never mind it." He tried to smile too. "It doesn't hurt yet, really it doesn't. We got a man in Richmond will fix me up right away. But—" he looked at the truck, "how are we going to get there now? I can't steer, or shift."

"How is he?" said Turner, joining them.

"I can't drive."

"I can. Drove a truck down the waterfront couple of times when the white boys took sick."

"Yes, but—"

"I know. Can't pass if they stop us." Turner scowled. "But we still got guns. Ain't hardly used them yet, either."

"That isn't the way through the Army, Turner. We got to go through quiet."

Turner snorted.

"Look," Leo continued. "We'll stay here today."

"Here?"

"Yes. But first we've got to get the boat out of sight. Can you sink it?"

"Not in here. Too shallow," said Turner.

"Then can you get it under cover? So that it can't be seen from the air?"

"I saw a creek back there by the road. Trees over it . . ." Turner waved to Finnick. "Hey, Bo. Come on with me. Goin' to move the boat." They walked together toward the water, and Vyry, left behind with Leo, remembered something else.

"What about the white major?" she said, in a low voice, pitched so as not to carry to Turner.

"What about him?"

"Can't just leave him tied up there in the boat."

"It's that or kill him, Vyry. I don't think Johnny would mind doing that, either. With his bare hands. That's the man who had him under interrogation, isn't it?"

"Yes. But he's not a—real bad type. Like some of them, the KKLs. I don't"—her eyes fell—"I don't want him killed."

The Railroad man's eyes searched her face. "I see. Well, we've got to keep Turner away from him, then. The others I can handle. Him . . . no. The best thing is just to leave him there."

"Get over here, you lazy black bastards," Turner was shouting from the beach. "Lean into her. She's stuck fast."

The men assembled, heaved, and the patrol boat floated free in a roar of motors and a flurry of mud and water from astern. Finnick steered it toward a thick copse of trees farther down the shore.

"We'll stay here today?" said Vyry. She looked up the lawn. It was full daylight now and she could see that the house was large, not palatial, but far beyond what any CE could hope to own.

Leo followed her gaze. "Yes. We'll stay there. Hole

176

up, get some food, some rest. It'll be a long night's drive to Richmond."

"But the people in the house—"

"They know we're here," said Leo, walking up the lawn. His useless arm swung, and he coughed briefly. "In fact, they're part of the Railroad, too."

Speechless, she followed him up the lawn.

Sixteen

The first things, for a long time, that he was conscious of were the small white pinwheels.

They came and danced at the edge of the darkness, daring him after them. For a long time—hours, it seemed —he resisted, preferring the friendly nothing and the ease of not-thinking. But at last the pinwheels were joined by nagging pain and the darkness in his mind dissolved gradually and he came back to himself.

He was lying on his side, in darkness, and all was quiet around him. The pain was principally in his arms, which were doubled behind him, and in his wrists, which were (his brain slowly interpreting the feelings) bound together rather too tightly for circulation. As a consequence he could no longer feel his hands, nor his right arm. His feet too were bound.

The last thing . . . the last thing that he remembered (though this seemed fuzzy; his mind did not seem to be working too well, everything seemed uncertain, drunken-edged) was struggling with Turner. Slowly being strangled. And now . . . he was lying tied up on a hard floor, in someplace dark and silent. And closed up; the air seemed stuffy, smelling of paint and diesel fuel.

He was still on the boat, then. But it was not moving, not even the tiny restless motion of a boat alongside a

178

pier. And he could hear no footsteps, no talking, nothing but, when he concentrated, a faraway scraping sound, a rustling.

How long had he been unconscious? He pulled himself upright, gasping as his head began to pound. Some nausea, too, he noted. Perhaps a slight concussion—hadn't his head struck something just before he went out?

Circulation flooded back into his right side with prickling agony.

I have to get free, he thought. If they've abandoned the boat then they've taken the shell off with them. To do what? To go where? Perhaps back North. No, that would be asinine.

The Railroad terrorists wanted the shell for themselves. In a way, even as he groaned and tested his bonds, he had to smile. It was such a neat reversal. Even now, according to the op order, Richmond would be telling Philadelphia that black terrorists had seized the freighter. Well . . . it was true.

His wrists writhed as he tried for a grip on the thin rope. One loop seemed to be high, caught on one of the fat brass buttons of his uniform jacket sleeve. He twisted in the dark, cursing the rolling oaths that too were Quidley heritage, trying to work the slick line free. At last he felt one of his numbed fingers slip under it and he pulled and twisted and worked it free.

A second later he was unwrapping the cord from his wrists and groaning as the rush of fresh blood brought new pain; but he kept working till he had his legs free as well. At last he was able to get the gag from his mouth. He ran it through his fingers in the dark. An oddly fine, silken fabric. It had a familiar feel. . . .

He tossed it away and rose. He staggered a bit, holding himself up by leaning against the invisible wall, but remained upright. *Good going, Aubrey,* he thought. He buttoned up his tunic and hooked the collar and pulled his uniform into place. Then he began feeling about the room, very quietly. At last he found the door and eased it open a crack. There was darkness on the other side. Another small room by the texture of the black. He took a step forward and stumbled over something and felt for it: a folded-down bunk.

Now he knew where he was. This was the bunkroom and the hatchway should be back in the first room but to the left of the door. He felt his way back and found the hatchway.

No. It wasn't locked. He slid it open cautiously, waited a long time, his ear to the crack, and then opened it the rest of the way and climbed up the ladder.

Night, still. Or was it, night again? Hadn't it been almost dawn when they'd left the *President McClellan?* Yes it had. He twisted his watch to catch a faint gleam of starlight. He couldn't read the date, it was too dim, but both hands pointed straight up. It was midnight.

He realized that he had lain unconscious below all through the day.

And the deck he stood on was obviously deserted. Trees bent low over it (he remembered the tapping, rustling sound) and underbrush grew close on either side. Up some narrow channel, to hide it from the air . . . even as he thought it his ears registered the distant drone of zep motors. Someone, then, was out looking. Perhaps they'd already caught Turner and his people. Certainly, with the kind of search Vickery and Norris would initiate when FPB-122 did not arrive, they could not evade capture for long. He walked toward the stern, ducking to avoid a low branch, and looked over the side. The hull was wedged against the bank and he wouldn't even have to get his boots wet to get off.

Thinking of that reminded him of his loss. Not the loss of the shell: that was too big for him even yet to grasp. But the loss of the Quidley sword.

He stood and thought. There was a bare chance they might have left it aboard. Certainly, a colored carrying a sword would attract instant arrest, and they couldn't, if they expected to get wherever they planned to go and do whatever they wanted to do, afford to be conspicuous. Hurrying below again, he snapped on the light and quickly went through the boat. His disappointment and anger grew. No sign of it. They'd probably dropped it over the side as soon as they'd taken it from him. The damned—

He stopped, and bent. There in the corner, where it had rolled, by the hatchway, was a metal tube, perhaps a foot long. He picked it up.

They'd left the fuze. A slow smile spread over his face.

He had to get in touch with Norris. He thought of the radio and looked into the wheelhouse but someone had anticipated him, and he saw it lying smashed in there. Well, there must be a house somewhere near. There he could find a telephone, and find out, too, just where he was.

He returned to the stern and looked over the side again. A slight stirring in the water: a snake? No, probably just a frog. He slipped the tube back into his tunic and threw one leg over the gunwale.

Mud sucked at his boots and then he was fighting his way through the underbrush to get up the bank. Thorns ripped in his uniform and he cursed as his bare face encountered them. Then he was out under the trees and the brush had thinned out a little. *Have to check for ticks when I get out,* he reminded himself. *And a nice hot shower would help . . . aspirin, this damn head. . . .*

He saw lights ahead, through the trees, almost at once. He smiled. A house, people. But then he caught himself. He had to be careful still. What if they were sympathizers? Or, worse still—what if Turner and the others were there, hiding? A momentary fantasy shaped itself of him bursting in, wresting away a gun, capturing them all.

Thinking of Turner reminded him of Vyry, too. And suddenly he realized that in what he had thought was the last moment of his life, with the black giant's hands crushing the life from him, he had felt something soft—something with her scent.

His lips drew back in a half-conscious snarl as he thrashed through the woods. She had been there with them, the bitch. Images of the fine porpoise curve of her back came unbidden to his mind. *And you thought you liked her, even loved her!* Sawyer had been right. Like belonged with like. He had been tricked, used. . . .

The dark underbrush ended just ahead. He crouched, listening. There seemed to be an open space beyond, for he could hear, all around him, the singing of the cicadas . . . but not from ahead.

After a moment he moved warily out, onto carefully kept lawn. Water sparkled to his right. The lights of a house yellow on his left, perhaps a hundred feet away, up a slight slope. He moved toward it, crouching, but after ten steps stumbled over an inequality in the ground.

It was a rut. No, a pair of them, just visible in the starlight. He bent and ran a finger inside of one of them.

Fresh, wet—an obviously heavily laden vehicle with knobby tires. He followed the ruts backward toward the water, curious, and found the torn grass and trampled mud at the shore, and the deep V depression that looked as if a boat had been run up on shore.

He nodded.

Trudging back up the lawn, toward the house, he moved more cautiously than before. The shadowy grounds seemed familiar, as did the pattern of tall windows in the house, but he just couldn't put them all together into a specific memory. He paused twenty yards from the house, by an ornamental tree, and listened intently. Nothing. Light streamed out quietly from the windows. The tire tracks led on past it to . . . that would be the driveway, and then this, the shadowy mass between him and the house, this would be the garden, and—

He was standing in back of Sharon's house.

Momentary doubt, then certainty. Now it was all familiar, though the night still made it mysterious. He caught his breath. If they'd broken in, used the house, harmed her—

The thought sent him running quietly round toward the front. The ruts turned into the driveway but there was no truck there, only a small low shape that he recognized as her Triumph. He stood for a moment in front of the familiar door, then slipped round to one of the tall front windows, the living room window, and raised himself on tiptoe and peered in.

The living room was brightly lit but empty. His eyes searched it from one side to another. Nothing was broken, nothing missing that he could tell, no evidence of violence or the presence of strangers. He moved silently to another window: the dining room. The big table shone softly in the light; it was cleared and polished and a cut-glass vase held slightly wilted peonies. One corner light was on.

Then, even as he watched, a figure appeared in the hallway beyond, and his heart leapt up. It was Sharon Sue in a red dress, with her hair up. She passed the door and he lost sight of her. He dropped to his heels. *Thank God she's safe,* he thought, and wondered whether she had seen them, reported them . . . she couldn't have ignored a truck rolling over the lawn, unless, of course, she had not been at home. He crossed to the front door and rapped on it sharply.

"Who is it?" he heard her call, from the inside.

"Me."

"Who? Aubrey?"

"Yes."

A pause. "What do you want?"

"Well, I want to come in. There's been, well—just let me in, please, and I'll tell you."

He heard the snick-snap of the electric bolt and then the door swung open. He smiled, envisioning how he must look to her, in bedraggled, torn uniform, black-smeared face, muddy boots. "Evening. I'm not looking my best, darling, but believe me, I've been through a lot." His eyes fell on two suitcases beside the door, and then returned to her. Besides the red dress she now had a hat and a small black purse. "You're going some-where?" he said.

"Jus' a little trip, Aubrey," she said coolly, fidgeting with a glove. "What is it you needed? I really haven't much time."

"I'd hoped for a shower, and—but I'd better phone in first." He saw the telephone on a stand nearby and started for it.

"Aubrey, dear."

"Yes, Sharon Sue?"

"Sit down."

"Just have to make one call."

"Aubrey, *will* you sit down and tell me what this is all about? Do you know what time it is, and you burstin' in here all crazy like?"

Slightly cowed by her tone, he retreated to the divan and perched on its arm tentatively. "Why—sure, all right, I'll explain. I was kidnapped, by coloreds—by the Rail-road. They took government property. The shell, I told you about it, remember? *Shiloh?*"

"The coloreds?" said Sharon Sue, looking suspicious.

"Yes." He was in a hurry to explain; the telephone sat on its stand and stared at him impatiently. "They took over the patrol boat somehow that was waiting for us. When we transferred the shell to it I was knocked out and left tied up in a boat that is right now in the woods out back of your place. I just got free and now I've got to call General Norris and tell him what I know. They're in a truck, and I know where they're going." He stood up and took a step toward the phone again.

"Aubrey—"

Her voice was soft, and there was even a little note of pity in it as he turned and saw the little automatic she held in one red-gloved hand.

"Sit down, Aubrey," she said.

And he was conscious of a sudden chill inside. It was not the sight of the gun, nor that it was being pointed at him. It was Sharon Sue Hunt herself. She was the same —no, looked the same, pale, lovely, teetering on high heels, faultlessly dressed—yet she was not the same. Though her west Tennessee nasality was the same, that coyness, the southern-belle archness, was gone, and it showed even in the way she held herself: straight, without the sway, the slight incline toward a man, the plea implicit for support. The change was indefinable yet definitely there, and he felt incongruously that he faced a stranger. He sank back into the divan, eyes fixed on her face and on the eyes that dominated the room.

"That's real nice now. You just sit there for a little while, while I think about what I'm going to do with you."

She looked around the room. "Poor boy. You look so tired. Can't hurt to offer you a drink, can it? Want one?"

He nodded, not trusting his voice. He was still in shock, still trying to convince himself that he was awake, that this was real.

"Joke," he croaked suddenly.

"What?" she poured bourbon from a decanter.

"This is a practical joke. Sharon Sue, it would be funny, but this is not the time for it. I really do have to call Norris. Now. You see, *they're on their way to Richmond*."

"Now, Aubrey." She set the glass down near him and backed away, leaning against the jamb of the door. "That's a natural response, I suppose, and it makes me feel bad, it really does, but I'm not playin' with you. Not anymore. Now it's all for real—though I never intended for you to get caught in the middle like this. Even when they told me you were out in the boat, I thought I could leave in time, before you got free.

"You're not a bad man, Aubrey. Not in your way. You were just—conditioned, in a way—and confused, and not all that bright. There are a lot like you in the

184

"Confederacy, I'm afraid. Not basically bad, but just held by the old unjust ideals." He watched her face set. "Of course, there are the others. The ones who *are* evil, in Castle Thunder, in the White Mansion and the Senate, the Leaguers, the Tredegar people."

It was all bypassing him; he couldn't see any of it, couldn't relate what she was saying to anything coherent. He reached for the bourbon and took a healthy slug for the pain in his head.

"Look, Sharon Sue—I'm just getting more and more confused. Are you—are you saying you're some sort of —of spy, for the North?"

"Does everything progressive have to come down here from up North? There are people here who think the CEs are human, Aubrey."

"That's ridiculous. Of course they're human. That's why they were emancipated, a long time ago."

"*Conditionally* emancipated. But did that give them their freedom? Bullcrap. They're assigned to work, they get inferior educations, poor food, they live in Colored Areas—that's not emancipation, it's only a prettied-over form of slavery. Which you know, Quidley, only you can't admit it, because then you'd have to admit that your life is a failure, you've spent it in the uniform of an unjust cause."

"State's rights—"

"Spare me that old Secesh horseshit. States have no rights. Only human beings do. And the Confederacy exists to stamp them out." She was flushed now, excited. "It would have been better for us, I swear, if we'd lost! Maybe rough for a while, but then we could have rebuilt, black and white together. They'd be no Almost War, either, we wouldn't be nose to nose with the Yankees. There would be peace in the world, real peace!"

"But, Sharon Sue—" he groped for words, scarcely aware of what he was saying; the shock was still too great for belief. "You—you're not a Yankee—"

"I talk like one?" she giggled. "No, I'm not."

She held up a fist. Staring at her, he could not believe what he saw, what it meant. Sharon Sue, on the Railroad?

And only then did his mind begin to function, setting the facts in their places. The first leak, about Shiloh itself; he had told her about it. Told silly brainless coy beautiful

185

Sharon Sue all about it. And never recalled that he had done so, when he had been busy suspecting Channing, Norris, the others—it hadn't been them at all. He had done it himself, with the aid of bourbon, soft lights, and the lips of a faithless woman.

"How—how did you get hold of the—the operation order? How did you know about that?"

"Nothing very complicated, Aubrey, believe me. In fact, all too simple. Jesse and Ella are both Railroad too, of course. Your briefcase was no problem for him—he started his career as a safecracker. Ella's a photographer. We had microfilm of everything in your briefcase on the way up within hours after you left the house."

"And the message?"

"Jesse showed me how to get into your briefcase. I found the message while you were in getting me a drink that night at your home. I took one of the carbons. You never noticed."

"I noticed later."

"Too much later." She smiled.

Suddenly it was too much for him: that familiar smile yet with so much treachery and falseness behind it. He clutched at the arms of the divan. "You betrayed me," he whispered hoarsely. "I loved you, and you—"

"Don't be an ass." She crossed the room and sat down on a chair opposite him, crossing her legs, ever the lady. "You never loved me. You never *saw* the real me . . . only something you constructed in your mind. You saw me as the right person for your fiancée—beautiful, wealthy, gay, rather witless. That wasn't love. I don't know if you've ever *been* in love, Aubrey—if you were, you wouldn't be smart enough to realize it—but you certainly weren't in love with *me*."

For some reason that rang in his mind, repeated itself. He stared past her, his anger thwarted and his emotions uncertain. *You never loved me.*

If you did, you wouldn't be smart enough to recognize it.

He had found the message gone and had been sure it had been Vyry. He remembered the moment when he had wavered between the two women in his mind and how his whole upbringing had colored the instantaneous decision that evildoing lay with black skin. He had suspected Vyry Lewis, destroyed her man, used and enjoyed her body.

186

But there had been that moment of doubt, a moment in which he'd felt something for her, some passing regret that he had been so thoroughly taken in. Yes, and more than that. Because he *had* felt something for her. Something that, *yes,* that he had never felt for coy simpering teasing Sharon.

Something that might even in his own heart have been called love in that moment of decision, except that she was black and he was a Quidley.

It was not possible that a Quidley could love a colored prostitute.

Sharon was watching him with an expression of intelligent interest that he had never seen on her face before. He saw that and straightened and put on a stern look. "Tell me something," he said. "You're Railroad, you say?"

"Yes."

"Then you're not really white. You're passing."

"Oh, Lord. In some ways you are just too naive, Aubrey. Do you really think the Road could have lasted for a hundred and fifty years without white people? White Southerners? Even before Secession there were plenty of whites who helped the escaping slaves get on up North." She laughed, then looked at Quidley and sobered—not really sober, but at least serious. "And if it was only blacks, then the Road would be nothing but colored terrorists. The way the government tries to portray us. But God help the South if there ever were a genuine colored revolt. We're the ones prevented it."

Quidley nodded. He hadn't really thought she was passing; her hair was too blonde, eyes too blue, skin too white. But it had cleared the uncertainty up. "Let me ask you something else. Do you know the people who took me? Took the shell, I mean?"

"Yes. They stayed here with me during the daylight hours."

"And you let them go on to Richmond with it?"

"Let them? I helped them. You still don't seem to understand what I am, Aubrey."

"I'm beginning to. But how could you do that, maybe not as a Railroader, but as a human being? Don't you know what they plan to do with that thing?" He leaned forward. This was his only chance to convince her that she was wrong, that Turner and his men had to be stopped. In the corner, barely four steps away, the telephone stood waiting.

"They won't use it. The man in charge is level-headed."

"Level-headed? *Turner?*"

"The big man? No, he's not in charge. Another man is, one from higher up in the Road. He's hurt, but still conscious, still in command. I can't believe he would . . . no, they won't really use it, Aubrey. But it's important that the government thinks they will."

But they can't, Quidley thought, feeling the stiffness of the cylinder under his tunic, against his heart. So that was a dead issue. What remained was to save himself, and to *use that phone*.

"Just what do you expect to gain, Sharon? The Railroad, I mean?"

"Equality, Aubrey. The same laws for black and white, for a beginning. Freedom to change jobs, organize, and vote."

"It'll be chaos. The two races can't live together! They won't even if they could!"

"Now you're just parroting the government line, Aubrey, and worse, the Kuklos League line. They *have* to live together, but the only way they can do that without fighting is if the coloreds are free, too. Conditional Emancipation, Dixie socialism—the same old hatreds go rotting on underneath the frosting. Aubrey, there's got to be a change, and this is our chance to do it quick and clean. If we don't the North is going to come down one of these days and do it for us."

She was persuasive, he had to admit . . . and, more than he liked to realize, she was expressing the very ideas that had stirred in him from time to time and which he had dismissed with a vague feeling of guilt as un-Southern, radical, unworthy of him as a Confederate officer and as a member of one of the first families of the state. He struggled to think. It was true, he hadn't loved her. He saw that now. But he *had* loved—loved Vyry.

Where did that put him? On whose side?

"You look poorly, Aubrey. You feeling all right?"

"I'm all right. What are you going to do? Where are you going now, Sharon Sue?"

"Leaving. I'm done here. Now I've got to be in Richmond, to act as an intermediary between the Railroad leadership and the government once negotiations start."

188

"And me?"

She twisted her lips in a moue that was almost that of the old Sharon Sue. "Oh, yes. You. Whatever am I going to do with you, Aubrey Lee Quidley?"

He waited.

"I can't let you go. Not before they're in Richmond. And I can't even let you get to a telephone." She rubbed her nose and looked at him. "Aubrey . . . now that you know about us . . . mightn't you want to join us? We could use an officer—"

"That would be dishonorable."

She rolled her eyes. "I should have expected that. The honor of a Confederate officer."

"And a gentleman. And a Quidley."

"I see. Well, I can't take you with me. I can't lock you up and take the chance you might escape again. As a matter of fact there's only one thing I can do with you, Aubrey. That's kill you. Don't you think that's a terrible waste?"

He had the fantastic feeling still that this was all a joke, but facing her eyes, eyes fixed on his with an irreproducible mixture of gaiety and regard and at the same time coldness and obvious resolution, he knew that it was not. She meant to kill him, with regret perhaps, with humor and without too much seriousness certainly, but she would do it. "Look," he said.

"It's no use, Aubrey darlin'. That's the only answer there is, and I can't say I'm happy to have you make me do it."

"*Me* make you do it?"

"You are, you know, Aubrey." She stood up, holding the little gun on him. Out of sheer habit, he rose too, and stood facing her, brushing ineffectually at the front of his tunic, where prickly seeds had stuck during his crashing career through the woods. "Because it is up to you. I gave you the chance. Now you've had time to think about it. I really don't want to have to hurt you, Aubrey. Won't you —change your mind—about joining us?"

He stood facing her and thought.

The Post. A younger Quidley, saluting the Banner for the first time, pride swelling in his throat thicker than grief.

Staring down at Turner as blood welled from his mutilated mouth.

189

His father, stern, commanding, uncompromising. A gentleman is defined by his word and by his actions—not by his speech, or by the size of his holdings. Remember that, son.

And another voice. Don't bother none about me, Major. You're one of a dozen I'll see tonight. And all white officers.

The tall dark portraits in the hallway.

Baylor's white-faced defiance.

The sword. The Stars and Bars.

The smell in the apartment in the Colored Area.

A salvo of thirty-inchers tracing white chalk across the sky.

The blind lost hate in Turner's eyes.

I, Aubrey Lee Quidley IV, do solemnly swear to support and defend the Constitution and way of life of the Confederate States of America; to defend State's Rights and majority rule; to . . .

Slowly, he shook his head, and dropped his hands to his sides. "No, Sharon Sue. I can't do it. I gave my word. Maybe the Confederacy isn't all I thought it was once . . . but I can't betray it now."

"Then I haven't any choice, Aubrey," she said, raising the little gun to the level of his chest. "I'll try to make this quick."

He stared back into her eyes, once so gay, so familiar, and now detached and cold and still somehow regretful. He forced himself to stand straight, closed his eyes, and found Vyry's name shaping itself on his lips.

It was in that tension-charged moment that they both heard the sound of the front door swinging open.

Seventeen

There were two ways, Vyry knew, to reach the capital from the vicinity of Norfolk.

The first, the fastest and most direct, led northwest across the two-mile-wide strait of Hampton Roads, past the outer works of the Union base at Fort Monroe, and on straight to Richmond through Carter's Grove, Williamsburg, Lightfoot, Providence Forge, and Sandston. Unfortunately, Leo felt that the thirty-five-minute ferry crossing at the Roads left them too vulnerable to detection, even after dark. There would certainly be guards on the ferry; and, since this was a well-traveled route, it would probably be roadblocked as a part of the government's overall response to the news of the utter failure of Project Shiloh.

The other route was quite different, and much longer. It led not north but southwest from Lynnhaven; then, across a downtown bridge over the Elizabeth, and on through Portsmouth and Suffolk. Somewhere west of Suffolk it became the old Petersburg road, turning northwest and paralleling the James River through Windsor, Zuni, Ivor, Wakefield, Waverly, and Disputanta to Petersburg. From there, via the new National Highway One, it was only twenty fast miles to downtown Richmond.

She had never traveled either route, naturally. Her

work assignment at the House kept her in Norfolk, and CEs did not travel for pleasure. Leo had, however, and he described the indirect route as a two-lane, gently rolling road through wooded country, almost deserted except for the occasional small town—all of which should be pretty well closed up at the hour they would be going through.

She turned her head to look at the Railroad man. In the darkness of the truck's cab he was slumped against the right window. To her left, she was crowded against Turner, feeling his warmth and the movements of his arms as he kept the heavy vehicle on the narrow road. He liked the windows closed and inside the cab it was very hot and Leo's loud rasping breath began to worry her. She twisted in her seat to put her hand to his forehead. He felt hot even in the stifling air.

"How is he?" grunted Turner, keeping his eyes on the road. Ahead, the truck's lights lit fence rows and the beginnings of scrub woods as the peanut fields and mills of Suffolk dropped behind them.

"Leo?" she said.

He moaned softly in reply.

"It's fever," she said. "That arm—he's got to have a doctor real soon, or he is going to die."

The arm wasn't all that worried her. His strangely altered breathing was another. She remembered how the shell had rested on his back. She didn't know much beyond first aid—one of the few things the colored schools taught that was any use in later life—but there could be lung damage, he could be bleeding inside. She just didn't know. All she could do was try to make him as comfortable as she could. And she had been doing that for the last twenty-four hours.

They had parked the truck, after getting the shell aboard, in the garage of the big house. The watermen—Nose, Willie, Ben, Finnick, the others—had scattered. They would show up on the docks in the morning, sleepy of course, but with no reason for anyone to suspect them of anything.

She, Johnny, and Leo had stayed the day in the garage. Sleeping. The white woman had brought them food, the bandages that wrapped Leo's arm, and what medicines she had—primarily aspirin and bourbon whiskey. As she lay there and waited she had considered going back to check on Quidley, but had decided not to. He'd

192

saved her life, she had saved his, they were even; eventually someone would discover the boat and he would be freed, if he didn't work himself free. And there was another reason. Johnny, in his odd way, seemed to have forgotten all about the white major. To mention him now might be to risk sending him off again into one of the strange attacks of violence.

At ten, well after dusk, it had been time to leave. With surprising gentleness Turner lifted the injured man into the cab. Vyry arranged pillows under his feet and head while Turner slid behind the wheel and started the engine and studied the gears.

"You drive careful now, Johnny."

"Woman, we run off the road with what we got in back and you never feel a thing."

Humor? She glanced at him as they swung out on to the road out of Lynnhaven. His face seemed more relaxed than it had been, less ridden by puzzlement and anger, less remote. Perhaps he was coming back. *I just can't mention the things that'd set him off,* she thought. *Keep him happy, keep him calm, he may get better by himself.*

And now, west of Suffolk, she felt the pull of the engine as he accelerated, sending the coffee truck hurtling along the ribbon of darkness that was State Road 460.

"What?" she said.

"Didn't say nothing," said Turner.

". . . Vy."

It was Leo, and she leaned over him. "Yes, Leo, I'm here. What you need, man?"

"Hurts, Vy," he whispered.

"I know. We'll get you to the Railroad people soon, they'll take care of you. Try to lie still now."

"Where are we?" He seemed to be waking up, but his voice was still weak.

"Just outside of Suffolk."

"Much traffic?"

Slumped down as he was, she saw, he couldn't see the road. She helped him sit up. "No. We see maybe three in the last ten minutes. It's getting late."

He sat painfully erect, breathing in his strange ragged tearing way, and said nothing.

"Want something? We got some of that whiskey the Hunt woman gave us."

193

"No. Got to be alert, in case someone stops us. Give me some of that aspirin."

"How many?"

"Six."

"That's a lot, Leo."

"Hell with that," he said faintly. "Maybe a short drink to wash 'em down. Thanks." He tilted the bottle up and liquor sloshed and she felt him shiver and then it came down, and he handed it back and wiped his mouth with his good hand. "Yeah, that's all-right liquor."

His voice was losing, she noted, the gloss of white speech as he grew more tired. That worried her. She glanced at Turner, but could see little of him in the dark but his silhouette against speed-blurred dim trees. If something should happen to the Railroad man, they'd not know where to go in Richmond, nor whom to see.

"I might not make it all the way," he murmured, anticipating her.

"Sure you will."

"Sure try. But if I don't, you and Johnny got to know what to do, you get there."

Neither of them said anything. She stared out of the window. Two brilliant points of yellow fire in the headlights: a cat. It loped across the road in front of them. Turner held the wheel steady. The cat hesitated, the light swept over it, and the slightest tremor came through the seat to her.

"First we got to get into the city, through any roadblocks, patrols they got out."

"We'll do that," grunted Turner.

"Drive in along Highway One. Now we can't go right in to the city center." He paused to breathe. "So we got to pick up some people. Guys who know the city. Couple to carry radios and guns, so when the Road makes the announcements, they can hold off the po-lice."

"Where'll we meet them?" said Vyry.

"That's what . . . I'm telling you. Listen now. Got to get off Highway One on Bells Road. That'll be maybe four miles before you cross the James, there'll be a sign."

"Bells Road," she repeated.

"Follow that to the left to Jeff Davis Road. Take a right, go a mile, you'll enter the Bellemeade Colored Area."

She repeated it.

"In Bellemeade you—well, better just stop. Ask some-one. LeLand Ray's. It's a dive. Don't talk to anyone but Ray. Nobody else."

"LeLand Ray. Bellemeade."

"He got the men there. They'll be waiting. Give him the shell, and the fuze."

"The what?"

"The fuze, the metal thing that major had on him. That was the fuze for the shell."

She glanced up at Turner, and felt his eyes turned toward them. In the dark the whites seemed to glow. "Johnny," she said, low, "Do you—?"

He shook his head, no.

"What's the matter?" said Leo.

"I don't think we have it," she said. "I haven't seen anything like that."

"Must have left it on the boat . . . It doesn't matter. Ray's got a boy can probably fix it to blow. Even if he doesn't—" Leo coughed weakly. "It doesn't really matter, I guess. Long as whitey thinks he can make it go bang, we get what we want."

Again she felt Turner move, this time to look at Leo. The truck began to drift toward the berm, toward the waiting trees.

"Johnny—watch the road," she said.

"Uh." He twisted the wheel. Headlights loomed far ahead, not yet visible, but lighting the night like a rising moon. They neared, dipped as Turner dimmed his own, and swept on by. Vyry breathed out; she had been holding her breath at each passing car.

Suddenly Turner spoke, his voice too loud, too harsh. "I thought the idea was, kill whitey. Now you saying we can't?"

"That wasn't the idea." Leo sounded very tired. "Not idea at all. Idea to get us our rights, man. Jus' our rights." He seemed to rouse himself with a great but flagging effort. "Where are we?"

Vyry saw the sign come up, glow briefly in the headlights, whip by. "Coming into Windsor."

Houses appeared, then crowded closer as the road widened with paved berms and sidewalks. A speed sign flashed by. "You better slow down," Leo said. "Don't want to get us picked up for speedin'."

"Keep going," Vyry snapped. "We got to get this man some help."

"Slow down, I said!" The Railroad man's voice was faint, but commanding. "Don't spoil it all for that! There's too much depends on this, girl!"

Turner took his foot off the pedal and the engine whined, slowing. Two streetlights, more white-painted clapboard houses, a huddle of small stores, and they were through the town and picking up speed again on an even narrower and more deserted and disused-looking road than before.

"Leo?"

When he didn't answer she leaned down to listen to his breathing. It was shallow and still slightly ragged, but it had subsided into regularity, and she decided that he had dropped off to sleep.

The whiskey, probably. He would be best asleep, she thought. Thank God for the aspirin and the whiskey and the bandages. And the house, a safe place to hide in through the dangerous daylight. The blonde woman, Hunt —she was strange. A white lady, but she was with the Railroad, and she'd served the CEs herself, with no hint of superiority. Strange to find a white person on their side. But it made her feel good. Maybe the white folks were not all bad. Maybe they could be changed. Maybe. . . .

As she nodded, half-asleep herself, a night vision of a new, changed Southland rose in her mind. A land where coloreds worked where they chose, where they had decent homes and schooling. Where they didn't have to obey, didn't have to fear, didn't have to scurry and hide in the friendly night. Maybe then there wouldn't be so much hatred of whitey, of the coloreds, of the North.

She dreamed on, sliding deeper. From time to time she was dimly aware of the truck slowing, and she opened her eyes for glimpses of frame and brick homes, lonely streetlights, worn-looking cars parked for the night. Zuni. Ivor. Then, again, long stretches of empty road, hills rising to the west lightless and vast. Again she dropped off, but was brought back some interminable time later by Turner's elbow.

She opened her eyes, and sat up. The truck was slowing.

There was something in the road ahead.

As the truck slowed, Turner flicked the lights to low

and she saw them: frame barricades, striped red and white, drawn across the right side of the road. In front of them two red fusees smoked and flared, drawing circles of flickering scarlet light on the roadway. Behind them—she was wide awake now, and shaking Leo—were two dark-painted pickup trucks. Several men stood motionless near the barriers. Her eye picked out details as the truck continued to slow. Flashlights. Uniforms—some of them; others were dressed like farmers. A shotgun, held carelessly, barrel drooping downward, the ruddy glare from the fusees etching it all sharply against the utter black beyond.

Leo stirred and muttered.

"Leo, *wake up!*" She shook him fiercely, not caring if it hurt.

He seemed confused, and his body felt hot under her hands. "Wh'm—"

"Wake up. It's a roadblock."

It seemed to take forever for him to drag himself up. Turner downshifted, slowed further. They rolled toward the barrier at walking pace.

"Bust through?" said Turner.

"Uh . . . no. Gi' me. . . ." Leo fumbled in his jacket. "Vyry, ah shit—help me here—"

She pulled something, a card, from the pocket and placed it in his good hand.

"Env'lope too."

Yes, there was a folded envelope at the bottom of the pocket, too. He took it and breathed hard and tried to hitch himself up in the seat.

"Get down, Vy. Don't want to let 'em see you. No, wait—they won't be expectin' a woman. Stay setting up. Johnny, stop the truck."

The brakes squealed softly, and the truck rocked to a halt a few yards from the barricade's crossrail. Vyry licked her lips and sat back, feeling her heart accelerate as one of the uniformed men stepped around the barrier, his hand at his belt, to meet them. Leo lifted his good arm lazily in a wave. "Evenin', Officer," he said.

"Howdy." The man, his face still in the dark to those in the truck, looked up toward the cab. He saw a white man in the passenger seat, a black woman, and a man at the wheel whose face he couldn't see. He looked up at the sign on the side of the truck. "Gill's, huh?"

"Yep. Runnin' a load up Richmond way," said Leo, his voice subtly changed, subtly, neither colored nor high-class white.

"Long way around," said the man. As he stepped closer to address Leo, Vyry could see his face more clearly in the reddish glare. He had a round, heavy face, with bushy light eyebrows, a dimpled chin, large ears. A name tag under a silver badge said WILLIAMS.

"What's the trouble?" said Leo. *He sounds so casual,* Vyry thought. Perhaps the weakness in his voice even helped.

"Don't rightly know. Army called us out this morning after some niggers, s'posed to stole some new gun or something." The man's eyes shifted to Vyry, and as they picked up the headlights they seemed to gleam. "See you got one with you there. Nice lookin'."

"Yeah, she is," said Leo.

"She, you know, she work for you?"

"Yeah," said Leo, his voice very casual, almost faint. "Leastways, you might say she works under me."

The inflection was just right; it took the deputy just long enough to get. He slapped his knee. "Yeah! Work under you, does she! I like that!"

"Oh, yeah," said Leo.

"It true 'bout them colored gals?"

"Ain't you ever had any?"

Some of the other men behind the barrier, some in uniform, others in drab dark cotton of farmers, a few with colored armbands, drifted closer, attracted by the deputy's laughter. As they heard Leo's question they snickered, and Williams glanced around. "Well, sure I have," he said. "Oh, sure." He looked at the other men and winked. "Anyway—they all pink inside."

The men laughed.

"All cats gray in the dark," said Leo, tired-sounding.

They laughed. One man put his foot up on the truck's fender.

"We got to get a move on," said Leo, coughing. "We got to get this shipment on into Richmond by dawn."

"Where you say you was from, fella? You not from around here, are you?" said the man with his foot up on the fender. Leo ignored him.

"What you say you was carryin'?" asked the deputy.

"Coffee. Carryin' coffee up Richmond way."

198

Vyry felt herself trembling. Leo's voice was growing fainter and fainter.

"Who that with him?" said one of the farmers, a small red-haired man. "That driver look like a nigger to me."

The officer came up to the window to peer in, stepping up on the running board. "Holy shit," he said, after a moment. "It *is* a nigra." He stepped down again and looked accusingly at Leo, who had his eyes closed. "What's this —say, fella, are you feelin' all right?"

"Just tired," said Leo, opening his eyes. "Real ass-busted tired."

"Is that a nigra you got drivin'?"

"What the hell's it look like? You act like you ain't never seen one before."

"Now don't get riled," said the officer, his voice becoming solemn. "No call to get upset, and I can see you tired. But I'm goin' to have to cite you. Even if he work for you, can't no nigra drive. Specially after dark. Lemme see your pass."

Lazily, Leo's arm held out the document. The deputy reached up to take it. Unhurriedly, Leo's arm came back in the cab again, fumbled around, came back out with an object that gleamed redly in the lights of the flares.

"You all care for a drink?"

The men looked at the deputy. Williams pursed his lips for a second, then nodded. "Go 'head, boys. Save me a swallow if it's any good."

"Think you'll like her," said Leo. "It's prime stuff."

"Where you get her? This ain't bonded."

"No. From farther on south. Private make."

Williams handed the pass back up. He looked at the men as they passed the bottle around and loosened the revolver at his belt and pulled his uniform cap down and wiped his mouth and said, "You boys go on back the barricade now. I wanta talk to this fella alone. Official."

"Sure, Denny," said the red-haired farmer. The circle of men dispersed and Williams came up close to the cab.

"How long you been drivin' tonight?" he said softly to Leo.

"Quite a while."

"All night? You sure look beat."

"You might say that."

"You ain't drivin' from Norfolk," said Williams. "And

199

you ain't got coffee in that truck." He cut his eyes up shrewdly to assess the impact of his words.

"That what you figure?" said Leo, sounding as if the deputy's opinion meant less than nothing to him.

"That's right," said Williams. "Ain't nobody drives from Norfolk to Richmond this way, on this road. It's hour, two hour shorter going up the peninsula."

"There's less traffic on this road," said Leo.

"There sure is," said Williams softly. "You know what I figure?"

"What do you figure?" said Leo, closing his eyes.

"Jesus, you're a cool one. But your bad luck tonight. You run into me."

"Could be," said Leo wearily. "Usually ain't nobody at all along this here road at night."

Williams chuckled and hung an arm from the truck's side mirror. " 'Ceptin' tonight. Yes, sir, I figure you doin' you a little smugglin'."

"Now what would I be doin' that for?" said Leo, in a bored tone. "You know that smugglin' is illegal, deputy."

"I figure," said Williams, looking at the barricade and his men, where the bottle, up-tilted, gleamed for a moment, "That you has got a truckload of cigarettes here. And you is just drivin' 'em up from Raleigh or Durham by dark so as not to pay the Virginia tax on 'em."

Vyry stared straight ahead, hardly daring to breathe. What would the man do? Would he check the back of the truck? Leo seemed to be sinking by the minute. But what could she do, except wait—and hope?

"I think I just better check the back of this truck," said Williams, but his tone was odd; there was just a shade of tentativeness, as if the statement were really a question.

And Leo's hand, dangling from the window, opened, and a bit of folded paper fell to the ground.

"You're pretty sharp, officer," said Leo. His voice was by now little more than a whisper. "There's two hundred in cash in that envelope."

"Yeah?" said Williams. He bent casually to pick up the folded envelope. "Two hundred, say?"

"That's right."

Leo looked down at Williams, who hesitated, looking at him. "Man, you really look dead," the deputy said.

"I am, man, I am. Do you mind if we get movin'? I got me a schedule, you know."

"Well, I don't know," said Williams. "This two hundred —it ain't a lot of money. And you know it's a crime to offer a officer of the law money like that."

"I can't pay you any more." Leo gestured wearily with his good hand. "Take that, or run me in. I only make eleven cent a pack, you know."

"Well . . ." the man hesitated, trying to gauge Leo's tone; then he nodded. "Well, you go on, then. Guess you been punished enough, been fined, sort of like. Hey, you boys!" he shouted to the men at the barricade. "Pull that out'n the way. He's all right, he's goin' through."

"Thanks," said Leo. "Oh, and look—you ain't goin' to be out here every night, are you?"

"I see what you mean," said Williams, waving to the men to hurry. "No, sure not. I guess you boys don't make too much doin' this."

"No, damn little," said Leo.

"But look, you oughtn't to have that nigra drivin'."

"I generally don't. But you just happened to catch me when I was tuckered out," whispered Leo. "So long, deputy."

"So long," said Williams. He stepped back and waved. Leo nodded to him, then to Turner, and the truck began to move forward. The flares flickered and dazzled as they moved past them, and then the road ahead was dark again. Vyry sat frozen for several minutes, still unable to speak.

A choking sound came from beside her, and she turned to Leo. "Johnny—turn on the inside light. I think—"

A thin thread of blood marked the side of Leo's mouth. His eyes were open, but distant, and he did not answer when she shook him. "Leo! Leo, are you all right?"

"He's dead?" said Turner.

"No, still breathing, but let's stop."

"What for?"

"Lay him down. We've got to stop this bleeding, Johnny, or he'll die."

"We've got to get into Richmond." Turner did not slacken speed; in fact, he increased it, and the roar of the engine shouted back at them from the dark trees lining the road.

Headlights glowed ahead, and Turner snapped out the cab lights. She kept her eyes on Leo. The oncoming car threw brilliant shadows across his face, half dark, half stark white.

"I said, stop!"

He didn't answer.

"Johnny, he'll die!"

Reluctantly Turner said, "Okay. In a little while."

"Little while, shit! You stop now!"

"Too close to the roadblock."

"Find a side road and turn off. Ain't nobody going to come along this time of night." She shook his arm and the truck swerved. Leo moaned.

"Johnny, now!"

A break in the trees showed ahead: a side road, unmarked, half-overgrown with brush and small saplings. The truck slowed, turned, and jolted over dirt ruts. Brush rustled and scraped along the sides of the cab, things snapped under the tires. When they were fifty or sixty feet away from the road Turner cut the engine and switched off the lights.

"Help me get him out," she said, jerking the door open and swinging herself to the ground.

Together they eased him out of the cab and laid him down on the grass in the road in front of the truck. It was very dark now that the lights were off and there were night noises from the forest around them. The engine ticked quietly to itself, cooling.

Leo breathed shallow, coughed, breathed shallow. She stroked his head with trembling fingers.

"We got to get going."

"Shut up, Johnny," she said, not caring if he hit her. "He's dyin'. Give him his time."

It seemed harder for the thin man now as he lay crumpled flat in the dark grass. He had to struggle for each breath, as if some heavy hand were squeezing down on his lungs. As if something soft and flowing was gradually hardening in his throat, cutting off air and life. She stroked his face gently. There was nothing else she could do.

When he didn't breathe anymore she sighed and stood up.

"He dead?"

"He's dead," she said. "Highway One, Bells Road, left,

202

Jeff Davis. Right, one mile, Belleville. LeLand Ray's. He's dead. Let's put him in the back of the truck."

"Just a minute," said Turner. "Listen."

From far down the road came the whine of a small engine at high speed. It neared, peaked in a high-pitched scream, then died away as it passed them and dwindled down the road. Vyry relaxed and turned back to Leo.

Then it grew again, neared. White light flickered through the trees, picking out the traceries of the foliage around them. The motor slowed and shifted downward in pitch. The light grew brighter, brighter yet, and she heard, behind the truck, the crunching of tires on the dirt road.

Eighteen

"Anybody to home?"

"Who's there?" called Sharon Sue, her voice high. She glanced toward the door, which was opening slowly, and then moved toward it, still holding Quidley under the savage black eye of the gun.

And Quidley stiffened. He recognized the voice. Slow, boisterous, Mississippian—

Earl Sawyer stood in the opened door, his hat in his hand. His eyes were on Sharon Sue, and he was bowing slightly, awkwardly. "Hello, Miss. You're Miss Hunt, I believe?"

"That's right." Quidley saw that her right hand had disappeared into a pocket of the red dress. "Who are you? What do you want here, sir, to come walking through—"

"Earl!" Quidley took two quick strides forward and seized her arm. She struggled, but he brought her arm out by main force and twisted it. The pistol clattered to the floor and he kicked it beneath the sofa. She jerked away, panting, but he held her, not gently.

"Damn," said Sawyer, staring at the divan. "Aubrey, what the hell is happening here?"

"I'm damned glad to see you here, Earl. Damned glad." He looked at Sharon Sue, whose long hair had

204

come down in the struggle and now swung forward, to cover her lowered face. "I've got a surprise for you, and for Norris. I've found our Railroad informant."

"Say she is?" said Sawyer, lifting her chin with one hand. "Pretty little gal. But look, Aubrey—what were you doing around here?"

Quidley blinked at him. "You found the boat. That's why you're here, right? Got men outside?"

"Matter of fack, no," said Sawyer. He looked slowly around the room, and his eyes stopped at the decanter. "Ma'am—Miss Hunt—could you spare a drop of that?"

She didn't answer, staring down at the floor, and he crossed the room and poured himself out four fingers of bourbon and half-turned. "Aubrey?"

"Just had one, thanks, Earl."

Sawyer replaced the stopper carefully.

"Look, Earl—if you didn't find the boat, then how do you know that—oh, I see. You captured the others and they led you back here."

"No," said Sawyer, taking his first sip and raising his eyebrows.

"Then how—"

"Look, Major. Let's put it like this. I come over to see Miss Hunt. I didn't expect to find you here. I'm havin' to rethink some things. That explain it to your satisfaction?"

"Oh, for heaven's sake. You think I'm Railroad, too? That's ridiculous. As a Southern officer you should know better than that."

Sawyer studied him over the glass, his heavy, red, short-necked face glowing already with the liquor. "No, sir, that was not my meanin'."

"Then let's get this woman into custody." The matter of the shell, almost forgotten, recurred to him and he straightened. "Colonel. You're looking for the shell, correct? Well, I know where it is. Or at least where it's going."

"Where is that?" said Sawyer, without, it seemed to Quidley, a great deal of curiosity.

"Richmond!"

"Say Richmond, eh?" Sawyer finished the drink and set the glass down carefully.

"Yes. The Railroad intends to blackmail the government into giving the—coloreds—equal rights." He shook

205

Sharon's arm. "And she's one of them, one of the terror-ists!"

"You're hurting my arm, Aubrey."

"Shut up."

"Why not let her sit down?" said Sawyer. "She can't hurt us now, Aubrey."

"Can't—" He choked on the sentence, and looked down at her. She had her face up now, the white small face he had dreamed about; the blue eyes he had thought empty and childish. The fire of passion, conviction, hate was in them now. He shoved her toward the chair oppo-site the divan. Sawyer, who had drawn himself another generous glassful, strolled over to stand near her, looking down.

"Is that right, Miss? You with the Railroad, the nigras?"

"I'm not answering your questions."

"Aubrey, how do you know they're takin' it to Rich-mond?"

"I overheard them planning the trip."

"That'll do, I guess." Sawyer spoke musingly to him-self. "So they'll be in the capital, with a live shell."

"Not live," said Quidley quickly. "Not that, at least."

"What?"

He fumbled with the fastenings of his tunic, and pulled the tube halfway out. "This is the fuze. They left it be-hind, probably didn't realize how important it was."

Sawyer's color had changed. He stared at the tube as if it were a live snake that Quidley had produced from his bosom. "That—that's the fuze? It needs that thing to go off?"

"That's right," said Quidley proudly. Sharon Sue shifted on her chair and her eyes sharpened, but she said nothing, only watched the two men. "Earl, I've got to call Norris now. They've got to get police out between here and Richmond, put a cordon around the capital, check every truck and van. Real police, and military too, not these rural types they depend on in the small towns. Patrol the roads by air, and the James too, in case they shift back to a boat again. We can finish this and catch them and keep it all quiet and no one will ever hear about it outside the government. And Shiloh will still be a success." He moved toward the telephone stand.

"Major."

"Sir?" he picked up the receiver.

"Don't make that call."

He stood still, not knowing what to think. Finally he said, "But, Earl—"

"I said, no need to call." Sawyer's voice was smooth, but with the tone of command. "It's all bein' taken care of, now you believe me. You see—I knew about Miss Hunt here. Have for quite awhile."

Quidley slowly replaced the handset. "Well, damn it, Earl, then why didn't you turn her over to the authorities? Even if we were engaged—you didn't hold off because of me, did you?"

Sawyer sipped at his drink and watched Quidley and did not reply.

"Oh. I see. If you knew about her—then you, and Army intel and the CBI, you've been using her. Passing false data, tracing people who visited her, cloak-and-dagger stuff like that?"

"You might say that," said Sawyer. "You're not all that slow to catch on, Aubrey. In fact, you're mighty quick. We might"—here he winked—"have a place for you up in Richmond."

"Oh, I couldn't operate on that level," Quidley said modestly. "But it's not that hard to figure out." He tried to think further, to impress Sawyer. "And since you'd been watching her, you know, I suppose, that they were going to bring the shell through here after they took it."

Sawyer's little eyes were intent on him over a refilled glass. Quidley paused, feeling almost as if he were under examination, and felt puzzled. "But if you knew about it—even if you didn't know what they planned to do with it—why didn't you stop them before they took it? That would have been so much easier—"

"He's lying," said Sharon Sue suddenly. The two men turned to look at her. She was sitting up straight, head high, her eyes on Quidley.

"What?" he said.

"Who is this man, Aubrey?"

"Now, look—"

"Answer me, Aubrey."

He grimaced apologetically at Sawyer. "This is Colonel Sawyer, a friend of mine from Army Intel, and a fine loyal officer."

"He's lying," she said flatly.

207

"Look." He felt anger return, felt its heat flood his face. "It's you who are the liar. I trusted you, and you've been, all this time, a Railroad agent."

"Whose agent is he?"

"He's no one's agent! He's a loyal officer!"

"This has gone about far enough," said Sawyer.

"I agree," said Quidley.

"Aubrey, think. If a loyal officer had known what this man says he knew, he would have had it stopped. The boat would have been alerted. Or there would have been soldiers here at my house waiting when you pulled in."

"That's about enough," said Sawyer, moving toward her.

"I'll call for the CBI," said Quidley, picking up the phone.

"Damn it, I said no!" Sawyer whirled on him, his face mottled with alcohol and fury. "Put that telephone down, Major, that's an order!"

"And why doesn't he want you to call, Aubrey? I think you'd better find out before—"

She stopped as Sawyer slapped her. She fell back on the chair, staring at Quidley.

"Now you keep quiet. Quid, I said put down the phone."

"I think I ought to call, sir."

"Put down the phone."

"No," said Quidley.

They looked at each other for a few seconds. Finally, Sawyer sighed and flipped open his holster and put his hand on his service pistol. "Major, you don't understand. This here is official, high-level. Now please get away from that telephone before I have to get mean."

"He's lying," said Sharon again, and her head rocked back as Sawyer's hand whipped across her face again.

"Don't do that anymore," said Quidley.

"You defendin' a Railroader, Aubrey?"

"I'm defending a lady, Earl."

Sawyer laughed. "This? This ain't no lady. This here is a nigger-lovin' white turncoat. Understand that, Quidley? That's the kind of people you been keepin' company with. Nigger-lovin' radical Republican abolitionist Railroad trash."

"She's not trash." He looked at Sharon Sue. "She believes in what she's doing." He folded his arms. "And I'd appreciate some explanation, Colonel, as to why you threatened me when I went to call my commanding officer."

Sawyer chuckled, but seemed, for a moment, uncertain. He tossed off the remainder of his glass and rubbed his mouth with his sleeve, keeping the other hand at his belt. "Sure, I'll explain for the gentleman. But, say—give me that fuze, would you?"

"I think I'll keep it."

"Aubrey, you sure are tryin' my patience." He looked down at Sharon threateningly. "I have good grounds for arrestin' both of you, you know. Findin' the two of you here . . . well, you could have been workin' together. Passin' information. I know she got a lot of it through you, Major. I ought to arrest the both of you."

"Go ahead, arrest me," said Quidley. "Don't talk about it, do it. The investigation will clear me. No Quidley would ever consider betraying a trust like that, nor have I. You know my family, we've been gentlefolk back to before the War."

" 'Gentlefolk'?" repeated Sawyer, with a sarcastic edge to his voice, which was becoming thick and rather slurred. "Gentlefolk? Even fine high Southern gentlemen have been known to sell out, Major. For money—for the love of a woman—" He sneered at Hunt. "Though there's not much meat on this traitor."

"You're an ignorant pig," said Sharon Sue.

"No, don't hit her," said Quidley, stepping forward as Sawyer swung his arm back. *How,* he was thinking, *could a Southern officer act this way . . . even to a traitor? She was still a lady. . . .*

His mouth dropped open, and he stared at Sawyer.

"What's the matter with you, Major?"

It was logical—it made sense of it all. Before he had fully considered it he blurted it out. "I know who he is."

"Who?" said Sharon Sue.

"All right, Quid," said Sawyer. He backed up a step and placed his hand on his hip. "I think you better sit down, too. Both of you, there, on the sofa."

He hesitated, then sat on the sofa as Sharon Sue settled beside him there. He felt her hand grip his. "Aubrey," she murmured, "there's only one reason he won't let you call in. He *wants* the thing to go to Richmond. Why, I don't know, but—"

"Oh, but you can reason it out, between you," said Sawyer. "The two of you are such powerful, original thinkers. From two such cultured, aristocratic families. Surely you can outthink a poor redneck cracker like me."

He stiffened, and then felt her hand on him holding him down, holding him back. "Don't," she whispered. "He'll kill you."

Me? thought Quidley, incredulously, but he forced himself to relax, to sink back into the divan. True—he saw that the big army automatic was only inches from Sawyer's hand. And that the Mississippi colonel's face was taking on, from the drinks and from some mysterious, deep-rooted source of anger, a strange, mottled, red-purplish color.

"Yes, you can reason it out," he spat at them. "You two *gentlefolk!* Now let me hear it, *Major. What* am I?"

"You're a Unionist," said Quidley. He clenched his fists and felt the warning pressure of her hand. "Why, I don't know. How you could betray your country, your oath, I don't know that either. But you did. You're a Yankee spy. You're the enemy."

Sawyer nodded heavily. "I'm the enemy, am I?"

"Aubrey," said Sharon softly, "he can't be—"

"Be quiet." He squeezed her hand back and stared up at Sawyer. "At least this woman is a Southerner. She thinks change is needed, but she's still loyal, in her way. But you—you're out to destroy us."

"Done, Major? Good, that's good." He laughed, short and bitter and humorless. "Because you're wrong, as wrong as you ever could be. I guess you're just not smart enough, Major. Well-bred—but just not very smart." He weaved a little as he stood and looked down at Sharon. "Why don't you tell him, pretty lady. Maybe you got it figured out better."

"Aubrey . . . I think you've left something out."

"What? It's pretty obvious to me."

"Aubrey, if he was a Yankee, would he have let us steal the shell?"

"Well . . . maybe."

"Let you take over a Union ship and kill all the crew?"

"I wouldn't put that past the Yankees," said Quidley stubbornly. "They don't think of life the same way we do."

"Would you have given the Confederacy the most powerful weapon you have?"

He had to think about that, but he saw a way out. "Maybe it isn't a weapon," he said. "Maybe it's only a trick."

"But why would they sacrifice a ship and crew to let a dummy fall into our hands?"

"Well. . . ." He hesitated again, and tried a random stab. "Maybe to let the Railroad have it in Richmond, to use it the way they intend to. . . ." His voice trailed off; he could see the end of that train of thought. If the Union wanted the Railroad to have anything, there were far easier ways to get it to them than by using the Confederate Armed Forces as a delivery service. But even on a political level it didn't make sense. Having the shell in the capital, with coloreds holding it over the heads of the government, would only make things worse between the North and the Confederacy. All of the South's ancient pride and stubbornness, which had carried it through three years of war to final victory, through war in the West and against Spain and then in Europe, would be aroused, and to fever pitch. There were plenty of "patriotic" and racist organizations that would be eager to jump on a bandwagon like that. No, it made no sense for the North to arouse the Confederacy and the Empire by such a provocation, not while their new weapons were still being prepared. If they planned war they would desire surprise and overwhelming power. If they desired peace they'd never have allowed a shell to fall into either Southern *or* Railroad hands.

Therefore . . . who was Sawyer? "You're not working for the Union?" he said slowly.

"Outstandin', Major!" said Sawyer, sarcasm heavy in his slurred voice. "I knew you'd come up with that sooner or later. Because you have got *blood*—and that's what counts." He leered liquor-purple at Sharon Sue. "Ain't that right, Miss Hunt?"

She did not answer, and he looked at Quidley.

"Blood tells, yes," he said, puzzled as to what the man meant.

"But your fine families aren't doin' *shit* for the South, are they?"

Quidley stared. Sawyer staggered across the room to the decanter, drained the last drops of the bourbon into his

211

glass, and then raised it. The facets of the cut glass sparkled. "To both your fine families," he said, drank, and threw the glass into the large mirror above the sofa, shattering it.

"You two are so damned clever," he resumed, pacing now. "So clever, so *re*-fined. So high and mighty with your swords and your *po*-traits and your fine whiskey and your *blood*.

"Well, they's folks with a sight more brains, and a sight more loyal to the real South, than your first families. Families," he sneered at Sharon, "that produce traitors —empty-headed fools—and both of you nigger-lovers clear through."

"Earl—"

"Shut up. You had your say. Now I'm havin' mine, at last. Same as the people, the real people of the South, the real patriots, is goin' to have theirs."

The liquor was working in him visibly. His face had darkened, and his steps were unsteady as he strode back and forth along the length of the room. Side by side, they watched as he paced the room, now waving the gun.

"We put up with you for too long, you know, Quidley. With people like you—planters, senators, governors, generals, diplomats, businessmen—put up with your swill and your re-fined ways and your cowardice too long. You aren't the real South. You just thought you were.

"We're the real South. The good white people of Mississippi, Georgia, Alabama, South Ca'lina. Maybe we don't talk so refined. Maybe we don't go to VMI and the Citadel, and maybe we don't have the money to dress in tailored clothes and keep yellow mistresses." Sawyer panted. "But we're Dixie, and we're sick of givin' the niggers everything on a silver platter and lettin' good white folks starve. We're sick of Dixie socialism and free food for 'em, and free houses—you know what kind of houses my people live in back home? That's why we burned that there project. These here city niggers got it good. But they won't no more!"

Quidley, watching him, was thinking, this is the real Sawyer. The other was just a pose, a sham—and not a very good one at that. Though the man was smart, he was clever, just as Norris had said. Clever enough to fool them all, right up till it was too late.

And the way he swaggered and the way he talked reminded him of someone.

Reminded him of Baylor.

"You're a Kuklos," he said.

"And damn proud of it," said Sawyer aggressively. He bent to wave the pistol in his face. "There's thousands of us, Major. Hundreds of thousands. In the Army, the police, the patrollers, just plain citizens—all over. We been waitin' a long time. We're sick of Richmond and them nigger-lovin' English queers they call a government. We aim to take over, Major. And when that there shell goes off —a shell set off by the nigras right in the capital—why, that'll be the signal. It'll all be over in one day." He paused to breathe. "And that day'll see all the radicals and all the uppity educated nigras and all their friends lynched, Major. The South will be purified—by the gun, the rope, and by fire. The Kuklos League will rule and the white race will be supreme." He swayed and stopped and eyed them, and then added, " 'Course, you all will have to take what I been sayin' on faith," and giggled.

"What do you mean?" said Sharon Sue.

"I mean, well, certainly I can't let you two fine people tell the gov'ment about us. Or about that shell. No, sir, we want that to be a surprise. We want that to shake the whole South."

"But why, Earl?" said Quidley.

"We been a puppet of the Empire too long, Aubrey. Now we goin' to be a nation, by God. One party—the Kuklos League. One leader. One flag, and one aim—the unshakable superiority of the white race."

Quidley sat stunned. The vision of it was too shattering.

Because it could be done.

Sawyer was right—and Hunt and the Railroad people were wrong. The men he knew in Richmond would never give in to Railroad threats. They couldn't—the country, led by the braying Kuklos reactionaries, would never forgive them.

And if they didn't give in, and the shell went off . . . *But it can't go off,* he reassured himself. *I've got the fuze.*

But the government would not know that. They wouldn't know the shell was impotent. They would be caught between the Railroad and the League, between the forces of change and reaction. They would have to play for

213

time, make concessions . . . and in the meanwhile, the League would strike. And with Richmond immobilized, they might well succeed in taking power. And if they did, it would mean a full-scale revolution. Lynching, burning. And there would probably be war.

Because the North could never tolerate a League-ruled Confederacy . . . and a revolution-torn South would be an easy, indeed an inviting, target for Northern invasion. The Empire—the Allies, would they interfere, faced with the awesome power of the new weapons?

If they didn't, the South was lost. And if they did, it would mean nothing less than World War Two. With the Confederacy, his beloved Dixie, as the battleground. *No, Quidley thought, I can't let it happen. I've got to talk to this man, convince him to let me call Norris and stop the shell from reaching Richmond.*

"Look, Earl," he began.

"Shut up," said Sawyer, waving the gun drunkenly.

"Earl, you have to listen to me. What you're proposing means war with the North."

"One of us can lick ten Yankees. Proved that twice. Let 'em come."

"It's not that easy anymore."

But Sawyer, it seemed, was no longer listening. Instead, he was staring at the ceiling, and then looking around the room, at the expensive furniture, the tasteful decorations, the deep-piled carpet. "Shut up, *Major*," he said again. "Get up. Both of you."

"What are you going to do?" said Sharon, and he heard in her voice the high note of fear.

"Get up. Outside." He motioned, and they moved in front of him to the door.

"Outside. And don't run. I don't mind shootin' traitors."

Quidley bit his lips. To be called a traitor, by a low person like this, and to do nothing . . . but he could wait. After all, Sawyer, with all his faults, could hardly harm a brother officer.

The Bentley stood outside. Quidley glanced around but saw no sign of Roberts. Sawyer must have driven it here himself. He suddenly missed the slovenly little sergeant.

"Stand there," said Sawyer. "Against the house."

He fumbled in his pockets for a long time and finally succeeded in finding the keys and opened the trunk. He pulled out one of the two five-gallon cans of gasoline that were kept, already filled, in every Army vehicle.

"Earl, look—"

"Inside you," said Sawyer thickly, waving the pistol. "Both of you blue-blooded nigger-lovers. Get back inside. Sit down where you was."

"Aubrey, what is he going to do?"

"I don't know, Sharon Sue." He patted her hand; it was pale and cold. "I'm sure he won't hurt us, though."

"No, I won't hurt you," Sawyer sneered. He had taken the cap off the can, and was sloshing the pink fluid over drapes, over the carpet, against the walls of the living room.

He felt her hand move to grip his, hard. The rich raw smell of gasoline filled the room. Sawyer, gun in one hand, can in the other, staggered toward them. Petrol sloshed out, over the sofa, over the gray uniforms of the two men, over Sharon's red dress. Quidley started up, but sat back down when Sawyer made a wild swing at him with the can, sending a dark stain down the colonel's arm.

"Earl—I think you're a little drunk."

"Drunk, hell. I'm just warmin' up." He grinned, tossing gasoline in a wide train into the dining room. "Like you will be, folks. Real soon."

Quidley blinked. The thick petroleum fumes were making him dizzy. It was so thick that the air seemed to shimmer between him and Sawyer, now in the next room. The can splashed busily. Sharon Sue stiffened. "My table! Aubrey—he's going to burn the place down!"

"I can't believe that," said Quidley. "He's an officer. He's just trying to frighten us."

"He's a Kuklos! Don't you understand? He hates us worse than he does the coloreds. You heard him talk. Aubrey"—and her voice rose, terrified, and not with coy terror either—"we've got to do something!"

Quidley felt his heart begin to pound. The fumes—her fear—Sawyer's drunken threats—*maybe she's right,* he thought. At any rate he couldn't sit here and wait any longer. No, he had definitely taken too much from this boor, colonel or not. He stood up.

Sawyer, busy in the next room, caught the movement and looked up. "Major—better sit down. You got a couple of minutes yet 'fore I get to you."

"Earl, I can't sit here and let you carry on like this,"

said Quidley firmly. He stepped forward. The carpet squished wet under his feet. He saw the telephone and moved toward it, and his first impulse, so long thwarted, returned implacable now. He would call Norris—and Sawyer would have no other choice than to kill him. He'd call the man's bluff.

"Sit down, I said. Or I'll kill you now," said Sawyer. The slurring was almost gone, and he spoke in a flat and deadly tone.

Quidley paused. The unthinkable began to take shape in his brain.

Sawyer meant what he said.

Sawyer was an officer.

He was also a Kuklos.

"Sit down, I said." Sawyer's voice was barely audible now. His eyes seemed to glow in the dimness of the dining room. Quidley could see wet patches on his uniform where the gasoline he had been tossing about had slopped over.

And something happened inside Aubrey Lee Quidley. All his anger and fear and bewilderment exploded and he said, "All right, you trash," almost in a whisper.

And began to run.

The colonel's head jerked up, his eyes widening as he saw Quidley coming at him. He brought the pistol up.

For Quidley, time seemed to stop. He felt himself hurtling forward, but too slowly, far too slowly. He saw the vast dark hole at the muzzle of Sawyer's .45 rise slowly into line with his eyes; saw the barrel dip as he thumbed the hammer back. And saw that he was not going to reach him in time.

"Aubrey!"

Something caught at his arm and he began to turn, to fall, caught off balance by the check. But his eyes were still fixed on the pistol . . . on Sawyer's face, broad, frightened, angry, behind it . . . as yellow flame burst from the muzzle. . . .

The room beyond was suddenly a white-hot hell, and he felt something strike his face and chest and hurl him backwards. He hit something behind him with such force that his head swam and he shook it and pulled himself upright, shielding his face with his arms against the terrible heat.

The dining room was like the heart of a furnace.

Drapes, furniture—including her prized table, he noted —the walls, all were covered by fluttering yellow-white sheets of flame, tentacles of which were reaching out into the living room.

But all this was only backdrop to a far more terrible spectacle. His eyes were held by the sight of a human figure—stocky, broad, and still grotesquely upright—standing in the middle of the room, bathed in flames from head to foot. As he watched, Sawyer raised his arms, standing for a moment with them stretched wide, like a man on a fiery cross. His eyes were fixed on Quidley. And then he fell, and the fire, fed by the can he had dropped, leaped up around him.

"Sharon," he whispered.

She lay midway between them, near the dining room entrance, and the fire was already in her dress and hair. He crouched and tried twice to move forward into the steadily increasing heat before he succeeded and got hold of her arm and was able to pull her back across the smoldering carpet. The sofa was catching too now, but he pulled a pillow from it and used it to smother the flames on her dress. When he was finished he stared at the red stains on the pillow.

The heat was increasing second by second and above him Quidley could hear the house creaking. Something fell and shattered in the next room and sparks cascaded through the doorway.

He had to get her out. And Sawyer? He could no longer even see his body for the mass of flames the dining room had become. He looked around the room wildly. The outside door had been blown shut by the explosion and he wrestled blindly with the lock for agonizingly long seconds before the bolt snapped back and the door sprang back at him and the wind came in. The fire began to roar.

Sharon . . . he tried to be gentle, fighting his own panic, as he lifted her. She seemed so light. He leaned into the draft that whistled through the door and stumbled down the stairs, blinking at the darkness outside; there were weird afterimages of the flames wherever he looked. He kept going, until they were a hundred feet from the house, and laid her down on the lawn and fell beside her. When he had caught his breath he rolled over to look back.

The house was going up rapidly. Already he could see yellow-white light flickering in the windows of the upper rooms, and the whole first floor was lit by tongues of flame streaming up from the shattered windows. Inside the thin brick sheathing was wooden framing and beams and insulation and furniture and all the beautiful things she had enjoyed so much . . . as he watched, something exploded in the back of the house with a low boom, and the flame rushed out of the windows, and light danced all around the burning house, on the lawn and the dark woods and the parked cars in front.

Sharon moved under his hand and he sat up and remembered the blood on the pillow. With trembling fingers he undid her blouse and pulled aside the clothing beneath, and swallowed. The big slow-moving bullet from Sawyer's Webley had taken her in the lower ribs, and he did not see anything that he could do at all. He stroked her face gently instead and saw her lips move and leaned down to her.

"Sharon Sue . . . I'm here."

"Aubrey. 'S it bad?" she whispered. He could barely hear her over the roar of the flames.

"I think it is, Sharon. I can't—I don't think I can help."

"That's all right," she whispered. "That man—"

"He's dead."

"Aubrey. Promise—"

"Yes, I will. Anything, Sharon Sue." He bent over her, not caring about his own tears.

"Don't—"

"Don't what, Sharon Sue?" His face hung above hers, waiting. "Don't what?"

At last he brushed aside the fire-blackened hair from her neck and kissed her. It was a long kiss. She no longer needed air.

When he drew his sleeve across his face and stood up he could feel the heat reaching out toward him. As he stood watching (yet not really seeing) the roof parted in one section and the flames broke free, soaring upward into the night sky. Small poppings and the deep crashing sound of floors collapsing punctuated the prolonged low furnace roar of the fire itself. There was little smoke yet, but from around the house a shroud of steam was rising from the bricks, the lawn, and the shriveling leaves of shrubbery and nearby trees, and the steam glowed, veiling the burning house in a light-filled flickering radiance like the full moon before a rain.

As he watched, staring childlike into the heart of flame, the front wall gave way and the steaming brick toppled slowly outward, over the gray Bentley, and it disappeared under bricks and flaming beams and glass and the fire-edged outline of an inverted four-poster bed. Now the whole interior of the house was exposed to the air and to his sight, and the flames soared upward and then the roof fell and then the rear wall, each making the low booming sound and sending myriads of swarming firefly sparks up into the night.

It was not until the fire had subsided, satiated, until only the two thick side walls and the chimneys were standing, until the space between that had been the house was only a low flickering and spitting amid dark heaps of smoking rubble and debris, and the unmistakable smell of a dead fire was beginning to creep out and the wind at his back had died, that he returned to where he was. He bent to touch her again. The smooth, small, triangular face was cold, her arms tossed out casually, her lips slightly parted. He straightened her clothing, buttoned her blouse and dress, crossed her arms. He looked down at her for a moment more and his lips moved, but he said nothing aloud.

He drew back at first from the heat the Triumph's metal retained; on one side, the side nearest the house, the brown paint had welled up in big dark blisters. But he finally got the door open and was able to slide inside. The key was there and he started the engine and spun the wheel hard and sent the little car out of the driveway without looking back. Behind him, after the sound of the motor had faded, the fire crackled and muttered to itself amid the rubble for a time longer, stirred, smoked, and finally, toward dawn, grew still.

Nineteen

Richmond, then, he thought.

The high whine of the car's motor ebbed for a moment and then climbed again as he shifted gears. He swung the Triumph out onto Lynnhaven Road and headed south. There were no other cars on it, no one on the street; he was alone. The dashboard clock read 2:45.

They'd left, Sharon had said, not long before. And the tire tracks, in her yard—the edges, when he had bent to touch them, had not yet softened, though yesterday's rain had turned the dirt into a near-mud. Say, an hour's head start? He nodded to himself and shifted up again. That could be recouped between Norfolk and Richmond, if he pushed himself and the little car to the limit. He shifted up a last time, into fourth, and watched the speedometer creep up over seventy.

But which road had they taken? He couldn't see their taking the direct route, over the Hampton Roads ferry. There were guards on that ferry and at both its terminals, and probably military there as well by now. Briefly, he wondered how the search was going, and whether Norris was missing him at all. Somehow he doubted it.

The roundabout route, then—west, through Suffolk and on toward the capital along the west side of the James River? That area was almost unpopulated, very rural, with only a few small towns between Suffolk and

Petersburg. From there on north it was more citified. But between the urban centers there might not even be roadblocks; Norris and the government, not knowing what he knew about the shell's destination, might assume it still to be hidden somewhere in the Hampton Roads area. Or even taken to sea again, to be landed somewhere farther down the coast.

He made his decision, and turned left at the first opportunity, toward Suffolk. The road widened somewhat and he pressed the pedal to the floor. Fortunately he had plenty of fuel; the needle showed near full.

I'll be using it up fast at this speed, he thought. At more than eighty miles an hour he rocketed through empty streets and left the echoes far behind. He passed two cars—neither of them, fortunately, a patroller—and slowed for the Elizabeth River Bridge. He hated metal-grated bridges and crept over it at fifty and then pushed the car back up near its top speed.

Gradually, as he drove on, his arms relaxed their choking grip on the padded wheel, and he felt the trembling leave him. The effort of concentrating on the road, on driving, was wiping clear his mind. Wiping it clear of the fire and of the memory of Sharon's eyes. And as he drove, as the houses receded from the road and the lights became fewer until the car sped screaming between great dark fields, he was able once again to think. He removed one hand from the wheel on a straight stretch to pat his tunic. Yes. It was still there.

Where are you going? he asked himself.

To catch up with Vyry. With Turner. With the shell.

And then what?

He had no ready answer to give himself, and that worried him for a moment. Maybe the coolest thing to do would be to stop at one of the silent farmhouses, awaken the owner, and demand to use his telephone for Army business. Get hold of the fort and tell Norris everything and let him decide, let him assume the responsibility for action. That was the logical way, the Army way, the smart way.

But you're not very smart, Quidley.

No, I'm not. That seems to be the one thing they all agree on, doesn't it?

That's right.

Do you mean you're not going to stop?

That's right. I'm not going to stop.

There were so many things now that were changing. Changing inside him. He could feel them slipping, like rock faces under titanic pressure, unchanging for millions of years yet moving now into new shapes. He could feel it happening, feel certainties that he had never questioned, givens that he had built his life upon, becoming open to the corrosive nibble of doubt.

He knew now—to take just one of them—that he loved Vyry Lewis. That was why what he had assumed was her betrayal of him had hurt so deeply. He had to smile at the idea of being betrayed by a colored whore. Yes, she was a whore—by government order—but that did not alter the fact that he loved her.

She had been the one he accused in his heart; but all the time it had been Sharon. Pretty, coy, witless Sharon Sue. She had used him. The one he'd smiled over patronizingly, thinking that she hadn't a brain that blonde head. He had typed her too, classified her neatly in his head as he had Vyry. And he'd been wrong. She was a fighter, she was strong, she was clever, and she too had a cause that she believed in.

And Sawyer. That did not surprise him as much, the fact that the Mississippian had been a Leaguer (he still found it more surprising that the man had become an officer, with such appalling manners). But the plans he had revealed did.

And driving west through Suffolk, Virginia, on a nighttime road, he had to admit to himself at last that it was not only the Kuklos League whose plans he hated and had to frustrate. They were the worst, certainly. But as the fault lines inside him shifted he could see more and more clearly that the principles and even the methods of the league were the same, at bottom, as those of the government, the Army, the Tredegar Works, all of Dixie socialism and the modern South that were . . .

Poorly planned?

Mistaken?

Wrong?

But if the Confederacy was based on wrong . . . if Sharon and Turner and the Railroaders were right, if inequality and separation were not natural but a monstrous wrong . . . then where did that leave Major Aubrey Quidley, CSA?

222

His hands tightened on the wheel as he remembered Turner. Remembered the Yankee captain he had killed. Remembered Sawyer, arms outstretched, a rigid figure dressed in flame.

He didn't know, quite yet.

But maybe, he told himself, not knowing was a form of progress, at least for him.

When he left the outskirts of Suffolk behind he slowed as he approached the fork. North, to Smithfield, along the winding ancient road along the banks of the river? Or northwest along the straighter yet less populous road that led through Wakefield? He tried again to put himself in place of the fugitives, but could not decide.

If he didn't know, the shortest route would be best: the straight road through Wakefield. He should be able to overtake them if he maintained speed, at least sixty miles an hour; they would be driving slowly, to avoid attention from the police or patrol. Just south of Richmond, where the roads joined, he could park by the road and wait. Whichever road they had taken they would have to pass by him there.

He hoped he would know them . . . he turned on to the old Petersburg road, 460, and accelerated again. The motor hummed and the transmission whined and air tore at the convertible top where parts of it had been melted through. He flipped the lights to high beams and roared after the light between what soon became unbroken forest.

He passed through small towns, sometimes identifying them from the signs, sometimes on and past them before his eyes could snap away from the road and read them.

It was almost the same, about a half hour later, with the roadblock. He saw the red light flickering ahead a long time before he reached it, and did not slow, thinking it a breakdown; only when the barricade loomed, and men suddenly stood and then scattered away from it as he bore down at ninety, did he see what it was and hit the brakes far too hard for the light car and send it skidding and turning half around, tires smelling of burned rubber and engine stalled, till it stopped broadside to the barricade only five feet away.

"Ho-ly *Jee*zus, man, you like to get youself killed drivin' like that."

Quidley looked up. A deputy sheriff stood beside the

223

car, arms aggressively akimbo. He sized the man up instantly: a bumpkin type, small-town poor white; overweight from grits and poor diet, loud because of his badge and his gun but easily cowed . . . and probably, yes, probably a Kuklos. This was their type of man.

The deputy—Williams, he noted from the man's badge —cleared his throat and leaned closer, then straightened up quickly and touched his cap. "Sorry, Major, I didn't see right away who you was. Boys, get that thing out'n the road, Army officer wants through."

Quidley beckoned him closer. "Thanks, deputy. You blocking this road against the shell?"

"Shell, sir?"

"Why are you out here, Williams? Or do you know?"

"Orders, sir—some niggers stole a truck, with some Army property, that's all I know."

So Norris had taken some precautions, yet without letting word out exactly what had been taken. Good, he thought. Sound thinking on Norris's part. "Anyone been through here last hour or so, Williams?"

"Not much, Major. Couple farmers in pickups, a carload of kids goin' up the conservatory. Drunk, of course." He chuckled and spat; Quidley noticed the bulge of tobacco in his cheek. "Oh, and one truck, 'bout a quarter of a hour ago."

"What kind of truck?"

"Coffee truck."

"Flatbed?"

"No, it was closed up in back. A reg'lar delivery truck, a Southern Motors, I think. Late model."

"You check it?"

"Sure I checked it," said the deputy, sounding hurt. "Think I'm just goin' to wave it on through? Sure I checked it."

Quidley stared up at the man steadily. Under the look he could see the deputy growing uncomfortable; his eyes slid away from the car, wandered to look at his men. "You can drive on through now, Major," he said, clearing his throat again.

"One more question," said Quidley. "Who was driving that last truck? Who was in the cab?"

Now Williams was visibly disturbed; he fidgeted, spat again, and finally said guiltily, "Hell, ain't no use lyin' to you, Major. Had them a darky drivin'. But there was a white man with 'em, and their papers looked all right."

"Them?"

"Colored gal, too, a real looker. All three of 'em up there in the cab together. Say, Major, I hope I didn't make no mistake, but it seemed to me——"

"No, it's all right," said Quidley automatically. It was them; had to be them. "Fifteen minutes ago, you say?"

" 'Bout that, yes, sir. Look—if you want, me and the boys can pack up here, get on the road—we can catch 'em afore they gets to Petersburg."

"You stay here," said Quidley firmly. "That can't have been them. They were all black men, no whites or women, and the truck was an Army two-ton."

"This here was a big SM," said Williams, sounding relieved. "It was no Army truck."

"Right then." He started the engine again and wheeled the Triumph around. The barricade had been moved and he saw that the right lane was unblocked. "You're only stopping northbound traffic?" he called to the deputy.

"That's orders, sir, but if you want——"

"No, no. You're doing fine, Williams." He touched a hand to his forehead as Williams snapped to a grotesquely rigid salute, his belly quivering far out over his pistol belt. "Carry on. Good night."

"Yes, *sir*."

Fifteen minutes ahead! He shifted up as fast as the car would permit, keeping the pedal to the floor. The motor growled and then hammered, and he wondered if it were overheating. He eased back to eighty and roared along at that speed for perhaps ten minutes, seeing nothing in his lights save the ruler-straight road and off in the woods the occasional double glint of animal eyes in the dark.

He was past it before his brain registered it: the dim glow of white light from the woods to the right, and the unmistakable yellow-orange flash of reflectors. There was something in there, probably off on a side road, and it was something big; the upper reflectors had been at least ten feet above the ground. He hesitated long enough that momentum carried him five hundred yards down the road, then braked, yanked the wheel around for a U-turn that would have toppled a larger car, and rolled back the other way at a little over thirty-five.

He saw no lights now. Perhaps they'd turned them off at the sound of his passing, or perhaps the underbrush was thicker in this direction. When he judged he was close to it he pulled on to the shoulder and crunched along at fifteen, leaning out to look.

There: a narrow, nearly overgrown dirt track leading off into the woods. He dimmed his own lights and pulled in, proceeding slowly. Bushes rustled under and around the body of the sports car.

He turned a corner and saw it, a towering, boxy shape. Its lights were out but its reflectors glowed in response to his own. This had to be it. He turned the key, and the engine stopped. The sudden silence seemed very loud and he could hear the cicadas very near, a low, ominous, pulsating buzz:

Au . . . brey. Au . . . brey.

He opened his door and stepped out. It was very dark. No sound or movement came from the direction of the truck and after waiting for almost a minute he closed the car's door quietly and began walking forward, shoving his way past the bushes that the truck's high sides had compressed. He came out in the open behind the truck and looked around. They might be hiding, he thought, and opened his mouth to call.

"Vy—"

The word was choked off in his throat. Someone behind him, without a rustle or a warning, had thrown an arm—a big arm— around his throat, and was tightening it. He wrenched at the arm, feeling the iron-hard muscles swelling under his hands but could not move it. Then someone moved in the dark ahead of him.

"Who is it, Johnny?"

He relaxed and stopped struggling. It was Vyry's voice. Somehow, he knew that she wouldn't let him be hurt.

"Don't know," the man behind him—Turner, he realized—grunted. "Can you see?"

She came up close and Quidley saw her start back as she recognized him.

"Kill him?"

"Maybe. Let's find out why he's here first." Quidley felt her hands move over his body; felt her unbutton the tunic, take out the fuze, and hold it curiously. "He's not armed . . . but here's something. Oh! It's that thing Leo was talking about—the part that makes it go off!"

"Yeah? Give it here, girl."

"Let go of him for a minute, Johnny, will you? We got to see if there's anybody came with him."

He felt the arm withdraw. He breathed, but did not turn when he heard Turner moving back toward his car. He remained facing Vyry and waited.

"What are you doing here?" she hissed. "You fool. He'll go crazy again soon as he sees who you are. Might kill us both. I thought I seen the last of you!"

"On the boat. It was you who rescued me, wasn't it? I have to know."

"Yes, and I guess I made a mistake. What in God's name are you *doin'* out here, Major?"

"I had to apologize," he said.

"You *what?*"

"I suspected you of betraying me. I was wrong; it was someone else. I had to tell you that I'm sorry."

"Major Cavalier . . . you're crazy. You're even crazier than Johnny," she said wonderingly. "You know that?"

"Yes. But that's not the only reason I came after you. Vyry . . . I know where you're going with this shell, and what the Railroad intends to do with it. And I've come to warn you, and the Railroad, to stop."

"No way we're going to stop, man. Not after coming this far with it. Not after—" and she motioned ahead of the truck and Quidley crouched and saw the body of a white man "—after he died doin' it."

"Who is it?" said Quidley, touching the man's forehead. It was stone cold.

"Railroad man."

"Oh." He remembered that Sharon Sue had mentioned another man, other than Turner, who was in charge; this must have been him. "He was . . . shot?"

"No. Had an accident while we was moving the shell. But I got to carry on with this, Major. For him—for Johnny—for all our people."

"I understand that," said Quidley, almost humbly. "And I want you to know that I haven't informed on you. I've not told the Army where you are or where you're going. I haven't reported in at all."

"Oh?" She moved closer to him, glancing apprehensively at the truck. "Why not, Major? Isn't that your duty?"

"Maybe it is. But I've found out some things." He took a deep breath. "Remember Baylor? The Kuklos?"

"Yes."

"There are more like him. They've infiltrated the Army and the government. They knew about Shiloh, and they knew about you too, about the Railroad's plans to take the shell from us."

"Then why didn't they stop us?" she said skeptically.

"Because they wanted you to succeed."

He could feel her stare, and hurried on; he had to convince her before Turner came back. "Listen. The Kuklos League wants the Railroad to threaten Richmond—paralyze it—even destroy it. They wouldn't mind that; Richmond to them is an effete, upper-class government, and Dixie socialism is a giveaway for the benefit of the darkies." She started to interrupt, but he didn't give her the chance. "They're poised now for a nationwide coup. If it succeeds, they will become the government. And their program,"—he swallowed and tried to put conviction into his words—"is to kill every black with a police record, every CE with education, every white with liberal convictions; to lynch everybody who doesn't meet their standards of a 'true Southerner.' And they can do it, Vyry, if the Railroad carries out its plans with this shell!"

She was silent for a moment, and he wondered if he had succeeded. "What about the Army?" she said at last.

"The man I . . . found this out from was *in* the Army, Vyry. I think Castle Thunder must be part of it, a military dictatorship along with the League. Vy . . . you know the coloreds are disorganized and unarmed. It'll be a massacre!"

"If it's true."

"It is; I swear it. On my honor as—" he faltered; the old familiar formula had turned bitter on his tongue. "As—"

"As what, Major? As a traitor, like us?" She chuckled. "How about just as a gentleman."

"No," he said slowly. "Not as a gentleman. Because a gentleman could not love you as I do. As a man."

She stared at him and he waited for her answer to that, but instead there was a rustling behind them by the truck and she grabbed his arm and whispered, "He's coming back. Get behind me now."

"Nobody else," came Turner's voice. "I looked up and

down the road, too. Nothing but that little car. Where'd he go?"

"He's here by me," said Vyry. "Johnny, he came to warn us. Says we can't go to Richmond."

"I want to see the fuckah try to tell me that. Who is it? Come over here, man."

"Johnny, listen. He says the Kuklos know 'bout us takin' the shell. Says they're going to let us go to Richmond and make our demands, even set it off, and then use that as an excuse to take over. And start killing people. Our people."

"Bullshit," said Turner. "Who's saying all this?"

"Never mind who," she said, and Quidley marveled at the steadiness of her voice as she faced a man who could turn berserk at any moment. "But he might be right, Johnny. What do you think we should do? Maybe go on in to Belleville, tell this LeLand Ray and let him decide?"

Quidley could hear grass rustle as Turner paced for moment.

"No."

"Then what, Johnny?"

Again, the rustle of pacing. Then, "You got the fuze now, right?"

"Yes, Johnny."

"Then we don't need this Ray."

"What do you mean, we don't need him?"

"We can drive into Richmond tonight. Right now. Plug that thing into the shell ourselves."

"Yes, but the negotiating—"

"And set it off," said Turner, his voice ice-cold. "That's it. Set it off. No negotiatin', no talkin', no begging whitey to give us poor loyal niggers our freedom. Just kill them. *That's* the way it's going to be, girl."

"Johnny, that ain't right," she said.

"Don't tell me what's right and what ain't, woman. You know what you get when you argue with Johnny Turner." He lifted his fist, half the Railroad salute, half a threatening gesture.

"That ain't the way to do it, Johnny. We got to negotiate, and for that we got to have the Railroad to help us."

"Fuck the Railroad."

"Johnny, think. You destroy Richmond and the whites will go kill-crazy. And it won't only be the Kuklos then,

229

either. Be every white man owns a gun." Her voice was pleading.

"Fuck them," said Turner again.

"At least think of the colored folk in Richmond. Over a million of them! At least—you can't—"

"Yes I can," said Turner, and they could hear his breathing, his panting, almost his sobbing. "Yes I can."

It was beginning now. Beginning. Inside his head.

Where there had been nothing, now a tiny flow was trickling through. A tiny flow of something almost as good, almost as right, almost as joyous as that something from the memory of which his mind still recoiled. Something that was not cobalt blue, but red. Orange-red, the red of rage.

He felt himself filling again, filling with a savage joy: the joy of killing. Killing whitey, who had done this to him, made him a husk of a man. Killing the thin-faced major . . . or had he already killed that one, back on the boat? He couldn't remember, quite. . . .

He didn't really understand all that she was saying about the Kuklos, about what would happen after they set the shell off. He didn't care either. It would kill them, kill them all, whites and maybe some blacks too, but that did not seem to matter as much as it once had long ago. For the red joy was filling him and he felt himself trembling with the thought of destruction and he was almost Johnny Turner again and save for the awful emptiness inside he was glad.

"Turner?"

That voice, he thought. *That voice.*

Quidley moistened his lips in the dark. He was frightened—terribly frightened. But he had to speak now that she had failed with the man.

"Turner," he said again. "It's me. Major Quidley."

He heard nothing; the immense shadow that was Turner neither moved nor spoke. He rubbed his hands on his tunic, feeling the sweat on them. He hadn't thought it would be like this. He had thought there would be others, that he would be welcomed and believed.

Still, he had to try.

230

"Turner, listen. I had to come after you to warn you. The Railroad is being used by its worst enemies. The League is going to make your seizure of this shell the pretext for a rebellion."

Still the big man was silent. Quidley heard the quaver in his own voice and tried to control it. "You've got to believe me—I've made myself a traitor by coming after you to warn you. Turner . . . Turner," he paused, bewildered at his silence, "Can you hear me? *Why don't you talk?*"

With a roar of rage, the waterman charged.

Quidley crouched and tried to feint aside. Turner didn't feint, or else never saw it. He drove straight on, slamming the lighter man against the radiator of the truck.

And again, Quidley found himself fighting, this time keyed up, ready, with the full knowledge that he was fighting for his life against slim odds. He kept his head down, away from the waterman's groping hands, and hammered his fists into Turner's stomach. But his fists felt as if he were pounding them into a wall, and even when he felt the opening and brought his knee up again and again Turner only grunted.

Then the hands found him and closed around his head and slid downward. He struck back, kicked, pushed—the truck rocked as his body was slammed back into it by Turner's sheer strength—but it was like fighting some irresistible machine, one that could not be hurt, or stopped, or moved—

For the last time the hands closed their hold again, and Aubrey Lee Quidley opened his mouth for a scream, but found he could no longer breathe.

"Johnny!" she cried.

Why had he said *that*—that, and nothing else, had finally and irretrievably pushed Johnny over the edge! She circled the two struggling men, hearing Quidley pant, hearing the thuds of blows—whose, she couldn't tell in the dark—and hearing Turner grunt—and she tried again to push herself between them.

She gasped as someone hit her, hard, on the left breast, and she staggered back, her whole side alive with pain; she held herself and moaned and went in again and was shaken off with a heave of Johnny's shoulder and fell backward on the grass. She lay there, smelling the night smell of the grass and the cool dirt.

Johnny.

The major.

Who was right?

Who was there to decide, except for her?

She forced herself to her knees and then to her feet. Her hands groped in the night-wet grass.

No more air . . . his arms were going weak, and he could feel that his blows were hardly stronger than a child's. But Turner was still above him, dark, enormous, invisible, implacable. . . .

This him, screamed in his brain. *This the bastard.* But the voice was distant and almost lost in the roaring flood of red tearing through his mind. Red . . . to kill, first this man, then all of them, and he knew at last suddenly but without particularly caring that he could not be at peace until he had killed them all and *they had killed him.*

A hollow, dull sound echoed from the boles of the trees.

And like a tree, one of the men stood rigid, swayed, half turned—and then toppled to the ground.

Vyry dropped the metal cylinder of the fuze and fell across Turner's chest.

Quidley sagged back against the fender of the truck. It was warm. He turned and hugged it, dragging in great lungfuls of irreplaceably sweet night air. Several minutes went by, with no sound in the little clearing of the road but his panting and Vyry's muffled sobs. At last he tried shifting his weight back to his legs. They held . . . barely. He managed a couple of steps toward the others, staggering like a drunk, and gave up and sank to his knees. He coughed for a while and then at the third try got his words past his bruised larynx. "Vy . . . Thanks."

"I didn't do it for you, Major *bastard,*" she sobbed.

"I don't care . . . who you did it for." He glanced around and got up again. This time he felt somewhat steadier and he walked carefully to the truck and turned the parking lights on and then walked back. He stood there watching until she looked up, hate written plain on her face.

"He's alive, Major."

"I'm glad."

232

"What you standin' there for?"

"I want you to tell me what to do," he said.

"Me?" She looked up again, surprised.

"Yes," said Quidley. He bent to Turner and picked up the fuze from where she had dropped it and held it out to her. "Every decision I've made so far has been wrong. Everyone I trusted was wrong. Everyone I mistrusted was right. Vyry . . . I think I'm getting a few things straight at last. I trust you. From here on in . . . it's up to you to decide."

Twenty

It was as if he'd shed it all—all the responsibility, the worry, and the guilt. He leaned back against the reassuring solidity of the truck, and waited with a quiet soul for her answer.

Her face was still upturned. "Major . . . you mean that?"

He nodded.

She looked down and touched Turner's head softly. "Poor Johnny . . . I don't know, Major. I'm not sure what to do either."

"Do you believe me? About the league?"

"Yes." She sounded uncertain. "And then, I never felt right about using this thing at all. To threaten them, sure . . . but not to use it."

"What are the Railroad's plans from here, Vyry?"

"We're supposed to drive it on into Belleville. That's just south of Richmond. Pick up a man there, some men, I'm not sure." She pointed at Leo's body. "He knew. But he's dead."

"We can do that," Quidley said, "if you want to. We'll put Turner and—him—in the back of the truck and I'll drive it. There won't be any trouble with roadblocks while I'm up front. Then I'll talk to the Railroad people there."

"You'd do that?"

"If you want me to."

She bent her head, then looked up. Even in the pale wash from the parking lights her eyes seemed to him night-dark. "And if they decide to use it?"

"Then it's between them and the government. I suppose I could volunteer to act as a go-between."

She shook her head slowly. "That's one thing we might do, Major. I'm thinking we might turn this whole mess back to the government, too. Give 'em their shell back. What you think of that?"

He thought. "Give it back and the Army will carry on with Shiloh. They'll take it to the labs and take it apart and study it and then copy it. And then make their own."

"Seems like that shouldn't bother you, Major."

It shouldn't . . . but it does, he thought. But he said only, "I'm letting you decide. But you're right. I don't think I want the Confederacy to have it either."

"We got to do something with it, Major. Can't leave it sitting here." She stroked Johnny's face. "And we got to think, the three of us, what we going to do, where we goin' to go."

Quidley chewed at his fingers, thinking. If they didn't want the Railroad to have it—and they didn't want the Confederacy to have it—

Couldn't give it back to the Yankees; that was impossible. They'd have to drive the truck all the way back, then up to Fort Monroe—either that or bypass Richmond, and drive on up to the old federal capital of Washington, now a divided city, and try to crash the Wall. No, he'd been right the first time: It was impossible.

But there was another idea, or at least he had the suspicion that back in his mind there lurked another idea. What was it? He drummed his fingers on the truck's hood.

"What time is it?" he heard her say.

"I don't know . . . three-thirty, I'd say."

"Any ideas, Major?"

"Just give me a little more time to think."

Then he had it. He turned the idea around, looking at it from every angle. It looked good.

"Vy?"

"Yeah?"

"Why don't we set it off here?"

"What?"

"We've got the fuze. I think I know enough about ordnance that I can arm it. Look. Say it goes off out here. The Railroad can't use it; the Army can't use it. And most of all the Kuklos League can't use it. It won't hurt anyone; there aren't any houses for miles around."

"How about us?" said Vyry.

Now that he had the key to it it all seemed simple. "You and Turner take the car. Go back to Norfolk. The deputy at the roadblock knows that car now, and he's not blocking the way south; just keep the brights on as you go by and all he'll do is salute. Oh," he said as a thought occurred to him, "Can you drive?"

"You'd be surprised, Major, how many of us know things we ain't supposed to. But what are Johnny and I going to do back there? They'd be looking for both of us, you know."

"Drive to Sharon—I mean, back to the house where you left the boat. Turner can run a boat, and that FPB will outrun anything that floats. You can take it North."

"North," she repeated.

"Tell them what happened. And why."

"Wait a minute now. Where are you going to be? Aren't you coming with us?"

"I'll come after. When I get it armed I'll follow you somehow."

"We'll wait," she said.

"You can't. I don't know how long this will take, and Turner . . ."

"Yes, Johnny," she said, looking down at the man. He was breathing regularly, lying completely limp on the roadway.

"Here," he stepped away from the truck, something in him touched by the sight of the big man lying there so helplessly. "Let's get him into the car."

Completely relaxed, he was too heavy to lift; Quidley compromised by dragging him, arms-first, around the corner of the truck. Vyry lifted his legs into the passenger's side of the little Triumph, and Quidley moved his trunk into position and propped his head carefully against the window and then closed the door on him and turned to Vyry. They faced each other in the dark.

"Vy?"

"Here, Major."

"Look—if I don't come—"

"But you said you will."

236

Quidley pondered her silhouette in the night. "Look," he said at last, "I know you don't love me. But could you —in case we don't get together again—"

She didn't answer; not in words. But suddenly he felt her arms around him and her lips hot on his, searching, open. Only after long minutes did she turn his head and murmur into his shoulder.

"What?" he said gently.

"I said—maybe it isn't too late to change my mind."

His lips found her neck and then her mouth again, and this time she moaned hungrily, deep in her chest. "Major . . . the door."

For a moment he didn't grasp what she meant; and then he did, and reached up to swing open the back of the truck. There, beside the dark convexity of the shell, he laid her down on a nest of blankets. He fumbled with her clothing; he was clumsy and she laughed and her hands moved and then things dropped away, and he was in her, and she was his.

There was no haste this time for either of them; and she seemed different; how he couldn't tell; could hardly think. Before she had been practiced and polished and perfunctory. Now—in the bed of the truck, in the shadow of the shell—she was his lover. And at the end when he cried out she pulled him into her and through his own joy he felt her shudder and move slowly under him.

They lay together, half-naked, warm, and listened to the insects and the rustling of the leaves outside and to the distant drone of an airship in the sky.

"Major . . . you know, I still love Johnny."

"I know."

"But I love you, too."

"Thank you," he said, leaning to kiss her one more time. "I love you, too, Vyry."

"But we got to go." She sat up and pulled her clothes together briskly and he had to smile at himself at the abrupt return of her old businesslike manner. "Dawn'll be comin' in a couple of hours, Major."

"Aubrey," he said.

"Say what?"

"Aubrey's my name, Vy."

She laughed. "Is that so? You never told me. Aubrey. I like it. But look, you've got to hurry. You sure you don't want me to wait for you?"

"No. You get going now. I'll catch up."

She hugged him quick, tight, and then jumped down. She peered into the car. "He's still out. I whacked him pretty good. Johnny's tough, though—he'll be comin' 'round later."

"Sure he will," said Quidley. "Maybe they'll be able to help him, up North."

"Maybe." They faced each other again.

"Well, so long," said Quidley.

"Major—I mean, Aubrey—"

"Yes?"

"One more kiss, just in case—"

This one was a long and deep one and he held it till he felt his eyes burning and the wetness on her cheeks against his own. He turned his head. "Go on now, Vyry. Get in the car and go."

He leaned against the truck and closed his eyes. He did not want to see her leave. He heard the quick scuff of her steps and then the sound of the door closing. The engine ground, then started, and he saw the headlights come on red through his closed eyelids and he raised his hand in farewell.

When it was dark and quiet again and even the hum of the motor had dwindled down the road to nothing, merging imperceptibly into the insect sounds of the forest night, he breathed a few times, deep, and then opened his eyes. She was gone.

Now it was time for the shell. He breathed a few more times, till the knot in his throat relaxed, and then climbed up in the cab and turned the dome light on and examined the metal cylinder, remembering and visualizing how it screwed into the base of the thing now resting, waiting, behind him. He turned it over in his hands and remembered all he knew of projectile fuzing. It had been a few years back, during the coast artillery assignment, but fuzing itself was relatively simple and not easily forgotten.

In a conventional heavy shell, whether nose- or base-detonated, the burst was triggered by the abrupt deceleration as the falling shell hit land or water or target. But there had to be safeties, mechanisms to prevent accidental detonation during transport, storage, and during the shock of firing. These safeties were in the fuze itself; it was far easier to maintain control of them, and to change

238

their characteristics if battle conditions required, than it would if they were located in the body of the shell.

In the weapons he was familiar with, two factors were involved in the shell's safeties: setback and rotation. First came setback. When the projectile was fired, the terrific acceleration within the barrel caused a movable element in the fuze to slide backward, against the resistance of a spring. A catch then locked this element back, out of the way of the exploder, which up till then blocked it from operating.

But a sharp blow or shock, such as an accidental fall from a loader sling, could also trip the setback element, leaving the damaged shell live. A second safety element was thus built in as two or more small spring-set pins, locking the exploder in place radially. When the shell was fired, rifling in the bore of the gun started it spinning. The centrifugal force of the spin, or rotation, moved the pins outward, disengaging them from the exploder.

After that, all the fuze needed was the sharp blow of impact to explode.

He frowned, looking down at it in the yellow glow of the dome light. This fuze didn't look all that different from Allied Joint Design Mark 47, the standard coast artillery impact fuze. Here were the lock-in prongs, the male threading at the head of the fuze body, and the central exploder cavity, with holes bored in it to allow the shock wave from a few ounces of detonator to transmit itself to the booster explosive in the shell itself. The Union fuze was slightly bigger, but all the elements were there; not too surprising when one considered that, to meet the same requirements, physical laws required both blocs' designs to be at least roughly similar.

Quidley lay the thing on the dashboard and relaxed in the seat, thinking. Obviously he could not accelerate or spin, a one- to two-ton shell hard enough to overcome the safeties. With proper tools, though, he might saw the fuze open and hold the safeties out manually; but, rummaging in the truck's tool chest, all he came up with was a crescent wrench and a couple of much-used screwdrivers. Disassembly, then, was out.

He sat and thought for a little while longer, then abruptly got out and popped the hood open and studied the engine for several minutes.

Maybe.

239

Setback could easily be duplicated by a sharp blow along the long axis of the fuze tube. But the rotational safeties were trickier. *Well,* he thought, *I can't lose by trying. Even if I can't set it off properly I might be able to damage it, set off part of it or something. Enough to make it useless. And that's the idea, after all.*

He broke out a flare from the truck's emergency kit and lit it and balanced it on the side of the frame so that it lit the exposed engine, and set to work. With the crescent wrench he backed off the fan belt retaining nut until the generator axle was bare. Using four feet of friction tape he fixed the fuze to the hub so that as the generator turned the fuze did also. He wiggled it and it held.

He got in the cab again and started the motor and got out and studied the fuze as it spun, then moved to the side of the cab and reached in and held his hand on the accelerator until the motor roared and smoked under the open hood.

It all depended on what rpm it was designed for. He could not remember what initial rotation rate was for a fired shell, but the generator was certainly whirling at a hell of a rate. *Should be enough,* he reassured himself. He wedged the gas pedal down and went forward again and stared at the silvery-red blur of the spinning cylinder. It would, he thought, take two axial accelerations to fire it, assuming that the radial acceleration being supplied now was sufficient to force the retaining pins out. Two; one, to mimic the setback as the shell was accelerated into flight; the second, in the opposite direction, to imitate the impact of a shell at the end of its eighty-mile flight.

He held the wrench carefully, eyeing the end of the spinning tube, and swung hard into it. The impact was satisfying. The tube, knocked off-center, began to wobble, then the tape loosened and it spun from the hub and whanged hard against the engine block and fell rattling to the ground. Quidley searched for it, holding the sputtering flare carefully, and found it under the truck. He held it up. It was dented slightly but essentially seemed unharmed, and he smiled as ruddy light glinted off brighter metal at the detonator end. The axials had tripped; the blow had set it back; one more blow, in the opposite direction, would fire it.

Except for one thing. It was dangerous to fire a shell

that armed instantly; it might strike a piece of ship's superstructure and go off close aboard. With a nuclear shell the danger would be even greater. Ergo, there would be a time-delay built into it, so that only after a given time—probably several minutes, considering the range from which this shell had to be fired—would an impact set it off. He cut the truck's motor and held the fuze to his ear. A faint ticking told him that he was right.

He laid the fuze on the hood and sat down on the running board, prepared to wait.

It was then, in the fitful light of the guttering flare, that he saw the ground moving in bits of shadow. He bent down, curious, and picked up one of the weakly fluttering things.

It was a cicada, one of the seventeen-year "locusts" he had seen a week before in Sharon's garden. The insects whose lurid wings predicted war. How long ago that seemed.

But this one was different. It buzzed weakly but barely moved as he placed it on his palm and held it close to the light.

There was very little left of it.

The foreparts, the head, seemed wizened, dull, and withered. The wings were no longer glossy but wrinkled and cloudy brown.

But it was the insect's body that made him frown. The fat thorax was almost gone, eaten away, ragged-edged. It was hollow and he could see within it the pulsing of the tiny drum as the creature rasped weakly, dying.

He tossed it back down among its fellows—coaxed into a final frenzy of activity by the roar of the engine, or the daylike glare of the flare—and watched it flutter its wings a few times and fall. Now, as he bent down toward them, he could see that they were all dying, all of them, the last survivors of the hordes that had milled thick as aphids on the trees, the crops, and lawns, that had called from the forests in waves of sound like the beating heart of doom. Survivors of birds and bats and the other predators that had feasted on the unnumbered hosts. Survivors that now were dying, eaten away from within, conquered only by the inexorable working of time and the decay within themselves. He stared down, tranced by the spectacle of their deaths, until amid their sporadic buzzing he sensed

241

the cessation of another, more regular sound; and he bent his ear toward the fuze. It was silent. It was ready.

Now, he knew, it was dangerous. A base fuze might go off only when the shell carrying it hit six feet of waffle armor and concrete ... or might explode with a relatively minor jolt. It all depended on how it had been set, and that, of course, he did not know.

He cradled it gently in his hands. It seemed warm. His imagination? No, he thought, might be it had picked up some of the heat from the engine.

Reaching for the smoking flare, he went to the rear of the truck and swung himself up into it and squatted respectfully beside the hulk of the shell. Curving, massive, it cast great moving shadows in the brilliant scarlet flame, reminding him of the worship of pagan idols. He held the armed fuze beside the base cavity and considered for one last time. Was there no way he could leave it? Rig it to detonate after an hour, when he might, with luck, be safely away?

No. He saw now that it was inevitable. His class, the finest of the Old South, had let it all happen. It had taken the Confederacy out of the Union for its own ends. Watched, with equanimity and even approval, the development of a system that destroyed humanity—not only in the colored, but in the poor whites as well; the Kuklos was the white shadow of the institutionalized injustice the Confederacy of the 1980s dealt out to all.

To all save its favored, aristocratic few.

He knew he was not very smart. Now, at this moment, or even in general. Aubrey Lee Quidley IV was not, he knew now, a clever man. He was not clever enough to deny what he realized; or to fool himself, like Turner or Sawyer, into believing that more injustice and violence could wipe out the results of the old.

No, he was not smart. But he was a Quidley. Old and eaten-out the line might be; but he had one thing left of it. However others might define it he knew it and held it before him like a shining sword. He had his honor; and what he was about to do, above all else, was a matter of honor.

He slid the fuze home, feeding it inch by inch into its fated cavity, its receptacle, its home, and when it reached the stopping-point he began to screw it in the remaining turns with his bare hands.

Postscript

When she saw the brilliance she braked, panicky, steering the little car to the side of the road not far east of Windsor. She turned round, ignoring Turner's groan, and stared west, shielding her eyes with her hand.

The first white, devouring flash, almost a second long, had dimmed to an orange glow even before she turned round; only that saved her eyesight. But as she watched, blinking back afterimages of the car's dashboard, something bright and appalling began increasingly to light up the road behind her and the trees and the houses, first eclipsing and then obliterating the growing glow of sunrise to the east.

It was light—pure, hellish, hot light, climbing like a hundred ascending yellow-red-purple writhing-together suns. She felt its heat on her face. Below it glowed a vast moving pillar of smoke and flame, lit from within by a twisting reddish radiance of its own.

As she watched, her mouth a little open in awe and fear, she saw a strange dark line, a shadow line, moving down the road toward her. The shock wave, mercifully attenuated in fifteen miles' travel, still was strong enough to tear the blistered convertible top over them to ragged shreds, skid the car sideways, which left her shaken and bruised and the car, with one wheel off the road, in a shallow clay ditch. When she was able to look back it was almost dark again; almost; but still she could make out a reddish glow against the sky and low down to the ground that seemed to be spreading, expanding, as it slowly was overtaken by the new light of sunrise.

"Vy—"

"You be quiet now, Johnny-Jo," she said.

There was something hard in her throat, but now was not the time to grieve, she told herself. "You be quiet now. Go on back to sleep. I'll get you up again pretty soon and we'll be on a boat, be on our way."

As he grew still again beside her she turned again in the seat, looking backward, westward, to where she had left him. Inside her she could still feel his warmth, she could still almost feel him, in the way a woman feels a man when she is his not by right, not by force, but by her own choice.

But he was gone. Bending forward, she felt for the ignition, blinking as tears stung her eyes. She did not want to cry. Not for him. She had never wanted to cry, not for him, not for Johnny, not even for herself. But in spite of that the tears ran hot on her cheeks as she groped blindly for the key, sobbing softly, softly, so as not to awaken Turner.

Good-bye, Major Cavalier, she thought, steering the little car back on the road. The wheel vibrated beneath her hands, but she judged that it would hold for the few remaining miles that lay between them and the boat that would carry them, at last, to freedom. *Good-bye, Aubrey. You were some kind of man, in your way. Good-bye.*

And . . . thank you.

Coming in January 1982

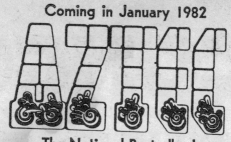

The National Bestseller by

GARY JENNINGS

"A blockbuster historical novel. . . . From the start of
this epic, the reader is caught up in the sweep and
grandeur, the richness and humanity of this fictive
unfolding of life in Mexico before the Spanish
conquest. . . . Anyone who lusts for adventure, or that
book you can't put down, will glory in AZTEC!"

The Los Angeles Times

"A dazzling and hypnotic historical novel. . . . AZTEC has
everything that makes a story appealing . . . both
ecstasy and appalling tragedy . . . sex . . . violence . . .
and the story is filled with revenge. . . . Mr. Jennings
is an absolutely marvelous yarnspinner. . . .
A book to get lost in!"

The New York Times

"Sumptuously detailed. . . . AZTEC falls into the same
genre of historical novel as SHOGUN."

Chicago Tribune

"Unforgettable images. . . . Jennings is a master at
graphic description. . . . The book is so vivid that this
reviewer had the novel experience of dreaming of the
Aztec world, in technicolor, for several nights in
a row . . . so real that the tragedy of the
Spanish conquest is truly felt."

Chicago Sun Times

AVON Paperback   55889 . . . $3.95

Available wherever paperbacks are sold, or directly from the publisher. Include 50¢ per copy for postage and handling; allow 6-8
weeks for delivery. Avon Books, Mail Order Dept., 224 West 57th
St., N.Y., N.Y. 10019.

Aztec 10-81

Coming in January 1982

CONGO

The National Bestseller by

MICHAEL CRICHTON

Author of THE ANDROMEDA STRAIN

"Darkest Africa. Strangling vines. Rain forest. Pygmies. Clouds of mosquitoes. Rampaging hippos. Roaring gorillas. Killer natives. Gorges. Rapids. Erupting volcanoes. An abandoned city full of diamonds, lost in the jungle. Maybe a new animal species, a weird cross between man and ape, but unheard of in 20th-century anthropology. Zaire. Congo. Michael Crichton's newest thriller. And of course: technology, which is what it's all about today, isn't it? Zoom!"

The Boston Globe

"A gem of a thriller!"

Playboy

"Oh, is this ever a good one!"

Detroit News

"The master of very tall tales plunges into the heart of darkness. . . . A dazzling example of how to combine science and adventure writing."

People

"What entertainment! . . . Crichton has created in Amy a 'talking gorilla' of enough charm to enshrine her in pop culture as firmly as R2D2."

Saturday Review

Available wherever paperbacks are sold, or directly from the publisher. Include 50¢ per copy for postage and handling: allow 6-8 weeks for delivery. Avon Books, Mail Order Dept., 224 West 57th St., N.Y., N.Y. 10019.

AVON Paperback

56176 • $2.95
Congo 10-81

"Ticks to an explosive conclusion!"
Chicago Sun-Times

#1 International Bestseller

THE FIFTH HORSEMAN

LARRY COLLINS
DOMINIQUE LAPIERRE

The President of the United States receives an ultimatum. Within hours, the world is convulsed in crisis, cover-up and panic.

America will surrender to impossible demands . . . or a major city will be obliterated. There is no time for a warning.

On the streets of a city preparing for Christmas, every agonizing minute now brings millions of unsuspecting Americans closer to annihilation.

63 hours of grueling suspense . . . The countdown to apocalypse has begun.

"Grabs the reader and does not let go."
Associated Press

"Chilling, tense, seizing, and providential. . . .
This is an engrossing, awesome and stunning book."
Vogue

AVON

54734 . . . $3.50

Available wherever paperbacks are sold, or directly from the publisher. Include 50¢ per copy for postage and handling: allow 6-8 weeks for delivery. Avon Books, Mail Order Dept., 224 West 57th St., N.Y., N.Y. 10019.

FiHorse 8-81